"I was so blind . . . so stupid," Stella murmured.

With his arms around her and his face near to her, she was conscious of a joy rising within her which was unlike anything she had ever known before, a joy so poignant, so thrilling that it was like a physical pain in its intensity.

"Your name means star," he said, "and to me you have always been like a star, out of reach, but making me yearn for it, making me long to find for myself the love and beauty it signifies."

Then he bent his head and his lips were gentle and tender against the softness of hers. . . . .

# TOWARDS THE STARS

## Barbara Cartland

PYRAMID BOOKS ▲ NEW YORK

'Man Struggles through his life,
Ignorant and fearful of his hidden powers.
Yet when Love lifts his eyes from strife,
His heart can rise towards the stars.'


**TOWARDS THE STARS**

A PYRAMID BOOK

Pyramid edition published September 1975

ISBN 0-515-03922-5

Printed in the United States of America

Pyramid Books are published by Pyramid Communications, Inc.
Its trademarks, consisting of the word "Pyramid" and the por-
trayal of a pyramid, are registered in the United States Patent
Office.

Pyramid Communications, Inc., 919 Third Avenue, New York,
N.Y. 10022

## 1

'There's a very bad case just come in, sir.'

The Doctor straightened his back and took out his handkerchief to mop his forehead.

'I know, I know,' he said testily; 'they're all bad. We're getting round as quickly as we can.'

Even as he spoke he deprecated the irritation in his own voice and glancing at the calm, almost imperturbable face of the man beside him, wished for the hundredth time that he was more like Clive Ross.

What he said was true enough; they were all bad—the men and women they brought in one after another, some blackened and twisted by the blast until they were almost unrecognisable as human beings.

The room was full of them, laid out on hastily procured mattresses, while there was the constant clanging of an ambulance bell outside as the cases which had received attention were moved to the hospital.

'Thank Heaven Ross was handy.'

Dr. Richardson realised he was grateful for Ross's presence not only for the help that he could give, but also because he himself could shelve much of the responsibility.

Clive Ross, head surgeon at one of London's largest hospitals, the man who had already performed miracles of surgery on war casualties, was not likely to find any disaster—whatever its magnitude—overwhelming.

But was it fair to expect as much from an unimportant, insignificant local doctor who before the war attended at most half a dozen accidents a year and the majority of whose patients died from nothing more virulent than old age?

Dr. Richardson, it was true, had never sought notoriety or, indeed, experience; he had been content with his small practice in a country village.

Medicine was his career but he looked on it only as the means to bring him an assured income, enough, anyway, to keep body and soul together.

Clive Ross was very different. They had been at Edinburgh University together and Dr. Richardson could remember how, even when they were first-year students, Ross had been picked out for special recognition.

There was something in the man himself which commanded attention.

Look at him now, for instance, calmly concentrating on each case in turn, quite oblivious apparently of the noise and confusion, of the cries of those in pain and the overwhelming horror of the whole catastrophe.

More than once Dr. Richardson found himself flinching as he looked down at a mangled, bloody mass of what had once been firm human flesh.

Once he couldn't prevent an exclamation passing his lips as he saw where the blast of the explosion had ripped not only the clothes from a young girl's body, but the skin as well.

He found himself echoing in his heart the words of an old stretcher-bearer who kept murmuring over and over again in a monotonous undertone:

'It's 'orrible, that's what it is, 'orrible.'

It was horrible right enough, and all the precautions which had been ready in this particular factory for just such an occurrence had been ineffective and useless when the moment arrived.

For one thing, the main first-aid post and sick bay had been blown up; for another, the explosion had taken place where it was least expected in one of the most crowded workshops.

It had happened soon after the factory started the morning's work—it was lucky in some ways, Dr. Richardson thought, that it had been at that time. He had been on the point of leaving his house for a case in the country when they had caught him on the telephone.

He had heard the dull roar of the explosion a few minutes earlier and thought nothing of it.

Pioneers had been blasting in the countryside all the

previous week and he had grown used to the dull rumble of their explosions and took no notice of this one until a breathless almost incoherent voice on the telephone had told him to 'come at once.'

Then, as he had snatched up his bag and hurried to the door he had seen the cloud of dark smoke rising in the distance above the spread-out roofs of the ordnance factory.

It was the sight of that smoke which had sent him back to the telephone.

Why it had made him think of Clive Ross he had no idea, but it had; and it had made him remember, too, that Ross had been speaking the night before only ten miles away at a conference of surgeons which had taken place at a big hospital recently opened by Royalty.

On an impulse, and perhaps there was a good deal of fear behind that impulse, Dr. Richardson had telephoned to the hotel where he knew Clive Ross was staying.

'Mr. Ross? I think he's left,' the clerk said at the other end. 'Hold on a minute, I'll see.'

As he waited, Dr. Richardson had been conscious that he was almost praying Clive Ross would not have left, for he was still hearing the terror in the voice that had spoken to him a few minutes before:

'There's hundreds killed, Doctor, hundreds!'

Hundreds! How was he—who was he, to cope with hundreds of injured people?

'Hello. Who is it?'

With a surge of relief Dr. Richardson had recognised Clive Ross's deep voice.

'Hello, Ross, it's Richardson speaking.'

'Oh, hello, Richardson, how are you? I expected to see you last night. I remembered this was your part of the world.'

Dr. Richardson had cut across the exchange of courtesies, telling Clive Ross what had happened and pleading with him to come at once.

There was no need to plead; Ross had promised to be with him just as quickly at his car could get him there.

'You can't miss the factory,' Dr. Richardson had said

eagerly, 'it's directly on your road and you'll see the smoke rising above it. . .'

He was conscious suddenly the line had gone dead; Clive Ross had already started and he hurried out to his own car.

The confusion when he arrived, the hysteria of several of the women who were awaiting him, the news that two of the factory nurses had been killed, and the first sight of the victims merely convinced him of what he had known from the first, that he was incapable of dealing with such an emergency.

When finally he saw Clive Ross's tall, broad-shouldered figure it was with difficulty he prevented himself from running towards him.

They had shaken hands gravely; then as Dr. Richardson started to explain, Ross had interrupted him.

'Is there anywhere I can put my things? I have my nurse with me.'

As he watched Ross washing his hands in the canteen sink, saw him using a nail-brush with unhurried precision as if a patient was waiting on the sofa in his consulting room, Dr. Richardson found himself thinking.

'The secret of Clive's success is that he is so sure of himself.'

He felt he could understand now why it was said that Ross's patients had an adoration for him that was almost idolatrous.

They clung to him, he was a rock in which they had absolute faith and trust. He gave the impression of being infallible and they were content to surrender both their bodies and their wills into his keeping.

All the time Clive was washing, people kept appearing at the door.

'The room's nearly full, Doctor; where are we to put the next lot?'

'There's a woman bleeding to death. What am I to do?'

'There's a man here, Doctor, who says he's found a leg by itself—what is he to do with it?'

At last Ross was ready. He seemed to have taken an

eternity of time, Dr. Richardson thought, and knew it had really been only a few minutes.

And then they had started. It was true that the big floor of the canteen was nearly full of casualties.

'We shall never get round them,' Richardson thought despairingly, alone.

But it was extraordinary how quick Ross was once they began. An examination, swabs, a dressing, in most cases an injection of morphia—he left that to Richardson—then:

'I should get this one to hospital as quickly as you can' or 'There's no hurry; she'll be comfortable for an hour or so.'

Once or twice they had nothing to do but to pull the blanket over some poor burned and twisted face.

'Do come to this one, Doctor. She's really bad and we don't know what to do.'

It was the same woman again. Richardson recognised her as an ardent First-Aider.

'Shall I go?' he asked.

For a moment he thought Ross had not heard, then Clive raised his head.

'I'll look at her. Morphia here and get this man to hospital at the first opportunity.'

He walked across the room with the woman who had been so insistent in her demands chattering beside him.

Dr. Richardson stayed behind to give the morphia injection. Ross's nurse, quiet and deft in her movements, tucked the patient round with blankets, then they hurried to where Ross was kneeling beside a woman lying on a stretcher.

There were no blankets and she was covered with a man's coat.

'A machine fell right across her,' someone was saying as Dr. Richardson came up. 'I had a job to get her out, she was wedged there.'

They had torn her clothing in moving her and Dr. Richardson noticed beneath the blue factory overall which all the women wore this woman's underclothing was very different from what they had seen before—soft shell-pink satin inset with coffee-coloured lace.

'Expensive,' he thought.

At that moment the nurse beside him gave a sudden exclamation.

'Why, it's Lady Marsden!'

Clive appeared not to have heard. Dr. Richardson looked at her in startled surprise.

'Lady Marsden!' he repeated, 'But it can't be!'

'It is—I'm sure it is,' the nurse insisted.

'But why should she be in the factory? I don't understand. Are you quite certain you're not mistaken?'

'Quite,' the nurse repeated. 'I nursed her once, a long time ago, but I should know her anywhere. Besides, her pictures are always in the papers.'

'Forceps,' Clive Ross said sharply.

There was a note in his voice which made both Dr. Richardson and the nurse feel as if they were rebuked for gossiping and yet if what the nurse said was true it was astounding enough.

Lady Marsden working in a factory, wearing the ordinary blue overall with which every employee was issued on arrival ... Stella Marsden, the wealthy, the beautiful, the acclaimed, injured in an explosion and, judging by a cursory glance at her, vitally injured.

Already Dr. Richardson could see the headlines, the photographs, hear the chatter and speculation.

He looked at the woman again. Could it be true? Despite the ghastly pallor of her face and the lines of pain or shock etched round the tightened mouth, it was obvious that the woman lying there possessed an unusual beauty.

Her underclothes were hardly those of the average factory hand and now he noticed her hands, slim, perfectly manicured, soft and unblemished.

'It's obvious she has not been in the factory long,' he thought, 'if it really is Lady Marsden.'

He tried to remember when he had last heard of her. Marsden House had been taken over in 1941 by the Ministry of Food.

He knew vaguely that some part of it had been retained

by its owners, but the neighbourhood was seldom honoured by the personal apparance of Sir Philip or her ladyship.

Sir Phillip had now been dead how long?—nearly a year, he supposed, killed in a flying accident.

The pilot had been off his course and the machine had hit the side of a hill; all the high officials inside it, among them Sir Philip Marsden, had lost their lives. Only the pilot had remained alive and he had died soon after the rescue party reached them.

'Yes, it must be nearly a year ago,' Dr. Richardson thought.

Perhaps Lady Marsden was still so unhappy that she had tried to find forgetfulness in war work. But why this particular work?

So far as he could remember she was President of the Red Cross and held various other official positions both in the county and in London.

He had a sudden vision of her five—no, six years ago. He had been eating his supper when an impetuous ring at the front door bell had made him start.

His housekeeper was old and half crippled with rheumatics, it would have taken her some minutes to come upstairs—easier to answer the door himself. A smartly uniformed footman stood outside.

'Sir Philip Marsden wishes to speak to Dr. Richardson.'

He had hurried to the window of the big grey Rolls Royce. Dusk was falling, he could just make out that there were two people sunk deep into the soft cushioned seats.

'There's a man with a broken leg in South Lodge, Richardson.'

'A car accident, Sir Philip?'

'I believe so; Crofton will give you all particulars, he was moving the man as we passed.'

The note of bored indifference in Sir Philip's voice was very obvious.

Instinctively Dr. Richardson found himself stiffening, he had always disliked the man although it was policy not to admit such a prejudice even to himself. It was then the other occupant of the car spoke:

11

'If there is anything we can do to help, please let us know.'

'Thank you—er—Lady Marsden.'

He had supposed it might be her though he had not met her before.

'Good night, Richardson. Drive on, Gates, we're late for dinner.'

Sir Philip was not prepared to be conversational.

Dr. Richardson had stepped back; as he did so he heard Lady Marsden exclaim:

'I've dropped my bag.'

The light inside the car was flashed on. He saw her bending forward, diamonds glittering in her hair, at her ears and round her neck, white foxes hiding her shoulders and framing the darkness of her head.

Then the footman sprang in beside the chauffeur, the car moved away.

A few yards down the road the light was switched off; evidently her ladyship had found her bag. Dr. Richardson had stood in the road watching the headlights pointing the way as the car went swiftly up the hill.

His mind was recalled from its wanderings by Ross's voice.

'Blankets.'

The nurse disappeared.

'This case should be operated on at once,' Ross said to Richardson, and gave him briefly in medical terms a quick diagnosis of what was wrong.

Richardson nodded and hoped Ross would think he was behaving intelligently. He admitted frankly to himself that not in a month of Sundays would he have known what had happened when the machine fell across that soft body.

'Extraordinary the whiteness of her skin,' he thought.

'Hadn't you better do the operation yourself?' he asked suddenly.

He realised that Clive Ross was interested in the technicalities of this case. This was something particularly difficult, something in which he knew Clive had always excelled.

'Perhaps.'

12

Ross spoke as if his mind was elsewhere.

At that moment the nurse came back with two blankets, pale green satin-bordered ones obviously borrowed from some adjacent private house.

'The W.V.S. are bringing in supplies,' she said cheerfully, 'there will be enough for everyone in a few minutes.'

'Good.'

As the nurse covered the woman on the stretcher, she stirred and opened her eyes.

'She's conscious, that's good,' Dr. Richardson said. 'Shall I give her morphia?'

'What has happened?'

Her voice was low and curiously sweet. The nurse answered her.

'You're quite all right, Lady Marsden.'

'Am I? I thought ...' She frowned in an effort of remembrance.

Dr. Richardson took her arm, the hypodermic ready.

'Now don't you worry, Lady Marsden,' he said. 'We're going to get you well again whatever happens.'

She looked at him frowningly and then up at Clive Ross. Her eyes widened for a moment and then quite distinctly and slowly she spoke to him and to him only.

'Can't you leave me ... alone?' she asked. 'Can't you understand I want to ... die?'


2


Hetty Hayton sat in front of her looking-glass gazing at the contour of her jaw.

'You'll have to get me an appointment next week with Madame Agnes,' she said. 'I'm looking a hundred.'

'I'll tell Miss Farley,' her maid replied starchily.

'Miss Farley's busy—better ring her up yourself, Watkins.'

Watkins sniffed as one who would say it was not her job

13

to make telephone calls, but before she could speak there was a knock at the door.

'Come in,' Hetty said irritably.

Alice Farley came quietly into the room. She was a thin, angular woman of nearly fifty with short-sighted eyes and a way of thrusting her head forward so that it came first round a corner before her badly-dressed body followed it.

'Mr. Ross is on the telephone. Do you wish to speak to him?'

'Of course I want to speak to him. Don't be such a fool, Alice. Put him throught at once and hurry up.'

Hetty jumped up from the dressing-table and ran across the room to the receiver by her bedside. She waited a moment and when a faint click told her that the connection was through she said in a noticeably sweet voice:

'Hello, Clive, how are you?'

'Good morning, Mrs Hayton. Sorry to disturb you so early.'

'But you aren't disturbing me—you never do.'

'Good. Well, I am sending three patients down to you today, two men—both R.A.F.—and the third is Lady Marsden.'

'Stella Marsden? I'd no idea you knew her. I read about the accident, of course. Why didn't you tell me she was a patient of yours?'

'Why should I?'

The question was abrupt, uncompromising.

'How secretive you are, Clive, even with your friends. Well, I'll forgive you and be ready to welcome Stella Marsden. I shall look forward to seeing her again. What time will they arrive?'

'About five o'clock. Lady Marsden has her own special nurse and I shall be down tomorrow.'

'How lovely! I've got a lot to tell you and a lot to show you, too.'

'Good-bye.'

Clive put down the receiver and Hetty replaced hers. Then she sat for a moment thinking, the point of one oval-shaped nail tapping her teeth as she did so.

'Stella Marsden! So she is coming here.'

Hetty's agile brain wondered how to turn the fact to her personal advantage.

She was also trying to remember exactly what she had heard lately about Stella, whom she had been with, what she had been doing. Strange she should be in a factory accident.

A factory and Stella Marsden!

Sitting on her peach satin and antique lace bedspread Hetty Hayton schemed and speculated. It was always the same; a new trend of thought, the mention of a new person set her mind revolving like an aeroplane propeller.

'Do you want me, Mrs Hayton?' It was Alice Farley again.

'For heaven's sake, Alice,' Hetty said, getting to her feet, 'do learn not to creep into a room like that, you give me the jitters. And where's Watkins?—she hasn't finished my hair yet.'

Watkins, who had retired discreetly while Hetty telephoned, entered the dressing-room.

'Let's get my hair done,' Hetty commanded, crossing the room to her dressing-table.

She spoke briskly, but her tone was not nearly so sharp and querulous as it was when she addressed Alice Farley.

Watkins was an experienced maid—they were hard to get in war-time—and she would stand just so much and no more from her employer. Hetty knew this.

With Alice Farley it was different. With her ill health and her shy, retiring personality she would find it hard enough to get employment.

She served Hetty as a whipping-boy, someone to bully when things went wrong, someone who would not answer back and who would never dare to give in her notice.

She was useful in other ways too—only Hetty knew how useful—for she had one gift which outweighed all others in her position of secretary-companion.

Alice Farley had a prodigious memory.

Her typing and shorthand were adequate, but any high school girl who had been through a commercial course could have done as well; she was bad at figures and, as

Hetty often reminded her, she was incapable of organising a Sunday School treat let alone a house the size of Trenton Park, but her memory was amazing.

She remembered faces, people's names and places; there was nothing particularly unusual in that, but she could also remember whole conversations, little details of gesture and deportment, a look, a glance—nothing seemed to escape Alice Farley's meek brown eyes, blinking apologetically behind the magnifying lenses of her glasses.

Hetty Hayton was no fool.

A few months after she had engaged Alice Farley she realised her value, but she kept the knowledge to herself and she kept Alice Farley in what she considered her proper place, while she made full use of the information Alice brought her.

Alice had been with her almost from the beginning—and by 'the beginning' she meant since she had come to England. Irish by birth, Hetty had started her career as secretary to an old man in the town of her adoption—Ohio.

'And a very good secretary I was, too,' she would say when she permitted herself to speak of those days, which was seldom.

True to all fictional stories of the business girl who makes good, she had married her boss, and when he had died after five years of temperamental married life he had left her enough money to ensure her being both comfortable and secure for the rest of her life—provided she was careful.

Hetty didn't intend to be careful.

She sank a year's income and a small part of her capital in buying herself some really wonderful clothes and settling herself in New York. She was pretty and extremely ambitious.

It took her two years to get what she wanted.

By that time her capital was exhausted; but she got Clement Hayton, proving for the first time, and by no means the last in her life, that a gambler's instinct could pay off.

Clement Hayton, with his oil mines and his railroad

16

tracks, his interest in the newspaper world and his almost uncanny knowledge of political nerve centres, was exactly what Hetty had been seeking.

He married and educated her; he taught her in fact what she had always craved in fancy—how to gain power and how to direct it to her own ends.

She learnt that it was almost impossible to fail if one was certain what one wanted in life and quite unscrupulous as to the method of getting it.

Hetty had always been ambitious—Clement Hayton made her fanatically so. He was a gross, diseased old man by the time she married him, but once he had been young, virile and dynamic.

All he retained in his old age was the ruthless driving force which had made an illegitimate child born in the slums of Chicago one of the richest men in America.

Hetty amused him.

He saw through her from the very beginning, summed up her rather too lavish flattery, her ingratiating attitude, and her stumbling, amateurish flauntings of sex.

'You would not,' he told her later, 'have deceived a boy just down from college let alone a man of experience who could, if I had wanted to, have brought up every bit of trash and half the virgins in New York.'

Clement Hayton knew that Hetty was out for marriage and because he was tired, old, and extremely lonely he was prepared to give her what she wanted.

He talked frankly to her and he liked it when she was frank with him.

'I'm not going to live long,' he said. 'I've paid the best doctors to tell me the truth and I'm not afraid to hear it. With the dollars I leave behind you can get anything in the world; but the point is, honey, you've got to aim high enough to keep the game amusing.

'The things you get too easily turn sour in your mouth—no one knows that better than I do—but even with money you can fail, unless you are one sharper than the other person, just that bit ahead all the time.'

Hetty listened to him and believed him. She met his friends and learnt from them just how cleverly Clement

17

Hayton had managed to keep one ahead of the other fellow all his life.

She learnt, too, to sum up a person very quickly, to find his weak spot and to exploit it so that every time it proved a trump card in her hand.

Now she had money Hetty looked round for the next step and it didn't take her long to tumble what that was.

Society! Deep down in her consciousness was the memory of a ragged little Irish girl crossing the Atlantic.

She could still smell that boat, the stench of the steerage, and feel the fear and horror of her childish heart; a fear that she could not express but sensed as it was communicated from her mother—fear of the future.

Not exactly of the starvation—they had been near to that often enough; not exactly of physical hurt—she had known blows and pain ever since she was a child. No, it was more than that—it was the horror of being the underdog, the fear of being trampled down, of being unable to rise, to keep going, to strike back.

Fear! Fear haunting her through all her childhood, and combined with it the smell of oil and sickness and the noise and vibration of engines!

Then New York! ... the sunshine on incredibly tall, glittering buildings ... pavements and people ... a ceaseless hustle and bustle ... and yet over it all the smell of crisp clean air.

It was all vast, imposing and magnificent, and there was born in that little Irish emigrant the desire to be magnificent too, to be on top of this wonderful new world rather than underneath—to be somebody.

'They're just people,' Clement Hayton had said to her once when she was poring over a magazine depicting important socialites at Palm Beach. 'Just people. Never forget that.'

And Hetty never had forgotten it.

Once in the London season, when she had been waiting, a Marchioness on one side of her, a Countess bearing one of the oldest names in English history on the other, she had seen approaching the most popular and best-looking of reigning monarchs.

18

That evening had been a climax in Hetty's career, she had worked hard for it; but it was Clement Hayton's dollars which had brought her a place in the line of those to be presented.

Clement Hayton's dollars made cruelly and often bestially, made by the shrewd hard dealings which had injured and crippled thousands of people.

Now being lavishly expended by his wife in bolstering up a charity whose main object was to care for destitute children—just such a child as Clement Hayton had once been himself.

And as Hetty waited, conscious for a moment of a sudden singing in her ears and a failing at her knees now that the occasion for which she had strained every nerve was upon her, she heard Clement Hayton's husky voice saying:

'They're just people, my dear, just people.'

How easy it had been really, once started, once one realised the greed of people, once one had found that inevitable weak spot. Money, money, and more money.

Was there a door in London that could not be opened with a golden key? If there was, Hetty had not found it. She became a legend.

'If you want to meet the new Ambassador, you'll find him at Hetty Hayton's.'

'They say the Shah of Persia has arrived in London?— ring up Hetty Hayton, she'll know. It's ten to one he's lunching there, anyway.'

Diplomats had found it convenient to use her and although some of the older aristocracy had tried to make it difficult at first, they, too had gradually capitulated.

'Your daughter has such a lovely voice ... what a pity she hasn't had it trained. But I must ask Signor Manuel to arrange it. Now don't you worry about the fees, I assure you he'll do it for me as a pleasure, and, anyway, how could one deny such a lovely child her chance—it would be a crime against art!'

Music lessons ... school fees ... stud fees ... subscriptions and allowances ... the things Hetty paid for those first years in London! Sometimes she wondered herself where they would ever end.

And the rubbish she bought, but which was worth its weight in gold in other ways—family pictures ... first editions ... ancient buildings ... silver ... brass ...

It was extraordinary how a badly faked Gainsborough could prove an open sesame into a circle which had done its best to bar her out, but nothing and nobody could eventually keep Hetty Hayton at bay.

Her parties became the vogue. Sometimes when she read the list of her guests brought to her every morning after breakfast by Alice Farley, she would lie back against her lace pillows and wonder if it was really true.

Hetty Hayton entertaining the Duke of this and the Earl of that ... Hetty Hayton at whose house a new European Ambassador would make his first appearance after presenting his credentials at St. James's Palace. ...

Hetty Hayton who would entertain casually and informally half the uncrowned heads of Europe and appear to think nothing of it.

It was funny, screamingly funny really, only she had no one with whom to laugh.

Sometimes it seemed to her that she missed Clement Hayton unbearably. How he would have enjoyed this—and yet she knew with that sound common sense of hers that this could never have happened while Clement lived.

Not all the gold in the world would have persuaded people to accept that coarse, diseased old man.

With her it was different, she had been educated in appearances as well as in manners, her clothes and jewels were just right—the choice of experts—her manner held just the approved note of arrogant insolence to appear discerningly well-bred.

She kept to the accepted social standard in public. It was only in private that she could cock a snook at the transfigured elegance of Hetty Hayton, the cosmopolitan who had once been Hetty O'Reilly of Ohio.

So much achieved! but there was more to come, and it was here that Hetty began to think about Clive Ross.

'Mr. Ross is coming down tomorrow, Alice,' she said.

'He is staying, Mrs. Hayton?

'Yes. The Lilac Room is empty, isn't it?'

20

'I'll put him there,' Alice Farley answered.

Hetty glanced in the mirror at her reflection, waited for some look or sign from Alice, but there was none.

'I wonder what she thinks?' she thought to herself.

Then realised it was odd for her to wonder what Alice was thinking. If she hadn't thought in the years that had passed, then she must be more of a fool than Hetty believed her to be; yet if she had thought she would certainly not have forgotten.

Alice never forgot. The last time the Lilac Room had been used by . . . but why think about it?

'Watkins, you're taking a very long time,' Hetty said sharply.

'I've finished now, madam. There's very little curl in your hair at the back—I think you will have to have another permanent wave.'

Watkins was hitting back. Hetty hated having a permanent wave and she knew it.

'Two R.A.F. men are coming today and Stella Marsden,' Hetty announced.

'Lady Marsden!' Alice exclaimed.

'Yes, Clive operated on her—didn't I tell you?'

'No—no, you didn't. How interesting. So she's better, is she?'

'Alice knows quite well,' Hetty thought to herself, 'that I didn't know that Clive had operated on Stella Marsden. Why did I say that? If I go on like this Alice will know I'm making a fool of myself about the man.'

'And aren't you?' something asked inside her.

'Which room is Lady Marsden to have?' Alice Farley inquired.

'Oh, she must be in one of the best.'

'The Dolphin room, then; I'm glad she is coming here. I expect Mr. Ross wants to use that new treatment on her that has just arrived from America.'

'And a nice lot of money it's cost me,' Hetty said sharply. 'Have I paid for it yet?'

'You paid the cheque last week—don't you remember?'

'How much was it?' Hetty asked, knowing quite well but wanting to have the pleasure of hearing Alice say it.

'Two thousand five hundred dollars.'

'Well, I hope Clive is pleased, that's all.'

'He ought to be,' Alice Farley said, 'indeed he ought to be.'

Hetty got up with a self-satisfied sigh.

'There's no convalescent home in the country that has the equipment I've provided here.'

'Everyone says that,' Alice said eagerly. 'Don't you remember the Prime Minister. . . .'

'Yes, yes, I remember,' Hetty said. 'But do you think that Clive realises all I have done for him?'

'I'm sure Mr. Ross is grateful.'

'He certainly doesn't over-elaborate the point.'

'Mr. Ross is a Scot.'

'What's that got to do with it?'

'The Scots are not demonstrative.'

'Hmm.' Hetty thought back. 'Do you remember Lord Borragh?—he was certainly demonstrative enough!'

She looked at Alice's face and burst out laughing.

She was always safe to tease Alice on this particular point which embarrassed and annoyed her.

It happened soon after Hetty had come to London and Alice had been with her only a few weeks. Hetty was only feeling her way from a palatial suite at Claridge's. A message had come up that Lord Borragh wanted to see her.

'Who is Lord Borragh and who has sent him?' she asked Alice who was as mystified as she was herself.

Lord Borragh had been announced. He was a charming young man who told Hetty that he had heard both of her charms and of her generosity.

He told her quite frankly that he had been advised to see her, as he was collecting for a special charity of which he was the Chairman—afterwards she could never remember what the charity was.

'Now we have met,' he said, 'perhaps you will do me the honour of dining with my family one evening?'

Hetty was fascinated and enthralled. Lord Borragh left with a cheque for three hundred pounds.

He forgot to leave his address and they never heard of him again save when the cheque came back from the bank, duly endorsed, having been cashed within ten minutes of his lordship's interview with Hetty.

Alice blamed herself.

'I ought to have known,' she said; and she bought a Debrett and a *Who's Who* the same day.

Hetty had learned her lesson, she was not in such a hurry to write cheques in the future. She paid, but she paid when she had received something in return. The word went round quickly.

'My dear, she'll give you hundreds if you ask her, but she'll expect to come to dinner for it first and if it's worth-while she'll often add another hundred—it depends whom you ask her to meet.'

That was before Hetty herself became exclusive. The gossip writers, the hangers-on and the aristocracy who were down on their uppers, had a fine time those first years in London and they made the most of it.

Then gradually—so gradually that outsiders hardly noticed the transition stage—Hetty became powerful. From asking favours she was dispensing them, from being easy she became difficult, from wanting things she had got them.

'Well, I hope Clive is grateful,' Hetty repeated.

She gave her reflection in the looking-glass a last glance. cessful woman.

At forty she was a very pretty, very smart and very suc-

3

Stella Marsden awoke early and lay quietly taking in her surroundings.

She had been too exhausted the night before when she arrived at Trenton Park to care where she was so long as she could close her eyes and sleep.

Now she looked round her and noted in the pale light

coming through the silk curtains that the room she occupied was both luxurious and beautiful.

The morning breeze blew the curtains forward and each time they moved more of the room was revealed to Stella.

The great bed in which she lay—of carved wood painted gold with chiffon and silk hangings suspended from a canopy composed of trumpeting angels and gilt dolphins; the furniture which matched the bed—marble table tops resting on a profusion of dolphins, cupids, and bare-breasted goddesses.

'It's florid, and yet it's lovely,' Stella thought.

Trenton Park! Stella made herself think of the name and then she remembered Mrs. Hayton.

Of course—it was she who had bought it some years before the war from a family who had owned it for many generations.

Stella remembered the comments about it at the time, the talk of how the ancestral homes of England were not only becoming Americanised but losing their historical significance.

Hetty Hayton herself, Stella thought, was a tiresome woman. She remembered meeting her once or twice and disliking her. She had always refused the invitations to her spectacular and much publicised parties.

Philip had gone to some of them but she had preferred to steer clear of 'the Hetty Hayton set'.

Funny how immeasurably long ago that sort of thing seemed—sets and cliques, social intrigue—how she had loathed every moment of it and yet how essential it was to most of her friends. And now here she was in Hetty Hayton's house.

That wasn't to mean that she was content to drift back into the same little world again.

Clive Ross had sent her here and Clive Ross would have to protect her—and yet supposing he didn't or couldn't, did it matter?

Stella let herself sink down into her pillows.

'What does it matter?' she asked. 'What the hell does anything matter?'

If only she had been able to die as she had wanted.

24

Death? Could anything in the world be more desirable?—to escape from everything and from oneself, to find release from the almost intolerable burden of feeling and suffering.

Stella shut her eyes.

Oh, to sink away into the darkness, to disintegrate, to desire nothing, to know that finally and irretrievably one had reached the end of a chapter. But her mind held her just as firmly as her body encompassed her mind.

She felt the freshness of the morning breeze on her face, there was the fragrance of flowers, the rustle of the curtains moving and far away in the distance the burr of a mowing machine cutting the grass. Life went on and—there was no escape as yet.

Stella heard the nurse enter the room and watched her draw back the curtains.

'You've had a good night,' she said cheerily. 'No pain?'

'Nothing very bad,' Stella answered. 'The sleeping draught you gave me last night was the best I've had.'

'Mr. Ross was sure it would suit you,' the nurse answered. 'I'll tell him when he comes today that he was right.'

'Is he coming today?'

'He is, and I believe he's going to prescribe a special treatment for you, something very new which has only recently arrived here from America.'

The nurse spoke as if she was offering her patient something particularly succulent and delicious. Stella turned her head away with a weariness which held in it something of dismay.

She didn't want special treatment, she wanted to be allowed to die without thought and without interference as she had lain for the last four weeks.

'If anyone but Clive Ross had attended me,' she thought, 'I should have died. It would be just my luck for him to be there of all unexpected places at that particular moment.'

She knew quite well that the nurses looked on the operation he had performed on her as something of a miracle.

'It's simply amazing what he can do,' her day-nurse had

told her in an outburst of enthusiasm which would not be repressed. 'He literally reconstructed your body inside. But then Mr. Ross has almost revolutionised surgery in this country, none of us have ever seen anything like it.

'He seems to mould the muscles and tissues back into their proper shape. If I was you, Lady Marsden, I wouldn't know how to begin to thank him.'

They thought her ungrateful, Stella knew that, and she supposed she was.

If she had to live she was glad that Clive Ross would eventually make her body serviceable, or—as one nurse put it—'almost better than new'.

But she didn't want to live and she resented his having been there to prevent her from dying. Poor little Richardson, white-faced and anxious, he wouldn't have known how to treat her. Clive Ross knew, and Clive Ross had apparently done the impossible!

'How tiresome, how interfering and obstructive of him!' she cried.

Yet she knew in her heart that it was nothing to do with her particularly, he would have treated any woman the same because there was some force within him which liked to defeat death, to snatch a victim away from the inevitable at the eleventh hour.

She remembered the first time, indeed the only time, that she had met Clive Ross in the past. One of Philip's 'friends' had had an accident while riding. Clive Ross had been called in.

Stella had met him on the stairs. She would have passed him with a formal greeting if he had not stopped.

'When I arrived here this morning, Lady Marsden,' he said, 'I nearly knocked down one of your dogs as I drove up to the door. It was a close thing, and if you will forgive my suggesting it, no dog ought to be allowed outside a London house except on a lead.'

Stella looked at him coldly.

'It must have escaped from the servants,' she said. 'I will speak about it.'

Her tone had been indifferent and Clive would have turned away; then he stopped.

'You are fond of dogs?' he asked.

He looked at her and it seemed to her that in that instant as if he looked deep down into her mind, as if he stripped aside the superficial beauty and elegance of her appearance, as if he saw what was in her heart.

Despite years of training, despite the building up of what she believed was an impenetrable reserve, she spoke impulsively.

'I used to be.'

'Get out more—take them for walks. If you can spare a week-end, give yourself and the poor little devils a run without their leads in the countryside.'

He was gone before she could answer him.

She had stood still where he had left her, feeling curiously shaken, aware that for the first time for years somebody had known the truth about her, had seen how near she was to breaking-point.

She hadn't even known his name until Philip had told her, adding a few words regarding his reputation.

Clive Ross!—she had never forgotten, and had known him in that first moment of consciousness when she had found him kneeling beside her and had guessed that he meant to drag her back by some magic of his own from what had been so very nearly a merciful release. . . .

'Mrs. Hayton has sent you a message,' Nurse was saying. 'She said if there was anything you liked would you please ask for it. She hopes to see you when you are strong enough to have visitors.'

'Thank her,' Stella said perfunctorily.

'And is there anything you would like?' Nurse asked cheerily.

Stella shook her head. She imagined there was a faint disappointment on the nurse's face.

'Perhaps she's wishing she could be asked the same question,' Stella thought.

She wondered what the nurse would ask for. Clothes? . . . diamonds? . . . 'Is there anything you would like, anything in the world?' What woman would not respond to such a question, except herself?

'Give me death.' What an answer to a simple question!

27

She had asked it of only one person, one man—Clive Ross, and he had refused it her.

The nurse came back into the room.

'Now we must make you look beautiful,' she said. 'What coloured nightgown and dressing-jacket would you like to wear today?'

Stella set her lips in a hard line.

'I won't be coerced into making decisions,' she thought to herself, 'it's part of their plan to make the patient interested'.

Then she had a sudden vision of herself with compressed lips, sulky, like a naughty child. It was all so humiliating, so unnecessary and tiresome.

'Pink will do,' she said, saying the first colour which came into her head.

Apparently Nurse was satisfied for the moment.

'I hoped you'd say that,' she exclaimed, 'it will go well with the room, won't it? There are the most lovely flowers waiting for you outside and a delicious breakfast, but you'll feel more like that after I've washed you.'

'If only I could be anaesthestised against all this!' Stella found she had spoken her thoughts aloud.

'Now, Lady Marsden, you've got to make a little effort you know, you can't make us do all the work for you. That's just what Mr. Ross said two days ago—"She's got to make an effort for herself".'

'And if I don't?'

'Oh, but you will; everyone does what Mr. Ross wants.'

'What an impossible person he must be at home.'

'Oh, I don't know, we all think he's wonderful. Sometimes he's abrupt and difficult with his nurses but then one can forgive anything of a man who is as brilliant as that.'

'Is brilliance in one direction an excuse for a lack of virtue in another?' Stella asked.

The nurse looked at her uncomprehendingly.

'I don't think Mr. Ross lacks any virtue,' she said.

Stella closed her eyes. She let the nurse move her about and wash her as if she were an inanimate form.

She knew if she lay with closed eyes she would not be

spoken to and for the moment she could not prevent her own thoughts flooding over her.

Brilliance! Brilliance of brain and intellect! How often had she made that an excuse to herself, listened to it as an excuse from other people.

'But then, Philip's so brilliant.'

'Of course, Sir Philip is brilliant; isn't he, Lady Marsden?'

The glittering surface, the dazzling tinsel which distracted one's eyes from what lay beneath.

And behind the lip service, the praise coming so facilely not from conviction but because it was the fashionable thing to do, she had sensed the cynical sneers and—what was harder to bear—the compassion and sympathy.

Brilliant! Brilliant! Brilliant!—how she loathed the word, it haunted her. Philip's brilliance, his amazing mental powers, his intelligence, his culture, his intellectualism—all that and so much more besides.

So much that she knew but other people only guessed at. So much which had drained all happiness from her at twenty-two and left her—a beautiful woman, but only a husk.

She would never gorget her first encounter with Philip's brilliance—that word must always be ineradicably connected in her mind with him.

Their meeting was conventional—a cynical prelude, perhaps, to unconventionality—at one of the first balls she had ever attended in London.

She had been so excited at receiving an invitation from a godmother who, with the exception of an expensively-bound prayer-book which she had received on her confirmation, had ignored her consistently since she had been christened.

It must have been by sheer chance that she had been asked on this occasion.

'Ethie has a daughter—let's ask her. We're a girl short and incidentally I believe she's my godchild.'

Just chance that she had been invited at all; perhaps her godmother, fashionable, casual, and with no particular im-

29

pulse of kindliness had been glancing through the K's in her address book.

There was no reasonable explanation why a little country bumpkin should have been invited to one of the most brilliant balls of the London season.

She had been reluctant to go at first—the usual excuse,

'I've got nothing to wear.'

But her mother had insisted—so gentle, so sweet, and so utterly unworldly in her insistence.

'Our little Stella would look lovely whatever she wore, wouldn't she, Arthur?'

'You'll be the belle of the ball, my dear, just as your mother was fifty years ago when I first saw her.'

She could see the dear old couple were planning such happy romantic things for her and somehow she had grown excited herself, reflecting their enthusiasm.

It was a mistake, Stella thought, to be the only child of old parents.

It had not been their fault, they had loved children, always wanted them, but a hunting accident had crippled her mother for years; then unexpectedly, when doctor after doctor had tried and failed, one succeeded in getting her right.

Quite a slight operation and Stella was born, but Lady Knowles was too frail to have any more children.

Their one ewe lamb, petted, cosseted, brought up in an almost overwhelming atmosphere for love and affection—they had taken it for granted that their child would be beautiful, but how beautiful they had no idea until after she married Philip.

Then the whole social world acclaimed what they had kept to themselves in the old Manor House among the orchards of Herefordshire.

It had been a struggle to find a dress for that dance, Stella remembered.

'You must have something really lovely,' her parents agreed;

The question was, how was it to be paid for?

Her mother's operations had eaten heavily into what remaining capital the family possessed. Generations of extravagant Knowleses had dissipated a fortune which had been founded in the reign of Queen Elizabeth.

Once they had lived in splendour, owners of vast estates and fine houses; now the Dower House and a few acres of land were all that remained.

The Dower House was small and home-like, sufficient indeed for Arthur Knowles and the woman he had loved all his life despite her infirmities.

Sufficient, too, for their daughter save that occasionally she wondered what the world was like outside.

Stella had not been ambitious or restless; she had her animals—three dogs who were her special companions, they seldom left her side—and when she felt that life at home was cramping or monotonous she would walk off her discontent.

Walk until they were tired and footsore, the wind on her face, the sun on her hair. She had been happy—how happy she did not know until years later.

The dress which when they finally chose—it meant a special journey to the big market town—had indeed seemed a dream of loveliness.

'A French model, modom,' the saleswoman assured them.

Stella learnt later how utterly English both in conception and design it had been, but at that moment she would have believed the saleswoman if she had been told it came from the moon.

What matter?—it became her well enough!

It was of delicate white lace and it transformed her from a sun-kissed, healthy-looking young woman into something ethereal and breath-taking.

Her dark hair—not so dark that it did not hold at times glints of burnished light—was cut and dressed by a local hairdresser; a manicure for the first time in her life.

Finally the transformation was complete, Cinderella went to London.

She was always to remember her first chaotic impressions of a London ballroom, her feeling of insignificance and her desire above all others that the ground should open and swallow her up, of the nostalgic longing for home, for places that were familiar, for those three uncritical friends who had been left behind whining miserably.

Then the amazing thing had happened.

Her godmother had sought her out as she had stood shyly beside a young man to whom she had been introduced at dinner, searching her brain for something to say to him.

'Stella, my dear,' the soft gushing voice claimed her attention, 'Sir Philip Marsden wants to meet you. Philip— my goddaughter, Stella Knowles.'

'Shall we dance?'

She had hardly formed her first impressions of him before she was in his arms.

Tall, thin, amazingly handsome, it was not surprising that she found herself gasping a little, looking up at him with wide blue eyes and his first remark took her breath away.

'You are very lovely, Star of the sea. Why haven't I seen you before?'

He had been like a comet flashing across her heaven, dazzling her, mesmerising her with his brilliance. He had talked brilliantly that night, at least so it had seemed to her.

She had felt intoxicated with the excitement of it. She had not realised what a sensation she was causing.

'Who is the girl with Philip Marsden? They've danced together all the evening! I've never known Philip to pay any attention to anyone as young as that before.'

'Of course he's brilliant, but I'm glad it's not my daughter.'

Two years later she would have known what they were saying—then she was concerned with nothing but the almost suffocating feeling of excitement which was rising in her throat. It was not surprising that her eyes were like stars, as Philip told her they were before the end of their second dance together.

She couldn't sleep that night—she had been blinded, intoxicated, dazzled by a brilliance such as she had never imagined, not even in her dreams.

## 4

Clive Ross finished his examination and with a slight gesture dismissed the nurse from the room.

When she had gone he stood for a moment looking down at Stella, then drew up a chair to sit down beside the bed.

'I want to talk to you.'

Stella looked at him and a faint smile touched her lips.

'You needn't say it,' she replied.

'Then why don't you try?' Clive asked. 'You know as well as I do that I can't do all the work for you. The operation has been successful.'

'Yes, I know,' Stella said. 'As the nurses have told me a thousand times—if it hadn't been for you I should have been dead ... if it hadn't been for you I should have been a cripple for life ... if it hadn't been for you I should never have been able to walk again! I have to thank you for living and for moving, but quite frankly. . . .'

'You don't want to do either.'

'That's right, you know the answers too, so don't let's worry about the little talk.'

Clive frowned; somehow it made him look merely non-plussed, not formidable.

'You puzzle me, Lady Marsden.'

'Does it matter?'

Stella spoke wearily.

'It matters to me very much. If you heard me talking to the students, telling how first and foremost it was important to gain the confidence and co-operation of their patients, you would understand. As it is, you are making me set a bad example.'

'So you are afraid of failing where I'm concerned?'

'I'm going to fail unless you help me.'

Stella smiled again, cynically this time.

'If the patient won't respond to one method, try another—there are various avenues of approach.'

This time Clive laughed spontaneously.

'If a doctor was allowed to be really human,' he said, 'I'd say—Die, then, and go to the devil!'

'I wish you would,' Stella retorted. 'It's what I've been wanting for a long time.'

'But why?—in God's name why?' Clive asked, speaking with an almost surprising violence.

Stella stared at him and then her eyes closed as if she was too tired to continue the conversation. Clive bent forward over the bed and felt her pulse.

'I'm going to be rude,' he said, 'and you won't like it. You're not nearly as ill now as you are making yourself think you are.

'You're not well by any means and you won't be for a long time; but we can't let matters rest as they are, we can't allow you to hold up your own recovery simply through some whim, some fancy of your own.'

Stella's eyes were still closed, she made no response, and yet he knew she was listening.

'You've got so much,' he went on, 'and so much to look forward to. You are a young woman with great beauty, an important position and, if popular rumour is to be believed, great possessions.

'You can have most things in the world and yet at the moment you are content to lie here deliberately fighting recovery because of some ridiculous fancy which makes you say you want to die. Nobody wants to die—nobody—or if they do I have yet to meet them.'

He paused but as she made no response, continued.

'You imagine you are unhappy; you may be, but unhappiness should not mean defeat; it should stir you to a desire to escape from it, to conquer it, to emerge stronger and more courageous. Forget about yourself for a little while and see if you can help other less fortunate people.'

Clive had spoken quickly and with a force which made his words so powerful as to be almost mesmeric even while he neither raised his voice nor made a gesture while speaking.

Stella's eyes had opened as he spoke and her glance was fixed upon him, her lips parted, her head thrown back against the pillow.

She was very beautiful as she lay there, but it was a beauty which lacked all animation; it might have been the mask of a face carved in marble by some skilful sculptor.

As he finished speaking Clive bent forward and after a short pause he said gently in a tone such as one would use to a recalcitrant child:

'What do you really want? Won't you tell me?'

Just for a moment it seemed as if Stella was going to speak, to pour out what was in her innermost heart; and then he knew he had failed, her reserve was impenetrable.

'You know what I want,' she said dully, and Clive was conscious of a sense of frustration.

He got up from the bedside and walked towards the window.

'Well, let's forget it,' he said at length, with his back to the bed. 'You are determined to be one of my failures, Lady Marsden—I do have them occasionally.'

Stella made no sign. A moment later he left the room and she was alone.

As he came into the sitting-room a little later where Hetty Hayton was waiting for him, he looked tired. Hetty rose to meet him and drew him over to the tea-table which was laid in front of a log fire.

'You've had a long week,' she said sympathetically.

'I am pretty tired,' Clive confessed. 'It's nice to think I can stay here tonight in the country air.'

'You know we love to have you.'

She poured out his tea in an extra large cup which was kept especially for his visits. Alice had a book in which were written all the peculiarities and specialities of the guests who came to Trenton Park.

People who liked two hot-water-bottles in their beds and those who liked no hot-water-bottles at all; whether guests preferred tea or coffee in the morning; those who started the day with orange juice; the men whose favourite reading was the *Financial Times;* the women who wanted

35

a special diet or hot drinking water brought to them at strange hours.

It was a useful book and, conscientiously kept by Alice, it had done much to gain Hetty her reputation of a perfect hostess.

'The most comfortable palace in Europe,' was how someone in the Diplomatic Service had once described Trenton Park.

It would be difficult for most guests not to find charming a hostess who gave them so much consideration.

'Your favourite scones,' Hetty said, passing them to Clive. 'Cook made them as soon as she heard you were coming.'

'You must tell her I appreciate them,' Clive smiled.

He split one open and added the thick yellow butter which came from Hetty Hayton's herd of pedigree Jerseys.

'It is hard to realise there's a war on in this house,' he added.

'Unless one looks at those poor boys upstairs,' she replied softly.

Clive nodded, instantly becoming the doctor again.

'I'm worried about Flight-Lieutenant Jarvis, he isn't reacting to treatment as he should.'

'But he will,' Hetty said cheerily. 'Don't you worry, Clive dear, he hasn't been here long enough yet. Trenton Park never fails.'

'That's true,' Clive observed with a noticeable sigh of relief. 'I keep my worst cases for you and you work miracles with them.'

'It is you who work the miracles,' Hetty replied. 'We merely try to help a little, but I think we succeed. That new equipment, for instance. . . .'

'It's good,' Clive interjected, 'very good. I want to try it on Lady Marsden as soon as she is strong enough.'

'And how is dear Stella? I'm longing to see her, but you see how scrupulous I am to obey your instructions. Nurse said you had ordered no visitors, and until you countermand the order even I keep away.'

'I don't think she wants to see anyone yet,' Clive said.

There was a pause while he appeared to be considering something intently, then he asked:

'Her parents are dead, aren't they?'

'Yes, fairly recently, there was less than a year between their deaths. But what about her very close friends, wouldn't she like to see them—or should I say him?'

There was an innuendo in Hetty's voice which could not be ignored, but Clive did not respond to it.

He had made the rule that he would not discuss his patients' health with anyone and he had extended this rule where his more social clients were involved so that their private lives remained private so far as he was concerned.

He picked up his cup which was now empty and held it out to Hetty.

'May I have another cup of tea?'

'I know exactly why you are changing the subject,' she smiled: 'but did you know that Stella was practically engaged to Bertram Armstrong?'

'The polo player?'

Hetty nodded.

'Such a charming boy. Everybody imagined that they were waiting the prescribed year of mourning after Philip's death. I can't understand what has happened now. Hasn't he tried to see her?'

Clive looked at Hetty with one of those sudden smiles which made him look his most attractive.

'You know I never discuss these things.'

Hetty sighed.

'You're inhuman.'

'I've been told that before. Must I apologise for it again?'

'I confess to being a very curious woman and I'm not ashamed of it; but if you want to know the truth, Stella's nurse told me you were worried about her and I wondered if the answer doesn't lie with Bertie Armstrong. She was crazy about him.'

'Did you know her well?' Clive asked.

Hetty shook her head.

'Not very. I always found Philip far the more amusing

of the two. A charming man of great intelligence—his death was a tragedy.'

Clive said nothing and Hetty went on:

'Of course there were stories about him; that wasn't surprising, one hears incredible tales about anyone in public life and Philip was too good-looking and too successful not to be shot at.'

Clive pulled out his cigarette case.

'Do you mind if I smoke?'

'Of course not.'

'You don't, do you?'

'No, I have no public vices,' Hetty said glibly, as she had said a thousand times before, and then as she watched him strike a match she thought suddenly:

'He's interested in Stella Marsden' and something cold and icy gripped at that part of her anatomy which she called her heart.

'Tell me what you have been doing this week,' she asked brightly, determined to take his thoughts away from the woman upstairs.

'I'm being ridiculous,' she told herself; 'Clive has never been known to like one of his own patients, there's never been a whisper of scandal about him. But Stella Marsden ... she's damnably beautiful.'

Deliberately Hetty shook herself of the imaginings poisoning her. She made Clive talk of his hospital in London, of the experiments he was making in the children's ward—a project which she knew was very close to his heart.

But all the time at the back of her mind a question was asking itself over and over again.

For the first time in her life Hetty was interested in a man because he was a man and not because he had something to offer her.

She could not remember now when she had first become aware of Clive as a person rather than a personality. She had heard of him long before she met him for it became fashionable to go to him.

Then when he was asked to operate on a royal prince

38

who had a bad motor smash, it carried him swiftly to the pinnacle of social fame.

Clive fed the legends about himself by being completely and un-self-consciously disinterested in his own reputation.

As he put it himself, he was an experimentalist; he didn't want simply to build up a huge following because he was a successful surgeon.

His job, as he saw it, was to restore battered and bruised tissues to health and well-being; whether he did it with his own skill with a knife or whether he found instruments and appliances to do it for him was quite immaterial.

There were doctors in Harley Street who thought him a fool because he would send away rich patients who wanted an operation and make them take a course of treatment which would produce the same effect without his help.

When he did operate, he was, as the nurses said, more of a sculptor than anything else; he moulded a body back to its true form, and his own colleagues averred that it was because of some genius within himself rather than the result of surgery.

As he grew more and more popular Clive refused to take any but the most serious cases.

It didn't matter how famous or how important a patient might be, unless he considered the operation warranted his special skill he would send the man or woman away to another doctor.

Instead of annoying people this merely increased their desire to be attended by him. It became not only the smart thing to be operated upon by Clive Ross but also it gave one the cachet of having been really ill.

Hetty had noted all this in the agile brain of hers which recorded anyone of importance as a potential ace which she might wish to use sometime in the future.

Then just before the war started she had met Clive at one of my luncheons,' she asked, 'luncheons to which all ing, and she thought him attractive.

They had talked and she had been fascinated by him so that afterwards she had found herself thinking and speculating about the tall, broad-shouldered surgeon with keen clear-cut features and long sensitive fingers.

Hetty asked him to luncheon; he refused.

She asked him again and once again he refused—a brief note of refusal written impersonally in the third person by his secretary. She was piqued.

'Doesn't this man realise it is an honour to be asked to one of my luncheons' she asked, 'luncheons to which all the most important people in London are delighted to be invited?'

She tried dinner with the same result.

It was then that Hetty Hayton became really interested. She had become almost satiated with the ease with which the social world had fallen at her feet in the past few years. She determined to get hold of Clive Ross, and when Hetty determined anything obstacles never proved themselves very formidable.

She was not ill herself so that could not be the obvious way of approach, but Alice was dispatched on a certain errand and came back with the information she required.

There was a child in the mews where Hetty garaged her cars; with some obscure affliction of the leg and thigh which the local doctors had found impossible to diagnose and still more impossible to treat.

It was exactly what Hetty required. She went to see Clive Ross, intent on her errand of mercy.

'A protégée of mine,' she told him, 'and I am determined that if it is possible the child shall be cured—it doesn't matter what it costs, I want her treated as if she were my own daughter—the daughter I have never been able to have.'

Clive was interested, as she had meant him to be.

After that he was not so difficult and it was comparatively easy when the war started to persuade him to take over Trenton Park and make it a convalescent home for all his more serious cases. Hetty paid for everything.

'My little contribution to the war effort,' she called it.

Clive was grateful to her in his own quiet, undemonstrative way, fondly believing, however, that she did it entirely impersonally and having no idea that he was the focal point from which all her lavishness emanated.

In other ways, though, Clive had proved surprisingly difficult.

To begin with, he was formal to what was to Hetty the point of exasperation. She called him Clive early on in what she termed their friendship. To him she remained Mrs. Hayton.

She addressed him affectionately and even coquettishly, but his courtesy towards her never altered—a courtesy cool and impeccable, but which was discouraging.

Hetty had been taught long ago in America not to rush her fences, but it appeared to her sometimes that she must be prepared to give up a whole lifetime if she were ever to win Clive Ross.

She admitted frankly to herself that she was falling in love, and her appetite was only whetted by the patience she must expend to win a man who apparently had no interest outside his work.

If only Clive had been ambitious Hetty would have found it easy—that she would understand; if he had wanted money it would have been still easier.

But he had enough for his requirements and although he was pleased to use Trenton Park and all the amazing equipment that she provided within it, she had always the uneasy feeling that if it were not her money which paid there would be other purses ready to give Clive what he required.

Restlessly Hetty had tried more than once to accelerate their friendship, to make Clive reciprocate in some little way her feelings towards him, but always she failed.

'Is the man human?' she asked herself more than once, and looking at her reflection in the glass felt that he was not.

'I can give him so much—so much!' she whispered, then knew that was not true.

There was little that she could give Clive that he had not got already. What was there about the man, not only that he should attract her, but that he should be able to resist her attraction for him?

41

Now as Clive lit a cigarette at her tea-table Hetty knew she was experiencing a new emotion where he was concerned—jealousy.

She was jealous of Stella Marsden, jealous of all the women in whom Clive was interested, on whom he spent his time and his skill.

Looking back over the years that were past she could not remember ever feeling quite like this before. She had been envious since she could remember of the good fortune of others, their wealth, their position, their fame, but not jealous as a woman is of the man she loves.

'Of the man she loves.' Hetty repeated the words within her heart and felt the pain of them.

She loved Clive—she desired him with a passion all the more volcanic because it had been denied so long.

'I will get him' she vowed, 'if it's the last thing I do.'

5

When Clive had left the room Stella lay very still.

'I won't think about him,' she told herself; 'I won't let what he has said disturb me.'

She heard the door on the other side of the room open and knew the nurse had come in. But she lay still, feigning sleep, so that she would not be talked to.

The nurse moved quietly about the room, the starchiness of her apron rustling as she walked, then she went away and Stella was alone.

'I'll sleep,' she thought.

She tried to compose her mind into an utter blankness, but suddenly, vivid against the darkness of her lids, she saw Philip's face.

He was smiling that cynical twisted smile of his which had become characteristic as he grew older when he lost a little of the spontaneity and easy charm that had been his when she first knew him.

She stirred and opened her eyes to dispel the memories that were pressing in upon her; but it was no use, she could not escape them, they held her captive, forcing themselves upon her attention.

Still she could see Philip's face, mocking her, it seemed, in her desire to forget him.

Her happiest moment had been when she had come down the aisle of the little country church on his arm. How confident she had been of the future then, elated with her happiness, with the wonder and the splendour of the life to which she was going!

But it was not only the glamour which uplifted her although that was enough, with Philip's wealth, ancient name, the treasures at Marsden House and his position in politics.

'He'll be in the Cabinet before he's forty,' people told her, and she had been ready enough to believe them.

Nothing could be impossible for Philip. But deeper than her appreciation of all that he was offering her was something else—a love for him which she could feel growing and blossoming beneath his kindness, his admiration and what she believed was his love for her.

'How young I was—how gullible!' Stella thought.

Yet she knew that any girl, even one more assured and sophisticated then she had been, would have been deceived by Philip's love-making. In all things he was an artist, in all things he was an actor.

In the years that she lived with Philip she never knew him do a gauche thing or make an unconsidered statement.

If he was rude, he was rude intentionally. People bored him and he ignored them; he grew impatient both with men and events; but he was intensely cultured, there was nothing gross even in his licentiousness.

He was fastidious to the finest point of good taste and he was a connoisseur of beauty. That, Stella learnt later, was why he had chosen her.

He saw beneath the unpolished exterior just how beautiful she could be, he glimpsed the elegance which was hers

43

despite the misleading efforts of the local dressmaker and the local hairdresser.

'A Sleeping Princess' he told her once but mockingly.

Already, on her wedding day, she had begun to blossom forth towards the loveliness which was to be hers in two or three years' time.

Philip had chosen her dress, Philip had given her the perfect jewels which accentuated the whiteness of her skin, Philip had bought her bouquet of white orchids, their petals powdered faintly with pink spots.

'Spots of blood—heart blood,' Stella was to think resentfully in the years to come.

Nevertheless her artistic sense must respond to the artist in Philip even when she hated and loathed him for the creature that he was.

A young girl in love!—

No wonder she had looked radiant that June afternoon; no wonder her father and mother, sentimental and adoring, had wiped away tears not of sorrow at her departure, but of gladness because their beloved child was so happy.

She remembered trembling with excitement as she changed from her wedding dress to her going-away gown of soft powder blue—again Philip's choice—and the ospreys of the same colour which haloed her head made her look absurdly young.

She had run down the stairs from the small single bedroom which had been hers since a child.

'I am ready,' she said to Philip softly.

He turned to look at her with that piercing glance she was to know so well, a glance searching and critical.

Then he raised her hand to his lips, a courtly gesture with something romantic in it which made her catch her breath.

Those standing by smiled wistfully and enviously.

'Such a good-looking young couple! What girl could ask for a better match, or, indeed, a better catch?'

How little they knew!

But really no one could be blamed. If Philip was an artist. he was also exceedingly clever—clever enough to keep his private life hidden to a large extent even from

44

the prying curiosity of those who were always ready to scent a scandal, to destroy if possible the reputation of the 'man in office'.

There were those who suspected a good deal but who were not prepared or were too decent-minded to voice their speculations above a whisper.

There were whispers, of course, how could it be otherwise? But Stella's parents were not likely to hear them. No one raised a voice of warning.

In the years which followed Stella was to wonder who knew, who guessed, who suspected. Had Clive Ross been one of those who knew? She thought so, remembering that moment on the stairs.

She had suspected that behind his casual words there was a deeper meaning. He had seen Philip, he had seen the 'friend' on whose behalf he had been called in—one of many 'friends'.

Had he pitied and felt sorry for her?

Or had he merely treated her on the face value, noting professionally the lines under her eyes, the pain which occasionally when she was off her guard was there for all to see.

A pain deeper and more virulent that any physical one could be—the pain of disillusionment and horror, of a humiliation which she knew was indeed an utter degradation?

How well she remembered the first time she was sure, the first time she became utterly certain of what she had suspected for a long while.

She had been courageous enough to challenge Philip with her belief.

He had not denied any of the things of which she had accused him, merely looked at her with that smile on his face which grew later to typify for her the personification of evil.

'And you?' he said. 'You haven't given me the son that I wanted.'

She had turned from him then and run in a dream-like horror to her own room.

The snatch of a conversation which had haunted her for

a long time was explained at that moment—two women talking at one of the big parties she and Philip had given at Marsden House.

She had gone up to her bedroom unexpectedly and had heard what they were saying before they realised that she approached them.

'But why,' one asked, 'did he marry?'

'They always want a son,' the other replied. 'It is part of the set-up.'

'Yes they always want a son,' the other replied.

It was what Philip had wanted of her and nothing more.

She thought of how she had loved him, how on their honeymoon she had surrendered herself utterly with a passion which, springing from tenderness and an awakening love, had been something too beautiful and fragile to be called by a word which has so often been debased.

Dry-eyed, she had picked up her coat and gone home. She had taken nothing with her, leaving behind every jewel she possessed with the exception of her wedding ring.

She had come to Philip empty-handed, she told herself, she would not take away even one of his gifts.

She had ordered the car and driven without a break the five-and-a-half-hour journey—home.

As she reached the lovely familiar undulating country-side she had felt a quiet peace descend upon her. She was free; she had left all horror and misery behind her; she need worry no more.

It seemed that the car could not go fast enough to bring her to her parents, into the arms which she knew would be outstretched in welcome. As the car turned into the drive gate, she said to the chauffeur:

'You can take the car back tonight or first thing in the morning, whichever you wish. I shall not require you again.'

She would not want any of Philip's possessions again, she thought exultantly.

She was home, she was back where she belonged,

among decent people, people whom she loved and understood.

She had not announced her arrival, and her father and mother sprang up with glad cries of joy at the sight of her.

'Why didn't you let us know you were coming, darling, and is Philip with you? What a pity! We were just writing to him.'

'Writing to him,' Stella echoed stupidly.

'To thank him, darling. Didn't he tell you? How like him to keep his kind action hidden even from you.'

'What has he done?'

Even to her own ears her voice sounded strange.

Her father and mother told her. The mortgage which had been on the estate for years had been paid off. Ten thousand pounds, not a big sum to Philip, but to the Knowleses it was a fortune.

There were other evidences of his generosity. A new car—he had laughed at the old ramshackle barouche which had carried them about for years.

Her father and mother were as pleased with it as a child with a new toy; they told her of plans to improve the shooting, Philip was providing an experienced keeper.

It was the one sport her father loved, and it seemed to Stella that he looked younger, his eyes sparkling in anticipation. It was Philip this and Philip that . . .

'Your wonderful husband, darling; I don't know what we've done to deserve such a splendid son-in-law.'

She had stood there listening, unable to speak, unable to break the spell which bound them, not her. How could she tell them, how could she find the words to dash their happiness to the ground, tumble it in the dust?

In a few sentences she could turn their child-like excitement into horror and disgust. They would be at first incredulous, then stricken. She could not do it!

Philip had beaten her and she was wise enough to guess by this time that he had done it intentionally, had been prepared for just such a moment of panic or hysteria which might threaten his security.

He had been forearmed so that she was defeated before the battle even began, defeated utterly and completely. She would go back.

She had returned, and it was her first and last effort at defiance.

She grew up overnight as she lay awake in the house which had once been her home but now was but another of Philip's innumerable possessions. Now he possessed her whole world.

'And me, too,' Stella whispered.

That was the truth; he had bought her just as he had bought all the antiques which made Marsden House more of a museum than a home, as he bought the jewels, furs, and clothes which made her one of the most envied women in society.

They were his, not hers; she was a puppet on which he hung his goods.

She never forgot this in the years that followed. The great emeralds which Philip gave her at Christmas she accepted as a present purchased for himself.

He was lavish in his presents, for he kept up appearances with such grace and such skill that sometimes she found it hard to believe her own thoughts about him.

But always, underneath everything he did, she knew there was shrewdness and the calculating thought of one who is prepared for any contingency, however unlikely.

'Do I do you credit?' she had asked him once, bitterly, as she came downstairs ready for a Court ball.

Her dress of gold lamé moulded her figure and against it she wore the pigeon-blood rubies which Philip had recently bought in India for her. She was an exotic figure and yet breath-takingly lovely.

Philip looked at her with the pleasure which he extended to all *objets d'art*.

He paid her an extravagant compliment, in the delightful tones which he always used towards her and which deceived everyone save herself. She had not replied.

With that new dignity which had been born in her after her marriage she had preceded him through the great ornate hall to where their car was waiting outside. They had not spoken again until they were half-way towards Buckingham Palace, then Philip had said:

'I chose well, Stella, when I asked you to marry me.'

It was then that she had thrust at him bitterly:

'Save in one particular.'

They both knew to what she referred and he had turned towards her, seeking in the light of the street lamps to read the expression on her face.

'Would you still like a child?' he asked.

She had not expected the question from him and she had shrunk away from him in horror.

'Not now,' she said, 'never, never—not now I know.'

Then Philip had laughed.

'Perhaps after all I made a mistake,' he said cruelly. 'I should have chosen someone of my own world—the world that accepts the unexpected.'

'I wish to God you had,' Stella answered, '—but it is too late.'

There was more of a question than a statement in her words.

There was just a faint hope in her heart that Philip would let her go, that there was some way out, some way that she herself could not perceive.

But he had echoed her words finally and irrevocably:

'Yes, it is too late.'

And she had known then that he would not let her go.

She was useful to him, she was ornamental and he was as proud of her as he was of his paintings, of his library, and of his collection of snuff-boxes—just another possession and one she was sure it gave him pleasure to look at and to own.

There was no way out.

She had thought then of that old couple down in Herefordshire; she remembered their excitement and their pleasure over the things Philip continued to give them.

The last time she had seen her father he had talked incessantly of the shooting prospects for the autumn. By such straws she was held, straws which had the binding force of steel chains.

The car drew up at the Palace door. With her head held high Stella stepped out on to the red carpet.

How strange it seemed now, looking back on those years, that she could recall very little save of Philip. Her hatred of him and her repugnance to his very presence had filled her mind to the exclusion of all else.

She had acted as hostess in London, Paris and the South of France, she met everyone who was famous or notable in at least three worlds.

There were Philip's political friends and enemies, the world of art in which he was looked on as a kind of patron saint, and the changing kaleidoscope called society which fawned upon him because he was both rich and important.

People, and more people—famous, notorious, regal, witty and talented; yet to Stella they were just faces; she moved in their midst like a woman in a dream.

'Beautiful, but dumb,' was how she once heard someone describe her.

It was one of Philip's particular friends and she agreed with him.

'Dumb because I have nothing to say,' she thought to herself: 'dumb because I am living a life that is utterly detestable.'

Few people guessed how lonely she was. Sometimes when she had an hour to spare between the engagements which were recorded for her so ably by an efficient secretary she would wonder what to do with herself.

At home she was always conscious of Philip, of his influence, of his taste, so that the very books she drew out of the book-shelves would lose their attraction because he had chosen and paid for them.

Once she had dismissed her car and walked into the coolness of a little church.

She had sat there, wondering if she could find some peace from her misery, and despair, but she had been unable to pray.

She felt as if every motion within her was frozen—frozen into a hardness and into a detached, one-point concentration which was merely a hatred of her husband.

Then when she was nearly thirty, when she had believed herself to have become merely a mechanical doll, a squirrel in a revolving cage which must go on round because there's no other course open, she had met Bertram Armstrong.

She had been at Ranelagh watching Philip's polo team mounted on the best and most expensive ponies beat good and sporting opponents who had not, however, the horse-flesh with which to compete with them.

As she had watched, a silent spectator, her sunshade protecting her from the hot rays of the sun, she had heard a man's voice behind her say:

'Of course there's no doubt that Marsden can ride, but I never have liked him and I never will.'

Someone shushed the speaker into silence and then as the chukker ended and Stella rose to go to the pavilion she turned to see a woman she knew slightly with a tall, good-looking fair young man.

She had smiled; but the woman, obviously uncomfortable in case the conversation had been overheard, had risen to her feet, talking gushingly in her desire to eradicate a bad impression.

'Dear Lady Marsden, won't you come to tea on Thursday?—it would be so nice to see you. I've got the Belgian Ambassador coming—such a charming man and I know he is one of your devoted slaves.'

Stella had refused, pleading another engagement; but as she turned to go, the woman, still insistently friendly had said:

'If you are going up to the pavilion we will walk with you. When the game is finished perhaps you and Sir Philip will come and have a drink.'

It was then she had made a gesture towards her companion.

'By the way, I don't think you know Captain Armstrong.'

Stella bowed, but Bertram Armstrong held out his hand and she had been forced to extend hers.

As she felt his touch something strange happened, something within her quivered and came to life again, some-

51

thing which she believed to have been dead for eight years.

She raised her eyes to his, he was much taller than she was, and it seemed to her that his blue eyes held something besides admiration in the glance that he gave her.

A message, or was it merely recognition?—the melting of two people who were predestined to love each other. She was certain of nothing save that she suddenly felt young and unexpectedly gay.

She laughed and talked with ease as they walked towards the pavilion and when Philip was found to be changing, she sauntered away beside Bertram Armstrong into the shade of the trees on the tea lawn.

A conventional beginning, as conventional as her meeting with Philip, and yet it had changed her whole life for her in the months that followed.

Within a week she had known herself to be in love, and in love as she had never dreamt that she could be.

Once spring had come and supplanted the winter of her being, she knew a happiness she had never known in her life before. She was as glad and radiant as a young girl.

For Bertram, satiated with the charms of many women whom he had loved neither wisely nor too well, she had an attraction which he had never experienced before.

He, too, fell in love and it was like the meeting of two strong rivers.

They could neither hide the joy they felt in each other's arms because they were drawn one to the other by a magnet whose strength would not be denied.

So far as Stella was concerned she lived only for these moments of the day when Bertram was with her. When he was not there she thought of him and at night she dreamed of him.

For some time she was content, too content to ask herself where she was drifting or what this could possibly mean in her life.

Despite the life she had led and the people she had known she was amazingly innocent, and where her own feelings were concerned completely unsophisticated.

Then just at the height of their happiness, when Stella

was blossoming because of it into a new beauty she had never possessed before, war was declared.

As she thought of that moment Stella stirred restlessly in her great gold bed at Trenton Park. A stab of pain rewarded her reckless movement.

But she told herself that it was but a pale shadow of what she had felt when she had realised that war must inevitably separate her from Bertram.

'How I loved him!' she whispered.


# 6


It was jealousy more than curiosity which made Hetty turn towards the south wing when she went upstairs.

Alice was hovering on the landing, waiting to give her a message from Matron. She waved her on one side and moving down the thickly carpeted corridors reached the Dolphin suite.

Stella's nurse was filling in some charts, but she jumped to her feet at the sight of Mrs. Hayton and smiled a welcome.

All the nurses liked Hetty—she took care that they should. She was the perfect Commandante from their point of view, always pleasant, always gracious, yet apparently without any desire to criticise or interfere.

What was more, Hetty was wise enough to see that the good things of life were provided in the staff room. When there were peaches and grapes for the patients, there was also some allotted for the nurses.

This was appreciated, for in many private convalescent homes those on whom the well-being of the patients depend are often forgotten.

Hetty Hayton was a clever woman; she had heard too many comments on the behaviour of Americans towards servants not to watch her step very carefully.

Actually, underneath a superficial self-assurance and

well-learnt poise she was afraid of those whom she thought of as her 'inferiors'.

'How are you, Nurse?' Hetty asked now, holding out her hand in what she believed to be a truly democratic gesture.

'Very well, thank you, Mrs. Hayton. It's nice to be down here again.'

Nurse Benson was one of Clive's special nurses whom he kept for his most difficult cases. This was not the first time she had come to Trenton Park and she hoped it would be by no means the last.

'It's delightful to have you; and how is your patient?' Hetty inquired.

'She had a very good night last night. Would you like to see her, Mrs. Hayton?'

'I don't want to disturb Lady Marsden if she is too tired to see me, but if she is feeling strong enough I'd just love to have a peep at her. I won't keep her long, of course.'

'I'm sure she'd like to see you, Mrs. Hayton,' Nurse Benson answered with an accent on the pronoun. 'Would you mind waiting a moment?'

She passed softly from her own room into Stella's.

As soon as she had gone, Hetty looked round swiftly noting the new additions to the rooms, charts, medicine bottles and equipment, and lastly two or three letters lying on the table ready for posting.

It was part of the training that she had learnt in New York under Clement which made her read the addresses on all three envelopes.

Such curiosity had in the past rewarded them over and over again when there had been a business deal to put forward, something to gain by learning a little about the private life of the man with whom they were negotiating.

Now Hetty was looking for a clue which would tell her of Stella Marsden's private life, but she was disappointed.

One of the letters was addressed to Nurse Benson's home, the other to fellow nurses at the hospital in London.

Hetty had hardly replaced the top envelope when she heard the door open behind her.

She was too well trained to start to do anything which might make her appear guilty; instead she bent forward over the table adjusting a picture on the wall and then turned with ease and a disarming smile to the nurse who was waiting.

'Well' she inquired.

'Lady Marsden will see you,' Nurse Benson replied.

Hetty had the impression that the nurse had accomplished something and she guessed that Stella had at first refused to see her and then been overruled by Nurse's insistence.

Nurse Benson held open the door and Hetty passed through it into the Dolphin bedroom.

The blinds were already drawn and the curtains pulled; the room was in semi-darkness, for with the exception of a fire there was only one light by the bedside and that was shaded.

Gently, Hetty moved towards the bed. As she grew accustomed to the dim light she looked into the wide, dark eyes which were one of Stella's most remarkable and beautiful features.

'She's lovely still,' was Hetty's first thought.

She knew that she had hoped Stella's illness might in some way have dimmed that loveliness which even her enemies had been forced to acknowledge.

'How are you, Stella? I am sorry that you have been so ill.'

It was characteristic of Hetty that she should use Stella's Christian name.

They had never been on such intimate terms in the past, but now that she knew Stella would be too weak to resent the familiarity or at least to protest against it, she established their acquaintanceship on a different footing.

'I'm better, thank you,' Stella replied.

Her voice was low and she made no effort to raise it.

'Clive has been wonderful as usual, I hear.'

Hetty could not prevent herself from speaking of him. What was more, she wanted to see Stella's reaction.

'So they tell me.'

Stella's tone was cool and impersonal and yet Hetty was

55

not satisfied. Because she was in love herself she must force herself not to speak of Clive even while it sharpened the pain of her jealousy.

'He's a splendid person and most attractive, don't you think so? I'm told that none of his patients can resist him.'

Even as she said the words she felt they were vulgar and ill-timed, but there was no change in the expression of Stella's face; it showed neither interest nor distaste.

She merely made no reply, lying there limp and inanimate, the dark shadows under her eyes seeming to enhance her beauty rather than detract from it.

Suddenly Hetty felt uneasy, she wished she had not come, wished—because in some ways she was peculiarly sensitive to atmosphere—that she had never made that last ill-judged remark.

'But I mustn't tire you, Stella dear,' she said quickly. 'If there is anything you want you know you have only to ask for it. We love having you here and Clive is quite certain that we shall do our usual good work by bringing you back to perfect health.'

'Thank you.'

There was a pause before Stella spoke; it seemed to Hetty as if she had to force the words between her lips.

Hetty turned towards the door, then came back.

'There's only one thing,' she said, 'which I have forgotten to ask you. Isn't there anyone with whom you'd like me to communicate, some member of your family? I'd be only too delighted to put them up.'

'There's no one, thank you.'

Stella's voice was so low Hetty had to listen intently to hear her words, then the light falling on her hand as it lay in the white sheet attracted Hetty's attention.

It was a lovely hand, slim-fingered, with oval nails, and it lay there limp and defenceless, but it aroused in Hetty a sadistic cruelty, a desire to strike and hurt the beautiful woman to whom it belonged.

'What about Bertram Armstrong?' she asked. 'Wouldn't you like to see him? Poor boy, he must have been desperately anxious about you.'

Just for a second she thought that her shot had missed

its mark, that Stella was going to show no more sign of interest than she had when Clive's name was mentioned.

Then she saw that slowly the fingers of Stella's hand lying there in the pool of light were pressing—no, digging—into the softness of the sheet.

Something hard and bestial in Hetty was pleased. Something within her rejoiced that she had at least roused some emotion in this woman of whom she was afraid.

She waited. The fingers relaxed again; it had been just a moment's tension or maybe a momentary panic.

'I don't wish to see anyone.'

Stella spoke uncompromisingly and she closed her eyes as if dismissing Hetty from her sight and from the room.

Hetty went quietly away, but she lingered to talk with Nurse Benson.

'I wish there was something I could do for Lady Marsden,' she said. 'She is an old friend of mine and I hate to see her like this. She tells me there is nothing she wants, but I can't help feeling she would like some of her own particular friends to come and visit her. You must try to persuade her to agree later on, Nurse; you know how pleased I should be to put them up.'

'You are so kind, Mrs. Hayton,' Nurse Benson replied. 'If anyone doesn't get well at Trenton Park they'd not get well anywhere—that's what I always say and I know Matron agrees with me.'

'It's my little contribution towards the war effort,' Hetty said; 'but war or no war, I hate to see suffering and unhappiness. I don't know how you can stand it, Nurse, year after year. I admire you more than I can possibly say.'

'Oh now, Mrs. Hayton, you mustn't talk to me like that when we know what you do.'

'Well, if you can think of anything Lady Marsden would like, let me know—it doesn't matter what it is, we must try to get it for her. The sky's the limit, as my countrymen say.'

'I'm sure Lady Marsden will be grateful,' Nurse Benson said in a tone of voice which told Hetty only too clearly that she was quite certain that Stella would be nothing of the sort.

'I must hurry now, Nurse. Don't forget—you and I must co-operate to get Lady Marsden on her feet.'

She paused at the door and, apparently as an afterthought came to the point of the whole conversation.

'I wonder if she would like to see Captain—no, I believe it's Major—Armstrong? He used to be a very dear friend of hers. He has telephoned, of course?'

'Major Armstrong,' Nurse Benson repeated doubtfully. 'No, I don't think so; I don't remember the name at all. There's been such a lot of enquiries, of course, but I don't recall anyone of that name.'

'Perhaps he's abroad,' Hetty said carelessly. 'That's the trouble with this war, all one's friends have disappeared into the blue and one hears nothing of them. Good night, Nurse.'

'Good night, Mrs. Hayton.'

Nurse Benson turned with a smile of self-satisfaction into her patient's room.

She would have liked to discuss Hetty's visit, but Stella was lying with her face turned away from the light, her eyes tightly closed, and after hovering for a moment hoping that she might rouse herself to speak, Nurse Benson went back to her charts.

Stella lay very still. She had no desire to talk to anyone and yet for the first time since her accident she was feeling more alive.

She was aware that her pulse had accelerated and that her heart was throbbing, throbbing relentlessly and with an emotion which could not be denied.

Ridiculous that Hetty Hayton's words should have this effect on her and yet the mere sound of Bertram Armstrong's name had been a shock.

She had believed these past weeks that never again would she be capable of feeling anything save a dumb despair, a desire to escape from herself and from the world; but there was nothing limp and languid in what she was feeling now.

It was many emotions in one—anger, hatred, helplessness, and an aching emptiness.

How childish, how utterly futile, she told herself, it all

was, and yet she could not prevent all this and much more besides being aroused within her like a leaping flame at the thought of Bertram . . .

Bertram, with his fair hair brushed back from a square forehead, his blue eyes twinkling with laughter—so easily, so quickly roused.

How he had enjoyed everything, how happy she had been to enjoy life again because she was seeing it through his eyes rather than through her own—prejudiced, cynical and disillusioned!

How ridiculously happy they had been, so happy that the remembrance of it appeared to be all glowing colours, gold and green, yellow and sky blue!

Summer days in the park when they had met and taken the dogs for a walk . . . moonlit nights when they had motored out of London to sit talking in some isolated little wood or in a field silvered and touched with magic by the moonlight.

They had been in love—in love as only two young people can love—and she had been young enough in heart if not in years. It seemed to her that Bertram was everything a man should be—straightforward and honest, unsubtle and true.

'Just an ordinary Englishman,' was how he often spoke of himself and she felt that it summed him up so perfectly, for that was what she desired.

A man who was neither brilliant nor exotic, successful nor perverted, just a man who wanted the real and decent things of life even as she wanted them, a man who loved her and whom she loved.

They were together for every possible moment before the war and after it had started, and because Stella was in love it completed her happiness that she could give Bertram some of the things that he had always wanted.

Bertram was poor. He had managed to enjoy luxury because he was popular and because people were always willing to entertain an unattached, attractive young man.

But there were many little things that he lacked and it gave Stella exquisite pleasure to be able to present them to him.

A gold cigarette case, sapphire and diamond links, a pair of Purdey guns ... she sought always for some way of expressing her happiness and her love.

When she found that it was possible for Bertram to hunt during the winter months she had not grudged the hours he must spend away from her but had been content to buy him the best hunters procurable.

'They are my present to you, darling,' she said, 'and by that I mean a real present not something that is a continual drain upon your pocket.'

He had demurred, but finally she had been allowed to pay for their keep.

Race horses were the next step. Stella had never been interested in racing, but when Bertram took her with him to race meetings she learned a good deal about the 'sport of kings' and was infected by his enthusiasm.

'We will own them together,' Stella said when Bertram protested that he would not allow her to purchase for him a horse which he admired and which had been pointed out to him as a future winner.

'My name obviously cannot appear, but *we* shall know. We will divide the winnings between us.'

These joint interests seemed to draw them closer, at least so Stella believed.

It was only a step from hunters and race horses to taking a really decent flat for Bertram. Stella had always hated the uncomfortable bachelor apartments where he had resided for many years.

'Think of the scandal,' Stella said, 'if I was killed in an air raid and we were both found dead in a bachelor building.'

Actually she did not care very much what was said or what was suspected where she and Bertram were concerned.

She was happy for the first time since her marriage; indeed for the first time in her life. She was learning what it was to be in love, and she was reckless with an unbalanced recklessness which comes from years of repression.

Neither of them ever mentioned the possibility of Stella

getting a divorce from Philip. Stella knew that she would never ask her husband for it and she knew, too, that even were she to beg Philip for one he would never grant it.

In his position even to be the innocent party in a divorce would be both damaging and detrimental.

The public expect their legislators to be like Cæsar's wife—Philip had no intention of involving himself in anything so unsavoury as the scandal and chatter of the divorce courts.

Only once did he make any reference to Stella's behaviour. She had come home in the early hours of the morning during a very bad air raid. Bertram was on leave and they had been together every possible moment.

He brought her back in a taxi. As she let herself in with a latchkey through the great iron and glass door she became aware that someone was standing in the doorway of the library.

She moved across the marble hall guessing who it was, at the same time uncertain because of the dim lights, shaded and darkened because of the black-out regulations. Then Philip had spoken.

'I was beginning to be worried about you.'

There was a sarcastic note in his voice and she walked across the hall to face him.

'You needn't have been. I am quite capable of looking after myself.'

'You were never capable of that,' he replied.

He stepped aside for her to pass him into the library where the fire was burning and where there were sandwiches and drinks laid out on a silver tray.

'How wrong you are,' Stella said.

'On the contrary I am right,' Philip replied, 'and, incidentally, I have your interests at heart, which is more than can be said of some of your friends and notably the gentleman with whom you have been tonight.'

'I have my own friends, Philip, as you have yours,' Stella said warningly.

'I am not quarrelling about that, but I would remind you, my dear, that you are also my wife.'

'Isn't it a little late in the day to remember that?'

61

'On the contrary, I have always remembered it most punctiliously—in public.'

There was a slight pause before the last two words. Philip was mocking her, she knew that, and suddenly she felt tired and weaponless. He was too strong, too formidable for her.

'What do you want me to do?' she asked, and despite every resolution her voice quivered. She knew that she was afraid.

'These raid are getting on your nerves,' Philip replied lightly. 'I want you to accompany me tomorrow to stay the week-end with the Prime Minister—nothing more formidable than that. We are invited together and I have accepted for us both.'

'Nothing more formidable than that'—

But Stella knew that she had been warned, and somehow, unreasonably and quite inexplicably, she was more afraid of her husband than she had ever been before.

The months passed, Bertram's regiment was not sent abroad; it was moved from one part of England to another, but always there were those ecstatic moments when he could get leave.

Stella had hinted to Bertram that they must be a little more circumspect and to her surprise Bertram became the more punctilious of the two.

'I've got to protect you,' he said more than once.

Although she believed it showed his love for her she was also vaguely resentful of the times when he would urge care and refuse to allow her to spend some precious time with him because of what people would say.

'They say! What say they? Let them say!' she quoted more than once.

But the argument was unconvincing for the shadow of Philip was ever behind her and deep in her heart she had the uneasy feeling that their idyll would not be so perfect were it not for the money she could and did spend on Bertram.

There were, however, still so many compensations that she was happy through the summer of 1941.

Marsden House was taken over by the Ministry of

Food; their London residence was first blitzed, and then a year later, when it had been repaired, commandeered by the Americans.

Philip had taken another house in London; it was smaller and she felt more at home in it. Bertram's flat remained untouched all through the raids.

Stella was at Marsden when she received the news of Philip's death. She was writing a letter to Bertram; she had dined alone and was sitting in front of the fire, a writing block on her knee, when she was told she was wanted on the telephone.

For some time she could hardly take in what they told her, it seemed unreal.

Ever since the beginning of the war she had been afraid for Bertram; there was hardly a night she had not wondered whether she might wake in the morning to find he had been either killed by a bomb or sent abroad.

She had hardly thought about Philip as being involved in danger.

His job at the Air Ministry was an exceptionally important one, but he seldom left the ground and he himself appeared to accept the raids with that cynical detachment which was, in these days, his outlook on life.

So much of what Philip enjoyed and liked had passed away.

His art treasures had been stored, his pictures placed below ground for protection, the famous carvings at Marsden House covered up to prevent their being broken or injured by bombs or carelessness.

Without the almost oriental splendour of his background Philip lost much of his personality.

Stella found that she had always pictured him standing at the head of the great marble staircase or sitting at the end of the many-leaved dining-room table, a handsome and distinguished host, witty in his conversation yet of an irreproachable dignity.

Philip working in an office, Philip spending his life at important conferences and meetings, was not the Philip she had known in the past.

It was difficult to remember that this stranger who hur-

ried in and out of the house at odd hours, carrying minis-
terial portfolios and followed by a flock of secretaries, was
the husband she had hated and loathed with a passion
which had supplanted all other emotions.

She had also a reluctant admiration for Philip.

There was no denying that he was magnificent in his
own way and now that he became more human, less
frightening to her personally, she found she could be indifferent even to the point of forgetfulness. But dead!

That seemed impossible, as impossible to believe as to
know what to do now that the martyrdom of herself had
come to an end.

A martyrdom which she had accepted and which had
become such an intrinsic part of her life as to become a
habit.

After the first bewilderment came the knowledge of
freedom, freedom from all she had loathed and all she had
shrunk from, from all that had turned her from a warm,
affectionate young girl into a hard, revengeful woman.

Then came another thought.

She was free, free to marry, free to have children, to
live a normal life, the ordinary life of an Englishwoman
with an ordinary Englishman—with Bertram.

There was such wonder and spendour in that thought
that for a long time she was half afraid to face it, half
afraid to express it even to herself.

It was Bertram who had no doubts in the matter, who
wrote to her in his usual plain way after hearing of
Philip's death and started his letter—

'My darling wife-to-be.'


7


No one would have believed, Stella thought to herself, that
she and Bertram were not lovers.

Yet although it had seemed to her that nothing could

bring them closer to each other, she had not surrendered herself to him physically.

She loved him, never for a moment did she doubt that; she wanted to give him everything it was possible to give, and yet some puritanical part of her upbringing, some innate purity within herself would not let her betray her own standards, her own principles.

All her life she had believed in her childhood's teaching that it was wrong for a woman to belong to a man without the blessing of the church, and the church, incomprehensibly, had blessed her marriage with Philip.

At first Bertram could not understand her point of view.

He had expected, because of the type of life she lived, because of the particular class of society that she represented, that it would be the natural and obvious thing for her to become his mistress.

When she refused him, gently and with tenderness, his passion became transmuted into something finer.

For the first time in his life Bertram wanted a woman who was unobtainable, for the first time in his life he reverenced a woman even while she could rouse his most passionate desire.

Perhaps deeper than any conviction of what was right and wrong was Stella's reaction against Philip and his way of life.

She would not stoop from the pedestal of morality on which she had placed herself.

Sometimes, as the years of war passed slowly, she fancied that Philip showed a new admiration for her in his courtesy and his attentions when they met.

Without any words passing between them she was aware that he knew she still kept Bertram at arm's length even while every fibre in her being cried out for him.

A part of Philip which had never withstood temptation, which had always given full reign to his lusts, admired the stalwart strength of her character which he would not attempt to emulate.

More than once she fancied that he would have spoken to her on the subject, but she shrank from any exchanges of confidences between them.

'It is too late now,' she told herself, 'after nine—nearly ten—years of married life, to become confidential with the husband I hate and despise.'

She had not wanted to confide in any one. The loneliness she had experienced during the years of her marriage had given her the strength to stand alone.

Unlike other women who must talk not only of their problems but of their happiness. She was silent.

Looking back she realised that even to Bertram she had remained silent about so many things. Once, laughingly, he called her 'my beautiful Sphinx.'

She resented the description at the time, assured him that she had no secrets from him.

But she had bottled up her emotions too long, imprisoned her feelings too closely behind a wall of pride and reserve; the barriers would not dissolve at will or even before the fiery onslaught of love.

When she was with Bertram she felt as if she was a child again.

There was sheer delight in playing the child with Bertram, in letting him tease her, in throwing aside her worldly airs as she might throw aside her jewels, in being shy so that her eyes fell beneath his when his love-making became too ardent, in feeling that catch in her breath, that suffocation in her throat when she loved him almost to breaking point.

She was very near at times to losing her resolution, to forsaking her own standard of purity.

The child in her would not have been able to withstand Bertram, he was too compelling, too magnetic and withal too irresistibly attractive.

But the woman who had suffered, who had watched her youth go by, was not so simple. She knew that it was easy to fall and far more difficult to rise again.

So the months passed. Moments of happiness came back to her as they flew by on wings.

A moment when they had been riding together over the downs in Sussex, the wind on their faces, both of them flushed and breathing a little quicker after a sharp gallop.

She turned to make some laughing remark to Bertram

and he bent across the intervening space between them to take her hand.

'I adore you,' he said suddenly.

As their eyes met it was a moment of wonder, a moment of transfiguration within herself so that she felt that the world could hold nothing more glorious.

Nearly all her memories were centred out of doors; they were in vivid contrast to the exotic atmosphere of Philip's houses and of Philip's own presence.

Stella fancied there was something oriental in Philip which must respond always to a superheated atmosphere, to a fragrance of hot-house flowers, to a too soft, too luxurious comfort.

Bertram brought with him a breath of fresh air. There was nothing sinister or subtle about him and being an all-round athlete he kept himself extraordinarily fit.

Stella learnt of his background. His parents had been poor but of a good family, his father had commanded a well-known Lancer regiment and was killed in the summer of 1918.

He was an only son, brought up by his mother, spoilt, and taught to believe that nothing in the world was too good for him.

Life without money was uncomfortable. Bertram never pretended that he did not want the things money could buy—his very frankness disarming.

'I oughtn't to take these things from you,' he kept saying to Stella, 'but I want them so much.'

'You know it pleases me to give them to you,' Stella would answer, 'and what is the use of money lying in the bank? I can't spend it all.'

Unspoken, the thought lay between them that it was Philip's money they used in such ways; and yet, thinking of what she had suffered, Stella told herself she was justified in doing what she liked with the vast sums he gave her.

'I'm not hurting him in any way,' she told a conscience which would not be entirely stilled, and she knew that at least was true.

So long as she behaved with dignity in public, so long as

she remained Philip Marsden's wife in name, he would not complain.

But Philip's death changed everything.

Stella knew then for the first time how heavy a cloud had always rested upon her, how subconsciously it had dimmed even her love for Bertram because, in the background, Philip was always watching, waiting like an adder ready to strike.

It took her nearly a month to realise to the full her position, to see with her own eyes definitely stated in legal documents the vast estates she owned, the sums of money which were hers.

It was not without irony that Philip had trusted her, and she found that he had left in her hands a number of personal requests.

Up to the very last he had kept up appearances, his Will was conventional and formal—splendid bequests to well-known hospitals and charities, generous legacies to servants, pensioners and impoverished relations, the residue *in toto* to his wife.

But for Stella a sealed letter telling her of things which were to be done for those 'friends', some she knew, some she had vaguely suspected.

It was a distasteful, degrading task, but she carried it out conscientiously, exactly as she was instructed.

When everything was finished she burned Philip's letter and felt, as she watched the flames lick greedily at his fine, educated handwriting, she was burning yet another trace of him from her life.

She could never be entirely free of him, that she knew—what he had been and what he had done was stamped upon her mind and soul as permanently, as ineffaceably as she carried for the world to see his name and his inheritance.

'The wealthy Lady Marsden!'

Already, a few weeks after Philip's death, she was inundated with requests for help; charities besieged her, importunate friends sat on her doorstep or hung on the telephone asking—always asking for something.

She was willing enough to give them money, that was

easy, but it was not so easy to escape from those who wished to lionise her now that she was an unattached woman of assured position with a very big dowry.

Within three months of Philip having died she began to sense the matrimonial attentions of mothers with eligible sons who pressed her to come and stay.

'I know you are still in mourning, dear, but Jimmy will be home on leave and would so like to see you. Just a family party.'

There were, of course, a large number of her friends who were quite certain—as Bertram was—that when the period of mourning was over they would be asked to a quiet but important little wedding.

Stella's women friends spoke of it quite openly.

'What are you going to wear, darling? I always think a second wedding's so difficult.'

It was hard to avoid being forced into a discussion, but Stella managed to remain aloof, to leave them guessing as to what were her intentions or plans. Only with Bertram were the barriers down at last.

'When are we going to get married?' he asked her, taking it for granted that she would be his.

'We must wait a year,' she replied, answering as frankly as he had spoken, neither prevaricating nor pretending.

It was so like him, this direct approach as he got out of the train at Victoria Station.

She had gone up to him among the hurly-burly of passengers, of troops moving to and fro, of families with luggage looking anxiously for a taxi—and without any other greeting save the clasping of hands, he had decided their future.

'A year!' he exclaimed. 'It's a long time.'

'It would be a mistake. . . .' Stella stopped.

She had been going to say 'a mistake to rush things' and then she realised that was not what she meant.

What she wanted to say was that Philip had been an important person and they must bury him decently, yet she could not bring herself to mention his name at this moment.

Philip must not intrude on this new happiness, this feeling of freedom and buoyancy.

She had come up to London to meet Bertram only a week after Philip's death had been announced.

Three days earlier she had seen Philip's ashes scattered in accordance with his wishes over the high ground at Marsden.

It had been a ceremony of great beauty and carried out entirely as ordered by Philip in his instructions to his executors.

It was strange to think that at forty-three he should have planned his own funeral service, should have anticipated that his death might be early—he, a man who had never been in any danger other than might happen to the most ordinary civilian.

'Perhaps he was prophetic,' Stella said, then shrank from the memory of their last meeting.

She was afraid to remember it, that was the truth, for recalling Philip's words she was afraid of the implication of them.

They had been alone in their private wing at Marsden House, the only part which had not been taken over by the Ministry.

Stella was surprised that Philip had come down alone for the week-end.

Usually he brought a party, telephoning the housekeeper or the secretary a few hours before he arrived. His guests were generally Cabinet Ministers or heads of the fighting forces.

Philip was a busy person and Stella had the idea that because he was busy he had little private life and little interest in anything save his work. When he arrived alone he complained of a cold.

'Would you like to go to bed?' she inquired; but he shook his head.

'We will dine together. It is a long time since I had the pleasure of your company to myself.'

She agreed with an indifference which for once was genuine, her thoughts were centred on Bertram and the

70

letter he had written her that morning. He had hinted there was a possibility of his going abroad shortly.

They had had these scares ever since the war started, but each time her heart beat quicker in anticipation.

She was just as much afraid for him as she had been when the declaration of war in September, 1939, had brought her fear for her personal happiness and for the love which was only just beginning to reveal itself.

When dinner was over, an excellent meal despite rationing, Stella and Philip withdrew into the sitting-room which they had converted for their joint use.

Each had a private room of their own. Stella's boudoir opening out of her bedroom while Philip had retained the great library, its valuable, unique books making it one of the show places of England.

The room they both used was beautifully finished but as impersonal as a railway station waiting-room. It was the meeting ground of two people who were as opposite to each other as the poles.

Although it was a warm evening, Philip had insisted that a fire should be lit and he stood in front of the fireplace warming his hands in a contemplative silence which somehow struck Stella as ominous.

'What is the matter?' she asked at length, wondering what troubled him and if it concerned herself.

She could think of nothing likely to implicate her. She and Bertram had been most circumspect on his last leave and actually most of their friends were too busy on war work for gossip.

'I was thinking about you,' Philip said unexpectedly, and Stella felt her heart give a frightened throb.

'Why?' she asked, her voice level and cold.

'You are a very beautiful woman, my dear.'

He looked down at her as she sat in the deep arm-chair, a dress of pale blue chiffon bringing out the colour of her eyes and serving as a background for a sapphire necklace and bracelets to match.

'Is that what is worrying you?' Stella asked, faint amusement in her voice, and with a feeling of relief beyond expression.

71

'I was thinking of your future,' he said, 'and wondering whether you would ever find happiness.'

'I have found it,' Stella nearly answered, and then somehow she was prevented from saying the words.

Was she happy, she asked herself, had she really found it in all truth? Yes, she knew the answer; then before she could speak, Philip went on:

'If one has too high a standard, Stella, the odds are against one's ever attaining happiness in this world. You will have to learn not to expect so much.'

'What do you mean?'

Stella wondered what he was driving at, what he was trying to say to her. Philip was always an enigma, but this type of conversation was unusual even for him.

'Wasn't it Somerset Maugham who said "You should never expect from people more than they are capable of giving"? You've always expected so much. People will always fail you because men and women, although you are not yet aware of it, my dear, are human beings.'

'You're cynical,' Stella exclaimed.

Then she was aware that Philip was looking at her with an expression which, incredible though it seemed, appeared to her to be one of pity.

Philip pitying her! How could he?

She was about to question him when they were interrupted—

'The Air Ministry wishes to speak to Sir Philip.'

He hurried from the room and she did not see him again that night. She went to bed with his words ringing in her ears.

'People will always fail you'.

She tried to forget them, tried to shake herself free from the spell of his voice, to forget that expression she had surprised in his eyes, but it was one of those things which she could not forget.

To whom had he been referring? To Bertram?—but Bertram had never been more than adoring during the months preceding his death.

He had not been sent abroad, once again it had proved

a false alarm; and when finally his regiment went, he had been given a special staff job at home.

He had been promoted and had rung her up, proud as any schoolboy with a games trophy.

She had been more than content that she was not to lose him; at the same time she wondered, before she could prevent the thought because it was disloyal, that Bertram did not prefer to be on the field of battle.

'He is so strong,' she thought, 'such an obvious man to lead men.'

She could not quite understand his gladness at remaining at home.

Then she knew the answer—he was afraid of leaving her.

They meant so much to each other, had grown so immeasurably close in these precarious years of war, that now she had supplanted everything in Bertram's mind—even his career.

'I am so lucky,' she told herself.

She felt that nothing she could offer would be too much for a man who loved her to the exclusion of all else.

'I love him ... I love him ... I love him!' she whispered into the darkness that night.


8


Hetty stopped at Alice's room on her way down to dinner. Alice was having her dinner off a tray and she looked up somewhat resentfully as Hetty entered.

She was used to her employer demanding her attention at all hours of the day or night, but when, as very often happened, she had her meals upstairs in the little sitting-room which served her both as an office and as a place of privacy, she did object to Hetty coming in and keeping her talking so that her food grew cold.

Yet, Hetty, considerate enough where it was worth her while, had a blind spot where Alice was concerned.

In her heart she believed that Alice adored her and she made demands, therefore, upon this quiet, elderly woman that she would never have dared to make on any other human being.

'Alice,' she said now as she entered the room impetuously, 'I want you to ring up Colonel Anderson at the War Office and find out if he knows anything about Bertram Armstrong. Tell him to discover where he is; and if it is in England, get me the telephone number.'

'Would Colonel Anderson be allowed to give you such information?' Alice asked slowly.

Not because she did not know the answer, but simply because she knew her question would annoy Hetty.

'Of course he will tell me—don't be so ridiculous, Alice! It isn't likely that Colonel Anderson will refuse me anything.'

That was true enough. The Colonel was what Alice termed in her mind 'one of Hetty's tame cats'.

She knew that was an Edwardian expression, but she could think of nothing in modern phraseology more apt to describe him and various other creatures like him.

They ran round Hetty like 'moths round a candle'—another of Alice's favourite idioms—because she could pay them to do so. They were useful to her and she never forgot to extort the last pound of flesh from them for what she did and for the kindnesses she rendered.

Colonel Anderson was a bluff, good-humoured sportsman who would have sold his soul to the devil any day for some first-class shooting.

Hetty saw not only that he was included among the guests at all the partridge and pheasant shoots at Trenton Park, but also that it cost him little or nothing.

Cartridges were provided for him, his first-class ticket to Trenton and back was sent to him in advance and there was often a cheque in the envelope as well towards such expenses as tipping the keepers and the servants and the high stakes he was forced to play at bridge with Hetty's more wealthy guests.

In return, Colonel Anderson became Hetty's devoted slave; he was hers to command, but Alice suspected that he was glad when she did make demands upon him.

To be useful made him in his own estimation seem less in her debt—and Alice felt that he was gentleman enough to dislike, if not resent, his financial dependence on a woman.

'I will ring the Colonel up,' Alice said with a sigh.

Her fricassee of chicken, which had been hot and succulent when she had taken off the silver cover, was now congealing upon her plate.

'Good—and tell him I want to know at once; don't forget—at once. And Alice,' Hetty paused. 'You've remembered everything I asked for this evening?'

'The champagne, the brandy, everything,' Alice answered, and realised with a faint inward smile that Hetty was nervous.

She was looking extremely attractive this evening. She wore a dress of black satin which had been made for her by a Paris dressmaker before the war.

It had always been one of her most becoming gowns and Alice suspected that Hetty regarded it as lucky, wearing it on those occasions when she particularly wanted to be favoured by the gods.

She had a marvellous figure, there was no denying that, and if it had not been for the almost defiant hardness of her expression she would have been pretty.

As it was she gave the impression of a sophistication and a smartness which could only have come out of Paris or New York.

Like many American women, Hetty had beautiful legs and feet and was wise enough to make the most of them.

Diamond clasps on her black sandals glittered as she walked, drawing the attention to the smallness of her feet and to the crimson toe-nails peeping through a gossamer-thin stocking.

'You look pre-war,' Alice exclaimed suddenly, and Hetty smiled.

'How tired I am of seeing nothing but uniform and dingy women with made-over clothes,' she said. 'If the war goes on much longer even my wardrobe will be exhausted.'

She smiled as if such a contingency was impossible and Alice remembering the row upon row of gowns, tailormade, dresses and coats which hung on the third landing near Watkins's room, could well believe it.

When Hetty was buying clothes she bought them as if for the sheer lust of spending, the sheer joy of possession.

Not in a dozen years of war could she have worn out all the things she had acquired before coupons were introduced.

Now as Hetty turned and twisted herself a little, watching her reflection in the mirror over the mantelpiece, Alice felt that she was like a young peacock spreading its tail, admiring herself.

'Why are you so anxious to know where Major Armstrong is?' Alice asked. 'Does Lady Marsden want to see him?'

'She doesn't!' Hetty stopped pirouetting before the glass. 'But there is something behind this, Alice, something which we have missed, and I am determined to find out what it is.'

She spoke earnestly and yet with a vehemence which made Alice suspicious.

She was used to Hetty's desire to know about people, to probe into their innermost lives, to drag out their most intimate secrets; but in most cases it had been only curiosity and a desire for power.

Alice somehow suspected that this new interest of Hetty's went deeper still.

'Can it be jealousy?' she asked herself, and wondered if she had found a clue.

Hetty stood looking at her for a moment—Alice thought she was going to speak, to confide in her, but she changed her mind.

She gave another look at herself in the glass and then walked away, calling over her shoulder as an afterthought:

'Good night, Alice.'

As she went slowly down the stairs, her black dress

moving behind her with a soft rustle, she thought of the evening ahead and then of the woman lying with closed eyes in the Dolphin room.

'I dislike Stella Marsden,' Hetty admitted to herself.

Dislike her?—no, she almost hated her. Stella had not come up against her in the past, she had done nothing to cause such an emotion.

Hetty knew that her hatred sprang from jealousy not only of Clive Ross, but also because Stella stood for so many of the things that she had wanted all her life and had never been able to obtain.

Hetty remembered seeing Stella move with an aloof dignity which was all her own through a thronged ballroom in London.

It was a hot night and flowers were wilting against many white shoulders, while men openly mopped their faces.

Stella looked cool—to the point of coldness: she looked bored and disdainful, too, as if the people greeting her with adulation made no impression on her.

That, Hetty thought, must have been before she knew Bertram Armstrong, for she remembered seeing Stella during the first months of the war and noting the change in her.

Then she had been like a statue come to life and her beauty had become a vivid, colourful thing impossible to be ignored.

But even when she was happy Stella could give an impression of hidden reserve, of good taste, or irreproachable breeding, and it was for that, if nothing else, that Hetty hated her.

They were rivals in the social world merely inasmuch as they were two of the small group of important and wealthy hostesses still existing before the war.

The 'Marsden House set' had a political significance greater than anything Hetty had ever managed to emulate in her circle, although she had succeeded in surrounding herself with an assortment of Ambassadors and Dukes, minor Royalties and other persons with some claim to note.

A miscellaneous collection of which any hostess might be proud, and for Hetty O'Reilly of Ohio a miracle beyond anything of which she had ever dreamt.

Yet with her fingers on the social pulse she had known even in the height of her power that Stella could, if she wished, beat her at her own game.

That Stella had wished to do nothing of the sort was more humiliating than the fact that Lady Marsden invariably refused the invitations of Mrs. Clement B. Hayton.

'The mills of God grind slowly, but they grind extremely small.'

Hetty had often quoted that to herself when she had been able to pay off an old score, to have her revenge for some slight or snub administered during her first years in London.

Now once again she was proving the truth of it. Stella Marsden was under her roof, was to all intents and purposes in her power, and she, Hetty Hayton, could exact the last ounce of retribution from the situation.

She found Clive Ross waiting for her in the drawing-room. He got up as she entered the room and she noted how well he looked in a dinner-jacket.

Cocktails were waiting on the table by the fireplace and Hetty, moving towards them, said in a voice into which she could when she pleased inject a large amount of charm:

'You must forgive me for being selfish tonight. I ought to have asked the County to meet you and instead I have chosen to keep you to myself.'

'If you had invited the County, I should have run away,' Clive answered. 'I'm tired, and—if you want the truth—tired of strange faces.

'That's the worst of my job; when one gets to a certain stage, one is always being called in for a consultation on strangers, while if one was honest one would prefer to do really good work with just a few, the precious few to whom one is really a life-line.'

He was speaking seriously and Hetty was warmed by his tone. He was being companionable, giving her his confidence—that at least was a step forward.

All her inquiries—and they had been many—about Clive Ross made skilfully and with her usual thoroughness, had resulted in very little information.

That he was a Scot, that his father and mother were poor and that he himself had earned his University fees was well known, but apparently when one had learnt that, one had learnt all.

Who were his friends, how did he spend his leisure hours, what other interests and hobbies had he beside surgery, were there any women in his life?

If so what were their names?—to none of these questions could Hetty find an answer.

Now, like a hunter tracking down some rare and strange animal, she was alert and watchful. She handed Clive the cocktail she had poured out for him and lifted her own glass in a toast.

'To our friendship,' she said gently.

It was a toast Hetty had often offered before and she expressed it with just the right degree of hesitant hope in her tone as if she longed for so much and yet was afraid to anticipate it.

Clive bowed, whether ironically or in all sincerity Hetty was left to wonder.

She drank her cocktail quickly and poured herself another, filling up his glass to the brim although he had only sipped at it.

'If you could only know,' she said softly, throwing back her head a little because she knew it revealed the lines of her throat, 'what it means to me to have a quiet evening here with you. I seem to be in a continual rush, day after day, night after night.

'It isn't only the running of this house—you know I love that, and it is actually the least of my difficulties, the nurses are so sweet and Matron a treasure. But there are so many other things—business and charities, all of which seem to need my attention.'

'And many of which benefit by your generosity,' Clive said.

' "Money is like muck—no good unless it is spread",' Hetty quoted softly, 'and that is one of the things I want

79

to talk to you about, Clive. Don't you think it is time that you had an experimental hospital of your own?'

She saw the sudden light in his eyes and knew that she had struck gold at last. So that was where his interest lay!

She had half suspected it and it was Alice who, as usual, had put the key of the door in her hand by repeating a few sentences she had overheard Clive say to Matron.

'Got him!' Hetty thought to herself.

It was at that moment that dinner was announced and they walked together into the dining-room.

Hetty was too clever to allow the atmosphere of the great empty baronial hall which was used on formal occasions to submerge the intimacy of a *tête-à-tête* dinner.

She had a table drawn up by the fire in her own sitting-room, the shaded candelabra casting a golden glow on the white cloth, the rest of the room in darkness.

Clive was tired, so tired that he was content to give his senses full rein, to enjoy the really delicious food which was handed to him, to savour the wine which he was connoisseur enough to recognise as being exceptional.

Also his hostess, whom he sometimes fancied was rather crude in her over-exuberant vitality, was talking gently so that her voice soothed rather than roused him from a pleasant and entirely physical lethargy.

'Funny,' he thought, 'how I have always remained on my guard where Mrs. Hayton is concerned.'

She frightened him, if it could be said that he was frightened of any woman, but his fear was not fundamentally for himself but for her.

She gave him the impression of a tight-rope walker swaying above the heads of the crowd, liable at any moment to miss her footing.

He did not know why he should think of Hetty like this—most people, he knew, would have laughed at him for being fanciful, for no one held a more assured place in the world in which she moved.

Yet he found himself watching her, waiting for the accident or collapse which he sensed with that part of him which his mother would have called 'fey'.

This evening he wanted to think of nothing but his own well-being, yet he found strange fancies crowding in upon him.

It seemed to him that the woman talking so easily and casually across the table was in danger, and he wondered what the danger was and if he could warn her.

Finally, as dinner came to a close, he shook himself mentally, cursing his own powers of perception, although he realised well enough how useful they were in his career.

Often, so often that he would never dare confess it to anyone, he diagnosed entirely by clairvoyance.

As he examined a patient he would know what was wrong instinctively and so surely that it was impossible for him to be at fault.

Sometimes he would fight this inner conviction, telling himself that there were no signs or symptoms that could be put on paper, that he could point out to another doctor.

Yet inevitably and without exception his diagnosis would be right; that inner sense, that sixth sense that he possessed was wiser than all the external evidences, all the proof of sight, feeling and hearing.

Often when he was tired Clive would know that this part of him of which he was half ashamed was getting out of hand.

Some conclusion would leap into being without even the direction of his brain to control it.

Once in the tube train he had known clearly and unmistakably what was wrong with the woman opposite.

She had been a fat, suburban housewife with nothing particular to distinguish her from the hundreds of other women clambering on and off the train at various stations and yet Clive had known she had some strange, unsuspected disease.

He had battled with himself as to how to approach her, common sense had told him to mind his own business, the woman would think him mad.

She might cause a scene, but the humanitarian and the doctor in him would not allow him to shirk the issue.

81

He had gone after the woman and, abruptly because he was shy and rather ashamed of himself, he had put his card into her hand and asked her to come and see him at the hospital.

To his surprise she came.

What he had suspected—no, what he had known—was only too true and she had died three weeks later.

But tonight this power irritated him.

'It is absurd,' he told himself. 'What could threaten Hetty Hayton?'

She was healthy enough, he was sure of that; her body was wiry and filled with the strength of the working class from which he guessed she came.

Her trouble, he was sure, was not that she had too much to do, but that she had too little.

Her muscles, responding to the call of generations behind her, wanted something hard and resilient against which to exhaust themselves; soft beds, luxurious food, idleness were all wrong for Hetty Hayton.

If she had been made to scrub, bake, and to delve into the earth for her food and keep, she might have been a fine woman.

Instead, what Nature was denied physically she achieved mentally.

Clive knew that the greed for power which was part of the Hetty Hayton legend resulted from a lack of work, from a life empty of children, and the affection and companionship which lies within a real home.

Dinner was finished, the table was taken away and Hetty drew her chair up close to the fire.

'Shall we stay here?' she asked. 'It is so much more intimate than the drawing-room and I want to talk to you.'

'What is worrying you?' Clive inquired.

He spoke with the good-humoured tolerance of a doctor who is used to patients getting a little advice on the side.

'Oh, I don't want to talk about myself,' Hetty said softly, 'But about you.'

'I'm afraid that's a dull subject.'

'That's where you are wrong. I wonder, Clive, if you realise just what an attractive person you are and how much you appeal to the average woman.'

She bent forward as she spoke and her low-cut evening dress revealed the soft hollow between her breasts. Clive Ross stirred restlessly in his chair.

For the first time he wondered if he had been wise in allowing himself to accept Hetty's pressing invitations to stay at Trenton Park.

He seldom stayed away and he had looked on this as a semi-professional visit, connecting Hetty in his mind with the patients he treated under her roof.

Now he wondered if he had made a mistake; but sensitive to his reaction Hetty changed her tune.

'Let's talk about your hospital. I've only a very vague idea of what an experimental hospital means. Won't you tell me?'

He was about to reply when the door opened. Hetty turned round sharply to see that it was Alice who was interrupting them.

She came into the room with the usual forward movement of her head, looking dreary and out of place in the shabby tweeds she had worn all day, her glasses flickering in the firelight.

'What is it, Alice?' Hetty's tone was sharp; it said more forcibly than any words that Alice was intruding where she was least wanted.

'I thought I ought to tell you, Mrs. Hayton, as Colonel Anderson says the news will be in the papers tomorrow morning.' Alice replied, 'That Major Armstrong has been killed.'

9

Clive rose to his feet.

'Are you quite certain of this?' he asked.

Alice answered before Hetty could do so.

'Oh, quite. Colonel Anderson was speaking officially.'

Alice's tone implied that she was eager to be helpful. She admired Clive Ross and was always pleased to do anything she could for him, even to the offering of a little information.

Then she caught sight of Hetty's face and knew she had made a mistake.

Instantly there swept over her that feeling of insecurity and apology which Hetty's anger and fault-finding invariably created.

She would lie awake at night wondering where she had gone wrong, and how she felt one part of her brain beginning to argue as though in defence of herself.

'But she told me she wanted to know at once. At once! Those were the very words she used. How could I know that she would mind Clive Ross hearing the news? Should I have sent in a note or rung her on the house telephone?'

Poor Alice's bewildered brain was seeking an escape, a way out like some animal in a trap. Then Hetty spoke:

'Honestly. I don't think we need worry ourselves; Colonel Anderson is an old gossip, he's often been wrong before in the things he told me and Alice should know him well enough not to listen to rumours.'

This was unfair to Colonel Anderson as Alice well knew, for although he was not over-gifted with brains he had proved himself on all occasions extremely reliable.

But Hetty knew what she was doing, Alice supposed, and wondered how she could escape from the retribution which she knew would be hers later.

'Perhaps you'll tell me who this Colonel Anderson is?' Clive asked.

His quiet voice seemed to break through the tension vibrating between the two women.

'Does it matter?' Hetty said, turning to him with one of her flashing smiles. 'It's very sad, naturally, if it is true about Bertram Armstrong, but I don't think any of us need be unduly disturbed.'

'I was thinking of Lady Marsden,' Clive answered, and his eyes met Hetty's levelly.

'Of course—poor Stella!' Hetty exclaimed, but lightly without emotion.

Alice, agitated though she was, could not help admiring the way in which Hetty was striving to give the whole thing an air of unimportance.

'Yes, poor Stella!' Hetty repeated again: 'but perhaps it would be wiser not to tell her yet but keep the news until she is stronger.'

'Who is this Colonel Anderson?' Clive spoke to Alice.

She hesitated before answering, glancing at Hetty for a lead; but Hetty, bending to take a heavily scented hand-kerchief out of her evening bag, gave her no help, and Alice, conscious that Clive was awaiting her reply, said dully:

'He's at the War Office.'

'And he told you the news was official?'

'Yes.'

'Thank you,' Clive spoke gravely.

Turning towards the fire he threw his half-smoked cigarette into the flames.

'What are you going to do?' Hetty asked.

'If you'll excuse me,' he replied, 'I'll go up and see Lady Marsden.'

'But why? Surely it's not your job to break the news to her?'

'Anything's my job,' Clive answered swiftly, 'that affects the well-being of my patients.'

Hetty gave an exclamation which might have been one of irritation or surprise.

'But surely,' she expostulated, 'we are taking this unnecessarily seriously. Even supposing that Bertram Armstrong is killed, are we not assuming that his death will necessarily affect Stella?

'I have reason to believe that he has made no effort to get in touch with her since her illness. Obviously, the whole affair—if affair it was—is finished.'

Hetty was speaking quickly with the strident note in her voice which Clive Ross most disliked.

He looked away from her towards Alice and it seemed

as if his eyes rested in relief on the shabby figure with greying hair and apologetic brown eyes.

'I think Lady Marsden should know,' he said patiently, 'and I would like to see her before she goes to sleep.'

He spoke to Hetty but he looked at Alice, and then as he passed the latter he stopped close to her.

'Thank you,' he said softly, and Alice gave a little gasp of relief.

Clive's understanding would not, she knew, excuse her with Hetty, but yet in some way she felt absolved from whatever sin she had committed. She looked after him as he walked out of the room.

'There's a real man,' she thought.

Then as the door closed behind him she braced her nerves for the inevitable scene that followed.

The night nurse was sitting before the fire reading a newspaper as Clive entered. She jumped to her feet, conscious of being caught wearing bedroom slippers and feeling in consequence rather embarrassed and ill at ease.

'Is Lady Marsden awake?' Clive asked.

'She was five minutes ago, sir,' the nurse replied. 'Shall I go and see?'

'No, don't bother, Nurse, I'll go myself.'

He opened the door into the bedroom and went in.

Stella had had her supper and was hoping it would soon be time for a sleeping draught when she could lose herself and her thoughts for a little while in sleep.

She thought it was Nurse entering and looked round to ask her the time. To her surprise she saw Clive.

He came forward out of the shadows at the door and as he approached the bed she noted for the first time that he was good-looking.

His hair was slightly grey at the temples and she wondered how old he was, thinking of him as a human being rather than as an omnipotent power which had prevented her gaining her heart's desire.

'I wasn't expecting you again,' she said, and then added: 'I thought I had offended you.'

'Doctors aren't allowed to be offended,' Clive answered

gravely, but there was a suspicion of a smile at the corners of his mouth and his eyes twinkled.

'Are they so inhuman?' Stella asked. 'Perhaps they ought to be as they are so powerful.'

There was a hint of bitterness in the last words.

Clive sat down beside the bed.

'How are you feeling?'

'Exactly the same. Did you expect much alteration?'

'Are you strong enough to bear bad news?'

Stella lay very still.

'Bad news?' she questioned.

He nodded his head.

'Who is it?' Her dark eyes were searching Clive's face; then before he could reply she whispered:

'Bertram '

Again Clive nodded. Stella's mouth quivered.

'He's dead?'

'I'm afraid so.'

There was a long silence before suddenly to her own surprise Stella found she had hold of Clive's hand. She was gripping it, holding on to it with a strength which surprised herself.

She felt detached, a spectator of her own emotions, then like a building which suddenly collapses before the blast of an explosion she crumpled up.

'Bertram dead.' She spoke hardly above a whisper and yet the words held an agony of suffering. 'I can't believe it! How could he be?—he loved life so, loved every moment of it.'

Bertram laughing and joking ... Bertram riding across the downs, the sound of his voice calling her name as she strove to keep up with him ...

Bertram catching her up in his arms, holding her high against his heart when he came on leave unexpectedly ... Bertram kissing her—in the darkness of his car, on a sandy beach, under the shade of a great oak tree, on the balcony of his flat....

At the last memory her hold on Clive's hand tightened; she couldn't bear this pain, the wounds conflicting within her heart.

Bertram in his life had injured her, so she thought, beyond reparation and yet now in death the agony was even greater.

She thought of that last morning, that morning when she had gone up to London to meet him, so happy, so radiant because she was about to see him.

Then like a dam breaking before a flood she began to speak. She was not conscious of her words, of how she phrased her sentences or indeed of what she said; it was not even thinking aloud.

It was feeling articulately, all the misery and unhappiness of the past months culminating in a passionate outflow which nothing could stop.

She was hardly aware that it was to Clive she was talking; her reserve was down, the bonds of repression were broken and she poured out her feelings as if it was her life-blood ebbing away and bringing relief in its flowing.

Clive sat very still and silent while she spoke.

It was not difficult to elaborate, it needed little imagination to understand behind the sparsity of the story she told and her choking whispers how much there was unspoken.

It was easy to conjure up how lovely Stella must have looked that morning when she set out from Marsden House for London.

She had received Bertram's letter the day before.

'I've got some leave, darling, and I'm coming to London on Wednesday. Will you meet me at the flat at twelve o'clock—not before, because if my train comes in a few minutes earlier I want to be spruced up and clean so as to look my best for you?

You know how much your approval of me matters to me. Incidentally, and this is a secret, I may be off abroad very shortly. The General is talking of taking a trip out East for a conference of big-wigs and he wants me to go with him. It would be rather fun if I hadn't got to leave you behind.

Wednesday at twelve, darling, and we shall have at least forty-eight hours together. Are you looking forward to it?—I know I am.'

She had hardly slept that night. Bertram had been in

the north for five weeks and she had not had the chance to set eyes on him.

She felt like a schoolgirl who has been unexpectedly granted a holiday.

Discarding her Red Cross uniform she chose her prettiest and gayest dress and coat adding a ridiculous little hat of tulle and feathers and two great blue foxes which hung across her shoulders framing the perfect carriage of her neck and head.

She went up to London by rail, regretting the days when she could have been taken comfortably from door to door in a Rolls Royce, but it didn't really matter—Bertram would be waiting for her.

She went up very early on a train that left the station nearest to Marsden at 7:30.

She, too, wanted to be spruced up before she saw Bertram and she telephoned to her hairdresser and made an appointment for 10 o'clock.

As soon as she had got Bertram's letter she sent for the head gardener and told him that she required peaches and grapes to be put into a basket, and she herself went down to the carnation house and picked a huge fragrant bunch of Bertram's favourite flowers.

It was difficult to get a seat on the train and leaving her maid to cope with the luggage Stella, laden with the fruit and flowers, finally squeezed herself into an already overcrowded first-class carriage.

The journey was hot and uncomfortable but she hardly noticed that there was anyone else in the carriages.

She could only think of Bertram and plan how they would enjoy every moment of the hours ahead.

'Forty-eight hours!'

It was not a long time in which to make up for the empty weeks when they had not seen each other, in which to steel themselves against the separation that lay ahead. The sound of the train seemed to echo his name; already her heart was beating fast in anticipation.

The train was late into Paddington and when finally she managed to obtain a taxi Stella realised that it was nearly time for her hairdressing appointment.

'I shan't have time to go to the house,' she told her maid. 'You can drop me in Bond Street.'

They were half-way there when Stella changed her mind. She rapped on the window and directed the driver to stop at the nearest taxi rank.

When he obeyed her she got out, telling her maid to drive on, and changed into another taxi, taking with her only the flowers and fruit.

She had ten minutes to spare before her appointment and she decided to go to Bertram's flat, to put the flowers in water in readiness for him and to leave the fruit arranged in a bowl on the dinning-room table.

While she had been travelling she had thought of him arriving at his cheerless, unopened flat, for the caretaker of the building did little in war-time, and she felt that she could not bear him to have so cold a welcome.

Bertram invariably managed to make himself comfortable; nevertheless, she knew how her flowers would brighten up the sitting-room.

She thought too that she might just scribble a note of welcome, imprinting on paper the words of love with which she would be greeting him herself in a few hours.

When she reached the block in which Bertram's flat was situated she told the taxi-driver to wait and then getting into the lift took herself up to the sixth floor.

They had chosen a flat at the top because Bertram said he must be able to breathe.

'Besides,' Bertram said, 'lovers should always have a room with a view.'

This had been a special joke between them for Bertram seldom took her up in the lift without saying: 'And now for our "room with a view",' and like all intimate jokes between two people who love each other it had a tender significance which meant so much more than could be expressed in words.

The lift stopped at the top floor and Stella got out.

'I shan't have any too long,' she thought. 'I wish I'd made my appointment with Antoine half an hour later.'

But then she might have been late for Bertram, for she

90

knew how long it took to be properly attended to in war-time, when there was a shortage of assistants.

She took the key of the flat out of her bag—she always carried it with her because from the very beginning she and Bertram had been wise enough to dispense whenever possible with the attention of servants.

'Half the gossip in Mayfair,' Bertram told her, 'comes from the chatter of servants who know everything. Let's be independent.

She had accepted his more experienced judgement without questioning it and had learned to love the times when they could be utterly alone without the fear of interruption or of curious ears listening to their conversation.

She inserted the key and opened the door. It was dark in the little hall and she put down her basket so as to use both hands to take the key from the Yale lock.

Even as she did so she heard voices.

For a moment she was too surprised to do more than think that someone had got into Bertram's flat by mistake, then she heard him speak.

So Bertram was back already!

Her heart leapt at the knowledge, but she realised that he was speaking to somebody and she checked her first impulse which had been to cry out his name, to call out a greeting so that he might know she was there.

'You are taking a time,' Bertram was saying. 'Hurry up—I'm ravenously hungry.'

There was a laugh and Stella knew that it came from the direction of the little kitchenette.

'Don't be so impatient, big boy,' a woman's voice answered. 'Your breakfast isn't ready yet; besides, I never was a good cook.'

'All women should be good cooks,' Bertram replied,

Stella knew now that he was speaking from the bed-room.

'Sez you!'

Stella stood very still, turned to stone.

She had been carrying the carnations in the crook of her arm and now they dropped to the floor, falling softly, a patch of vivid scarlet against their white paper and the dark carpet.

'How much longer are you going to be?'

It was Bertram calling out again and once again the laughter, gay, young and exhilarated, came flooding out of the kitchen.

'If you aren't a good boy you shan't have breakfast in bed. Besides, if you're hungry it's your own fault as you well know.'

'And you had nothing to do with it, I suppose.'

'Nothing at all, of course. I was only the accessory to the fact.'

'If I wasn't so lazy I'd come and spank you for that.'

'Well, you'll have the opportunity in a moment. Breakfast is served, m'lord.'

Stella pulled herself together with a sudden jerk.

She was aware of her own position, of standing eavesdropping in the dark hall, of feeling bitterly cold, of trembling so it seemed to her as if her teeth must chatter.

She slipped out, shutting the door behind her almost noiselessly, then for a moment she leant against it quivering all over and covered her face with her hands.

She could not think, could only stand there wondering why no merciful oblivion took her into its keeping.

Then she realised that faintly, very faintly, almost inaudibly, she could hear voices through the door.

She fled into the lift, got down to the ground floor and ran down the steps into the waiting taxi.

'Paddington,' she said.

She sat waiting on Paddington platform for the next train home.

She did not remember to telephone her maid until late that evening and the poor woman was worried as to what could have happened to her.

She could think of nothing, remember nothing save that gay, inconsequent laughter and Bertram's voice answering it. After that everything in life that mattered seemed to stop short as if she had died.

For she wanted to die, it was the one thing she did want—to be dead and at peace within herself.

Bertram had known she had been there as soon as he found the basket of fruit and the flowers from Marsden House. It was not difficult for him to guess exactly what had happened.

He had telephoned her, but she had refused to speak to him; he had written her passionate imploring letters, pleading for her understanding.

'Be reasonable,' he said. 'You tried me too high. I have loved you a long time and I failed you only because I am a man.'

Philip's words came back to Stella as she read this letter.

'Never expect from people more than they are capable of giving.'

She had expected too much and been disappointed. But she could not resurrect what had died within her heart.

She read Bertram's letters and his protestations of love with a feeling only of utter despair. All desire for him had ceased, she was encompassed about by her own misery and a sense of failure and of desolation.

She knew it would be impossible for her either to forgive him or to forget what had happened.

If he had taken a mistress anywhere else, perhaps it would have been different; but in the flat which had played such a big part in their lives, in their own 'room with a view'—that she could never forgive.

A doctor would have told her that she was suffering from extreme shock; she only knew that she was tortured by her feelings every waking hour of her life.

She felt that she could not go on living at Marsden House, doing the same things she had done since the beginning of the war, playing her part as Commandante of the Red Cross, as chatelaine of Philip's vast possessions.

Someone spoke of the factory and she decided to go there as an unknown worker. She had given a false name and started her apprenticeship.

The explosion had torn aside her anonymity.

'Can't you understand, can't you realise,' she asked Clive now, 'that I must get away? You have brought me back into the type of life which I have always lived, which

93

is so filled with memories of Bertram and with memories of Philip that is a crucifixion.

'These people know—they all know what Bertram meant to me, I can guess what they are saying. I've finished with them once and for all.'

Her hold on Clive's hand tightened until her nails dug into him.

'I hate my money,' she cried passionately, 'I have it! I lie awake now wondering whether Bertram would ever have loved me if I hadn't had any. I shall never know for certain but I do know one thing—he would never have wanted to marry me if I hadn't been rich. Do you think I want to go on living in a world of that sort?'

Clive said nothing and after a few moments she said dully:

'If I've got to live, and it's your fault that I have, take me away where there are real people. They must exist somewhere. This way of living is finished, it's dead. I know that for the truth because I, too, have died.

'I'm dead—can't you understand?—Stella Marsden is dead just as all the puppets who move round here, who once glittered and shone in that empty aimless life which we call society are dead too.'

Then in a tone which had something childlike in it and was infinitely helpless and pathetic, she whispered:

'Somewhere there must be people who are ... worth preserving ... those are the people I want to meet. Take me away ... please take me ... away.'

She still held his hand and now she tried to raise herself in the bed as if to compel his attention, but the weakness of her body prevented her and for the first time since she had begun to speak Clive moved.

He pressed her back gently against her pillows and taking a glass from beside the bed held it to her lips.

She was very exhausted and her breath was coming quickly, but now it was no longer the statue of a woman who lay there but a woman suffering and feeling.

Her face had changed, its look of immobility had gone.

Instead it was ravaged with emotion and tears glistened

on her cheeks where they had run unchecked from her eyes as she spoke.

Gently Clive wiped the tears away with his own handkerchief, and then he said quietly in that voice of strength and resolution which had so often brought comfort and peace to his patients:

'I will do what is best for you.'

'Then you'll take me away from ... here?' She pleaded. 'You ... promise?'

'Promise,' he answered gravely.


## 10


Miss Ongar, watering the geraniums blooming in her windowbox, leant out of the window to shout at a small girl who was in charge of a baby in a perambulator.

'Doris,' she called, 'take the pram off the road immediately. You are to keep on the pavement, you know that.'

The child, absorbed in watching a game of hop-scotch, looked up in surprise at the commanding voice coming from above her. When she saw who it was speaking she dimpled and smiled at Miss Ongar with the confidence born of affection.

'Orl right, miss, I won't forget again.'

'That's a good girl.'

Miss Ongar watched the little group for a few moments with a benign expression, then shut the lower half of her window and replaced the now empty jug in the tiny kitchen.

She was an enormous woman, so large that it seemed almost awe-inspiring that one human being could carry such a mountain of flesh. Her hair was streaked with grey, but her face was curiously unlined and it was difficult to guess her age.

People had even been known to aver that she was on

the wrong side of seventy and that she remained young and active by means of Yogi exercises or black magic.

Miss Ongar neither denied nor disproved the gossip about herself; she was in all things singularly uncommunicative save when it concerned the well-being of her patients.

Now, as she stood for a moment in her small sitting-room, her thoughts far away, she instinctively moved her fingers as a masseuse will, exercising them.

Her hands were surprisingly small in proportion to her amazing girth, the fingers short and well shaped with exquisitely-kept nails.

They looked like a child's hands and it was impossible without experience to recognise the power and strength in them.

As Miss Ongar stood pensively inactive there was the sudden burr of an electric bell at the front door.

She turned eagerly at the sound as if she had been expecting it, moving quickly across the room and into the little hall. As she opened the door she gave a sigh of satisfaction.

'Come in,' she said, 'I was expecting you.'

Clive entered the room, wiping his feet on the mat more from habit than necessity for it was a dry day.

'You were expecting me?' he repeated, puzzled, then as he turned to meet her wide smile he added: 'Get along with you—you and your heathen tricks. In any other century but this you would have been burned as a witch.'

'I can well believe it,' Miss Ongar replied complacently. 'The ordinary man has always fought knowledge and been afraid of it.'

'I don't fight it,' Clive answered. 'But the longer I live, the less knowledge I seem to possess.'

Miss Ongar led the way to the sitting-room.

'Sit down and tell me what's the matter; there is something troubling you or you wouldn't be here.'

Clive laughed.

'You always go straight to the point, don't you, Oggie?' he said, giving her the nickname by which she was known to all the children of the neighbourhood.

'Well, what is it? Out with it and get it over,' Oggie replied. 'I don't suppose you've come to see me because of my *beaux yeux*. There's enough smart society women running after you these days, from all I hear.'

'What have you heard?'

Miss Ongar merely laughed at him.

'That's touched you on the raw, eh? But you beware—you are still young and attractive and many a good man's career has been ruined when the wrong sort of woman got hold of him.'

Clive got to his feet, disconcerted, with a look on his face which his colleagues knew so well when he was faced by something difficult, something for which he could not for the moment find the right formula.

It was typical of Oggie, he thought, to throw him out of his stride the moment he arrived. She was uncanny and he had not been far from the truth when he had called her a witch.

She invariably seemed to sense what was happening before it had happened and he was quite sure that she had the power of thought-reading.

Now he looked out through his spotlessly clean window on to the narrow, sordid street below. The East End slums!

God knew they were bad and in some ways one could be grateful to the *Luftwaffe* for sweeping away at least a proportion of the worst of them.

'Out with it,' Oggie barked behind him.

Clive, feeling for a cigarette in his pocket, turned away from the window.

'The next time I want to send you any patients,' he said, 'I shall merely dispatch them by ambulance. You'll be expecting them and have everything ready.'

'Indeed I shan't,' Oggie retorted, 'for I'm not taking any more patients at the moment. You know that, Doctor.'

She invariably called Clive 'Doctor', disdaining the fact that as he was a surgeon it was not etiquette.

'There's no higher title to be had in the medical profession,' she would say. 'A doctor you are and a doctor you will always be to me.'

'Whom are you treating now?' Clive asked.

He knew quite well but he was playing for time.

Oggie reeled off a list of names, a formidable one, the majority of them children.

'And whom have you got here?'

'In the flat?' Oggie questioned. 'You know as well as I do—little Mary Robinson. You'll have a look at her before you go?'

'Of course I will, but we shall have to move her. I'll send her down to the home in Cornwall, she's well enough for that now.'

'Indeed she's not, I'm keeping her another month at least.'

'Now listen, Oggie.'

Clive sat down, his arms resting on his knees. He knew this old woman. She was as determined and as obstinate as a mule.

In her own way she loved him, and she would make any sacrifice, do anything he asked up to a point, but always her patients came first.

He had discovered her quite unexpectedly nearly fifteen years ago. There had been a street accident and the injured child on whom he had operated in hospital had been insistent that he must see her mother himself.

Weak where children were concerned, Clive had spent a precious hour in going to see the mother.

She was bed-ridden, the child told him that, and when he had arrived at the tiny over-crowded house he had found Miss Ongar massaging her.

It had not taken him long to learn about and to recognise the work that Oggie was doing in the particular neighbourhood and he had used every possible persuasion within his power to move her nearer to the hospital, to make her work for his own patients.

She had laughed at him.

'My work is here,' she said, 'and I have as many patients as I can take. Why should I move, and why should I look after strangers when I can tend my friends?'

Nothing would alter her decision and Clive, capitulating, had been forced to send his patients to her.

He had almost to go down on his knees to get her to accept them, but it was the children who finally won her over.

It was a difficult situation and one which tried Clive's patience hundreds of times during the year.

Children whom he believed must be treated by Miss Ongar had to be billeted out in mean streets, in houses with inadequate accommodation.

He had tried to provide a private nursing home in the neighbourhood, but no matron would tolerate her for more than a week.

She was difficult, she was unconventional, she was a rebel against nearly all the accepted forms of medical science, but she got results.

Patients who had been given up by every doctor except Clive and who had failed to respond to every known type of treatment were brought back to health and strength by Oggie's magic fingers.

Clive honestly believed that most of it was faith healing. She inspired her patients, they believed in her and she made them believe in their own power of recovery. Whatever it was, they got on well.

She loved the people amongst whom she lived, their troubles were her troubles, their difficulties her difficulties. They paid her what they could afford.

Sometimes Clive's patients in gratitude for what she had done for them gave Miss Ongar large sums of money; in nine cases out of ten she returned it to them, in the tenth she would pass it on to some deserving family.

What she lived on it was hard to know. Clive felt that she must have some tiny, but secure source of income and yet he could be certain of nothing where Oggie was concerned. She was a mystery woman even to him.

Now, tentatively, he started to fight her.

'I've got someone I want to bring here,' he said. 'The child is well enough to be moved. You know it, although you have grown fond of her, as you do of all of them.'

'I don't like having people here, you know that,' Oggie replied. 'I told you last time I wasn't taking any more. I'm getting an old woman, Doctor, and I've got to have a few minutes' relaxation to myself every day.

'Sometimes I feel my patients aren't getting well as quickly as they used to. If they don't, whose fault is that?—mine, of course. I'm tired and can't give them what I haven't got within myself.'

'I know,' Clive said gently, 'but I've offered you a bigger place, I've offered you servants or nurses to help you.'

'Servants!' Oggie snorted scornfully. 'What would I want with servants waiting on me? I'm a servant myself, the servant of those who are suffering, and when I'm so decrepit that I can't look after myself you can put me under the sod.'

She chuckled suddenly.

'But there, I was forgetting you'll be wanting this body of mine up at the hospital to see what's given me such a fine figure all these years. That's the truth, isn't it?'

She chuckled again as Clive looked slightly shame-faced and almost capable of blushing.

'If you'd only let me examine you and take a few tests.'

'What a chance you've got!' Oggie retorted rudely like a small boy. 'I'm as the Lord made me and that's good enough for me and as far as I'm concerned, Doctor, it will have to be good enough for you, too.'

'All right, all right,' Clive answered; 'have it your own way. But Oggie, I've got a favour to ask you. Will you listen to me for a moment?'

'I'll listen, but I'm not promising anything, mind.'

'Well, at least hear what I have to say. There's a woman, Oggie, and she has been through a pretty good hell of her own. She was married to a man of the type which you and I most abominate—

'We've talked of them before and we know that while they degrade themselves it is nothing to the degradation and humiliation they bring to others. She was young and very innocent when she married.'

His voice seemed to deepen, then he continued.

'Later she fell in love and when her husband was killed looked forward to marrying again. The man was unfaith-

100

ful to her and the shock when she found out made her seek escape from the empty life she had lived so long.

'She went into a factory. Two days after she had started work there was an explosion and she was injured—badly injured.'

Here Clive went into a mass of medical details. Oggie nodded, but when she would have spoken he stopped her.

'I haven't finished yet. Last night we heard that the man she had loved, the man perhaps she still loves, had been killed in action. I was going to try a new appliance on her which has just come over from America, but Oggie, that woman is as sick in her mind as she is in her body. I'm bringing her to you.'

'I won't take her!' Oggie snapped. 'I'll do a good deal for you, Doctor, but I'm no fool. This woman's got money, she can go to the best homes, the best hospitals in the country, she can have nurses, she can have masseuses and appliances.

'Why should I deprive the people who can have none of these, the ones who are too poor and to frightened to go into your hospitals? If I could do them all, you know I would, but I can't.'

She paused then snapped at him—

'Is this woman's life more important than that of some child mowed down by disease or crippled by an accident before it has ever begun to savour life? No, Doctor, take her elsewhere. I don't want her here.'

Clive got up from his chair and walked towards the window. He stood with his back to the room as he had done a few moments earlier.

Oggie, sitting in her chair, looked at his broad shoulders blocking out the light, at his head towering so high in the tiny room that he almost touched the ceiling, and as she looked she saw that he was beginning to turn grey.

Suddenly she knew, knew as surely as if he had told her, that this woman meant something to him personally.

He had brought her so many cases in the past, he had turned to her often enough when he was troubled and worried about someone who would not respond to treatment.

He had brought her children who had only a few weeks to live, men who desired only suicide and must be taught to take up the threads of life again, to look trouble in the face courageously.

He had given her bodies which seemed as if only a miracle could make them whole, could force those torn and lacerated muscles to work.

She had never failed him; only occasionally she had refused a patient whom she had known she could not help.

She loved Clive, loved him as a mother might love her son; she loved the humanity in him, the gentleness, but above all his skill.

Oggie's whole life was a mission, a crusade, and she had learnt to recognise the same quality in others. Clive was dedicated to his career, but now for the first time he was interested in a woman.

She knew it and her first reaction was one of fear—fear lest the woman should fail him. But whatever the future held, she knew that she must help him if she could.

Grudgingly, in her own way, she gave in.

'Well, if you're so set on it, I suppose I must consider it. You'll drive me to my grave and then you'll be happy.'

'You'll have her?'

Clive turned swiftly, a gladness lighting up his face.

'What choice have I got?' Oggie grumbled. 'Tell me first, what is the name of this all-important patient.'

'Stella Marsden . . . Lady Marsden,' Clive said hesitatingly.

'I've heard of her,' was all Oggie said brusquely, but her heart cried out: 'Poor boy! the poor boy!'

They talked for a little while, fencing with each other, for Clive guessed the reason for Oggie's sudden change of heart and Oggie was curious about the woman who was to come under her roof.

Finally she rose with a sigh, but whether from the exertion of moving her vast bulk or from the preceding conversation Clive was in doubt.

'Come and see Mary,' she said. 'I told her you were coming.'

'How did you know that?' Clive asked, and Oggie shrugged her fat shoulders as she replied:

'I just felt it in my bones. Maybe there's negro blood in me some way back.'

Clive knew that she did not like to be questioned further and together they went into the small badroom opening off the sitting-room, which was to be Stella's.

It was only a tiny room with a brass bedstead and white-washed walls ornamented with three gilt-framed texts.

As they opened the door, the child, who was sitting up in bed playing with a shabby, battered doll, held out her arms with a glad cry of surprise.

'Doctor Clive! Doctor Clive! I can walk. I can, can't I, Miss Oggie? Let me show you.'

Clive sat down on the bed and pinched her cheek.

'You've got well quickly, young lady,' he said; 'that is why we are going to send you to the seaside. You would like that? In a very short while you will be swimming, swimming in the sea like a small fish.'

The child gave a whoop of pleasure, then she looked troubled.

'I'm not going away from Miss Oggie, am I?'

'I'm afraid so,' Clive replied; 'but, as I have said, you are going to the sea and you've got to be kind and give up your bed to someone else who is very ill and will never walk again unless Miss Oggie looks after her.'

The child's lower lip trembled for a moment, then with an effort she controlled her tears, but they shone in the eyes that were unnaturally large in the small peaked face.

'You'll come and see me, Doctor Clive, when I'm at the sea?'

'I'll try to, my dear. You will be very happy there with lots of other girls and boys all learning to walk. You will have to have a race and I will come down and give a prize for the one who can go the fastest.'

'I'll win it, I will really, Doctor Clive. You look. Help me, Miss Oggie.'

Oggie helped her out of bed and with the aid of a chair she took a few faltering steps.

It was a pathetic sight, the child striving to move, trying to walk, flushed with excitement in her eagerness, the leg only half responding to the impetus given it by the brain.

But to Clive and Oggie it was the triumphant result of months of hard work.

The leg had been condemned, the doctors decided there was no chance of saving it, and yet Clive had taken that chance.

He had operated and they had told him that the child would never be able to use it, that it would waste away, a useless limb which could well have been replaced by something artificial.

He had proved them wrong as he had so often before, but it was Oggie's skilful fingers which had made the blood flow, which had developed the unused muscles until undoubtedly, slowly but surely, the child could walk.

'Bravo, Mary,' Clive said, when Oggie put her, pale now from the exertion and excitement, back in the bed and laid her down against the pillows. 'In six months you'll be as good as new, and what do I get for that?'

Mary held out her arms and he kissed her gently.

'You'll come down and see me, won't you?' she whispered against his ear, and again he gave her a half promise, hoping inwardly that he would have the time to fulfil it.

'The child seems happy enough,' he said to Oggie when they left the sick room.

'Happy! She's never known the meaning of the word. Her stepmother beat her and her father was seldom sober. What are we going to do with her when she's cured?'

'I'll find something,' Clive said, 'or maybe you will.'

'I wish sometimes I could adopt them all. There's too much suffering in this world where the children are concerned. If people paid as much attention to them as they do to their wars, the world would be an easier place.'

'That's true enough. Now, Oggie, I'll send Lady Marsden down tomorrow afternoon. Mary will be picked up first thing in the morning. Is that all right?'

'It will have to be, I suppose,' Oggie admitted grudgingly.

She said good-bye from her doorway and watched him

104

as he ran down the stone staircase which served all the flats in the block.

She listened and heard his car drive off from the street and then she shut the door and went back to her little sitting-room.

She stood in the centre of the room as she had when she had awaited his coming, moving the fingers of her hands, exercising them, keeping them supple.

There was a troubled look on her face.

After a moment she sighed heavily and turned towards her own bedroom. She had an appointment some streets away and already she was late for it.

'I'm an old fool!' she said aloud, as she struggled into her huge, enveloping overcoat.

## 11

Someone knocked at the bedroom door. Stella said, 'Come in,' and a small girl entered carrying a large tray.

' 'Ere's yer lunch,' she announced, 'and Miss Oggie said I was ter tell yer she'd be back about two o'clock. Yer was asleep when her went out.'

Stella looked at the child in surprise. She might have been eleven or twelve and the clothes she wore were of poor quality, patched and darned, but surprisingly clean.

Her long hair was dragged back from her forehead into two neat plaits which stuck out on each side of her head and were tied at the ends with tape.

She had lost a front tooth which gave her a lisp and she spoke with care, slowly, as if she had memorised every word she uttered.

'I don't think I want any lunch,' Stella said.

She felt a sudden wave of resentment that Miss Ongar was not there to attend to her, at having been left alone since breakfast, in spite of the fact that she had fallen asleep naturally and slept dreamlessly for at least an hour and a half.

'Miss Oggie said yer was ter eat it, and look—I've cooked the fish for yer just as she tell me.'

The child took the china cover off the dish and Stella, looking at the neatly arranged tray, could not help but notice that the dish did look surprisingly appetising.

'What's your name?' she asked.

'Elizabeth,' was the reply; 'but everyone rahnd 'ere calls me Liza—except Doctor Clive. 'E always says Elizabeth.'

'So you know Doctor Clive?'

'Know 'im! I should say so. 'E operated on me 'e did, three years ago and if it 'adn't been for 'im I should have been a goner. Me muvver says 'e saved me life.'

'What happened?' Stella asked.

Not because she was really curious but because somehow it was a relief to talk after being alone.

She remembered how often she had craved to be left undisturbed in hospital and at Trenton Park, how the idea that the merest movement would bring Nurse Benson rustling into the room could fill her with dread so that she would feign sleep.

She had hated being spoken to, and yet the morning had seemed unnaturally long while she had lain alone and apparently forgotten.

'Have I been crazy to come here?' she asked herself more than once.

She did not know quite what she had expected when she had begged Clive to take her away from Trenton Park; yet when he had given her his promise she had felt at peace, trusting him utterly not to fail her.

She shrunk with every nerve in her body from the knowledge that those around her knew what had happened.

She had refused to see Hetty Hayton to say good-bye despite Nurse Benson's pleadings.

She had known instinctively that Hetty Hayton wanted to hurt her, to torture her with her references to Bertram, to drive deeper the wounds which were agonising enough in themselves.

106

Nurse Benson knew about Bertram. Stella could see the sympathy in her face although she said nothing. She lay awake all night imagining long conversations between the two nurses.

She thought they watched her, looking for her reactions, for any expression of sorrow and misery that might fulfil their expectations.

'Get me away,' she had pleaded with Clive.

She felt that, if she did not do so soon, she would go mad.

She had heard the surprise in Nurse Benson's voice when she came into her bedroom the following evening to say that Mr. Ross wished to speak to her on the telephone.

There was something disapproving in the way she handed the telephone across the bed—Doctors should send messages through nurses, not speak to the patients themselves!

Stella lifted the receiver to her ear.

'Hello.'

She heard Clive's deep voice respond.

'You are leaving tomorrow morning. Does that please you?'

'Of course it does. Thank you for remembering.'

'You'd better not thank me until you know where you are going. You are quite certain that you wouldn't rather stay in comfort and luxury?'

'I don't mind where I go so long as I leave here.'

Stella's voice was strained now and as if that particular note reassured him Clive said:

'Good. Well, you won't be keeping Nurse Benson.'

'Am I going to a Nursing Home?'

'Not exactly. You see, Lady Marsden, your case is rather a peculiar one. I particularly wanted you to be at Trenton Park so as to try out a certain electric appliance which has just arrived from America. It's the only one of its kind in the country.

'But if we can't use mechanical help, then we shall have to use the human sort and there's only one person I can trust to do what I want done. She's a friend of mine and I think that you will learn to like her, too. But be prepared for surprises.'

There was a hint of laughter in Clive's voice as if it amused him to make her curious.

He certainly succeeded, for when she would have asked more he bade her curtly "Good-bye' and the line went dead.

All the time she was being got ready for the journey Stella was acutely conscious of Nurse Benson's resentment and disapproval.

She said little and Stella gave her no encouragement to talk; but anything she may have felt then could not be compared with her feelings when finally she got Stella into bed in Miss Ongar's tiny flat.

Even Stella had been slightly disconcerted as she arrived at her destination.

She was tired, for the journey was long and any movement hurt her; but as they neared London and turned into the narrow squalid streets of the East End she wondered if Clive was playing some inhuman trick upon her.

When finally the ambulance stopped outside a block of flats which seemed even less prepossessing than the surrounding buildings, Stella had a momentary impulse to refuse to be removed from the vehicle; then pride kept her silent.

She had asked for this—very well, she would show him that she was not afraid, that she was not to be taken off her guard by his surprise, however formidable.

Miss Ongar was waiting for her and something in her smile and the soothing touch of her hand reassured Stella.

Despite her amazing appearance there was a hint of authority in the way she directed Nurse Benson what to do, and the manner in which without fuss or saying anything that should have been resented she whisked the disapproving woman off the premises.

When the nurse had gone, with a last almost sentimental good-bye to Stella as if she was leaving her in prison or under the penalty of certain death, Miss Oggie came back into the bedroom.

'That's better,' she said. 'Now we are alone and can get to know each other. I never can stand hospital nurses. If I had to have them about me I should die and quick about it.'

'But aren't you a nurse?' Stella asked in surprise.

'Me! Good heavens, no; whatever put such an idea into your head? I'm a masseuse, my dear, and proud of it. The good Lord didn't give me much, but he gave me hands and I've learnt how to use them. Now are you comfortable?'

She adjusted Stella in the bed, pushing the pillows into just the right place beneath her back and against her shoulders.

'You're tired, that's what's wrong with you,' she went on before Stella could reply. 'I'm going to make you a cup of tea and when you've had it I want you to sleep.'

'Is Mr. Ross coming to see me this evening?' Stella asked a few minutes later when Oggie returned with a tray.

Oggie shrugged her shoulders, a gesture which seemed to make her whole body ripple in sympathy.

'He may and he may not; you never know with Doctor Clive. Sometimes I've a feeling that he's coming, but tonight I can't tell one way or another.'

'A feeling?' Stella questioned.

Oggie looked at her with twinkling eyes.

'You evidently haven't heard about me yet. They suspect me of witchcraft in this part of the world—when they don't think I'm a saint who can work miracles. Sometimes I can be seeing things and sometimes I can't—that's what it comes to.

'Most people have the faculty one way or another, but in some of us it's more developed. Doctor Clive's one of them, but he won't admit it—oh no! He tries to give chapter and verse for every conviction he has, but I'm not deceived.'

Stella, sipping her tea and looking round the bare, poorly furnished bedroom, felt this could hardly be true. The change from Trenton Park was too overpowering.

How long ago was it since she had slept in such a tiny

room, and this was poorer than anything she had ever known in her life!

Everything was spotlessly clean, but the linoleum had lost its pattern, the rug was threadbare; the curtains of bright, cheap material were the only patch of colour and in contrast to the whitewashed walls.

And Miss Oggie herself?—Stella had by this time learnt her name and nickname.

The latter suited her, she thought, it was as queer as the woman herself with her great body, tiny hands and ugly face which somehow inspired confidence and trust.

Suddenly Stella felt overwhelmingly drowsy; the bed, poor though it might be, was comfortable and warm. She slipped down in her pillows.

She felt a hand touching her forehead, smoothing away her hair.

It was mesmeric, the rhythm of the fingers at her temples seemed to soothe away the tenseness of her muscles and the querulousness of her mind.

She closed her eyes and slept. . . .

She had opened them to find Clive looking down at her. It was quite late in the evening; she must have slept for a long time.

'Hello, it's you.'

She greeted him sleepily and was not aware of the informality both of her exclamation and of the smile she gave him. It was the first time Clive had ever seen her smile.

'I came to see if you'd decided to stay,' he said, and she fancied he was teasing her.

'I haven't been here very long.'

'Long enough to make up your mind. Do you realise how honoured you are?'

He spoke seriously.

'Honoured?'

She was puzzled by the word.

'That Oggie would take you in. She refused flat at first.'

'Why?'

'She has no use for my moneyed patients or the social ones.'

'How did you persuade her?'

'I almost went down on my knees! But it was a question of here or Trenton Park and you seemed to have taken a dislike to Trenton Park.'

'Are you always so considerate of your patients' likes and dislikes?'

'Generally, when I want them to get well.'

For the first time since she had woken from her sleep Stella thought of her own well-being and was astonished to discover that she was feeling immeasurably better. It was ridiculous, of course, a mere illusion of the mind.

'I like Miss Oggie,' she said after a moment's pause. 'Thank you for bringing me here.'

She spoke with conviction and Clive smiled in response.

'Good,' he said, 'that's what I wanted you to say.'

'Is she such a marvellous masseuse?'

'She works miracles, literally and continually.'

'Then why,' Stella asked, glancing round the room and choosing her words so as not to give offence, 'doesn't she have bigger premises where she could accommodate more patients?'

'If you could persuade Oggie to move you would indeed remove mountains,' he said.

Although he smiled at the play on words Stella knew that he was speaking seriously.

'You'll find it all out in time,' he went on, 'and Oggie will give you the answers. I'm not going to tell you too much about her, I want you to find out for yourself.'

'Yet another way to arouse the interest of the patient?' Stella asked, but before Clive could answer she added:

'And I hate to admit it, but you are succeeding.'

They were both laughing as Oggie came into the room.

'Now we will get to work,' Clive said. 'I'm going to show you what I want you to do, Oggie, and I am sorry, Lady Marsden, but this is going to hurt you.'

It did hurt her so much that Stella felt the sweat break out on her forehead and she had to clench her hands to-gether to prevent herself screaming.

Yet in some extraordinary way the pain was nothing

111

like the agony she had experienced only forty-eight hours earlier at Trenton Park.

She had slept peacefully after Clive had gone, although she fancied that it was not entirely a natural sleep but induced by the hot drink which Oggie had brought her after a light supper.

In the morning she had a treatment from her hostess and then was left alone, a prey to her own doubts, to the feeling that she had been hasty in deciding that she liked this strange new life.

Now as she ate her luncheon, watched by the wide-eyed child with the plaits, the humorous side of it suddenly struck her.

Here was she, rich, socially important, acclaimed, choosing to live in a slum with a peculiar old woman, half witch, half faith-healer who, however, could allow her only a small portion of her valuable time.

'I'm crazy!' Stella thought to herself.

She then realised she had eaten every bit of the fish and that it had been delicious.

'I've got some rice puddin' fer yer now,' the child Liza said, taking away the empty plate.

A small pudding was brought in, browned crisply in its basin, and the plate on which to serve it was hot.

'Do you often cook for Miss Oggie?' Stella asked.

'I give 'er an 'and when she's busy,' Liza replied. 'Muvver spares me, but it ain't always easy because of the kids—six of 'em.'

'Six?' Stella questioned.

'Yes, six and me—that's seven altogether and Bert's only four months old.'

'How does your mother manage?'

'Oh, we manage orl right now Farver's in the army. It used to be a bit 'ard when 'e was on the dole, but now with the Club money we gets four pounds a week. Things are fine, I can tell yer—I only 'opes the war don't ever end'

Stella stared at her. Four pounds a week and seven children! She remembered how often she had paid five pounds and more for a hat, for dinner at a restaurant, for a bag

112

to go with some special suit—and this family thought four pounds a week luxury.

She pushed her plate away with a little gesture of disgust, not at the food but at herself.

'Have you had your lunch?' she asked Liza.

'Oh yes,' Liza said; 'we 'as it at 'alf past twelve.'

'Do you have enough?' Stella asked. 'You're not hungry?'

'No, I'm not 'ungry,' Liza said; 'we're never 'ungry now Farver's in the army.'

Then, as she picked up the tray, she added:

'Sure you're finished? 'cos Miss Oggie lets me finish up the bits so there'll be no waste.'

Stella lay back against the pillows and shut her eyes.

She thought of the fruit at Marsden, of the great bunches of grapes in the vinery, of the peaches, nectarines and greengages which often rotted on the trees because there were not enough people to eat them and Philip would not allow the gardeners to sell outside the estate.

Looking back through the years Stella tried to remember the people she had helped, people to whom she had been kind.

She had written cheques for charities, of course, but somehow it didn't seem the same thing, there was nothing personal about that.

Was this why Clive had brought her here, to show her a world she had never known?

'I'm ill,' she told herself. 'Things seem to matter so much more, to get out of all proportion when one is not well.'

Her eyes were closed, but she felt as if Liza was in the room; she could see her little peaked face and under-nourished body.

'I wish I'd never come,' Stella thought. 'I don't want to know about such things, I want to be left alone with my own feelings, my sorrows, not to have other people's thrust upon me.'

The door opened abruptly.

'I'm off now, miss. Anything else you wants?'

'Come here,' Stella said.

113

As Liza obeyed her she pointed to the drawer of the dressing-table.

'Look in there, you will see a handbag. Bring it to me.'

Liza did as she was told and Stella, opening her note-case, took out several notes.

'Will you give these to your mother and tell her to buy something you want?' she asked.

Liza's eyes glistened, but only for a moment. Then she shook her head.

'Miss Oggie wouldn't like it,' she said. 'There was a lidy 'ere once—oh, a long time ago—and she wanted to give me five shillings for what I done while she was ill. Miss Oggie wouldn't 'ave it.'

'We needn't tell her,' Stella pleaded.

Liza looked shocked.

'I mustn't do anything Miss Oggie wouldn't like.'

Feeling curiously ashamed, Stella put the money back in her note-case. She had tried to buy herself peace of mind and had failed.

'I'll tell you what I'll do, Liza,' she said. 'I'll buy you something you want. I don't believe Miss Oggie would mind that, but I'll ask her first. You think of something you want very much indeed and I'll send to the shops for it.'

'Ooh! 'Onest yer will?' Liza exclaimed. 'Yer won't forget?'

'I won't forget,' Stella said. 'But you must tell me what you want.'

'I'll tell you right enough, but gimme time to think. Yer won't be going away before termorrow, will yer?'

'I don't think it's likely.'

'Then I'll tell yer termorrow. Will that be orl right?'

'That will be all right.'

'Oh, I 'ope Miss Oggie don't say no,' Liza said; 'but if she do, we can't do anythink abaht it. She's like that—even the boys rahnd 'ere does as she tells 'em.'

'And you?—do you always do what she tells you?' Stella asked.

'Betcha life. She's a wonderful person—'er and Doctor Clive.'

The door slammed behind Liza and Stella was alone again.

Funny to think how isolated she was and yet somehow she felt more at home at this moment than she had felt anywhere for a long time.

It was cosy, and yet she thought of the horror with which her so-called friends would view the room in which she was laying and the street outside.

Somewhere in the distance a barrel-organ was playing and there were shouts of children playing, high Cockney voices yelling defiance or shouting a warning. It was noisy and yet Stella preferred it to the peace of Trenton Park.

There was the rumble of traffic, the sudden shrillness of a policeman's whistle and the continual hoot of motor-horns and ting of bicycle bells.

For the first time since that ghastly moment in Bertram's flat Stella felt the load of misery, the ice which had bound her heart, lessening a little.

The world went on; whatever happened, whatever one suffered, the world went on. Whether she liked it or not, she must go on too, there was no escape, no relief from oneself.

She heard the front door open, heard footsteps crossing the sitting-room and then her own door swung back.

Smiling a greeting as she entered, Oggie came into the room like a ship in full sail. Stella turned on her pillows and felt a sudden impulse of gladness as one might feel at meeting an old friend.

'Oh I'm glad you are back.' she said.

12

Hetty looked up from her writing-desk as Alice put her head round the door.

'Lady Danvers is on the telephone. She wants to know whether you will come to tea this afternoon.'

Hetty hesitated.

'I'd like to go, but I don't know how long this man is going to stay. Are you quite certain, Alice, he didn't tell you what he wanted?'

'Quite certain,' Alice replied firmly.

'Then tell Lady Danvers I'll come if I can. I ought to be able to manage it.'

Alice disappeared with the message while Hetty put down her pen and sat thinking.

Vernon Wrighton—somehow the name seemed familiar and yet irritatingly she could not remember how or where she had heard it.

For once Alice was of no use to her, all she knew was that a Mr. Wrighton had rung up from the Foreign Office and said that it was essential that he should see Mrs. Hayton. He was arriving by train and Hetty had arranged to send to the station for him.

Vaguely, for some unknown reason, the appointment disturbed her.

She always disliked having an interview with anyone about whom she knew nothing; she liked to be prepared, to have her answers ready. She was sorry now she had not spoken to the man himself.

'He was very insistent,' Alice told her.

She tried to dismiss the uneasiness of her premonitions by thinking of Clive, but that brought her no peace of mind. She was disturbed about Clive, worried about him. First and foremost their evening together had gone wrong.

That was due to Stella Marsden and Hetty registered yet another score to be paid by the woman who had jeopardised all that she most valued.

For when Clive had told her that he was sending Stella away, she had, for the first time in their work together, challenged his authority.

'It's ridiculous!' she asserted angrily. 'You send her down here for a cure and before she even commences it you remove her. Give her a chance, give her at least the opportunity to find out what we can do for her. Besides, what are people going to say?'

116

There lay the real cause for Hetty's anxiety on Stella's behalf and Clive knew it.

He had been well aware ever since Trenton Park was opened as a Convalescent Home that Hetty hankered after the most important patients, the ones who had big names and assured positions in peace time.

Clive, in his own quiet unobtrusive way, had taken no notice of what Hetty wanted or did not want.

He decided from the beginning to use Trenton Park only for his most serious cases and the patients he sent there were only those he considered would benefit from the treatment they could receive, whether they were important or unimportant from their hostess's point of view.

Hetty, in her desire to win him, had been careful not to allow her social ambitions to obtrude themselves or to show through the mask of mercy and loving kindness which she invariably assumed in Clive's presence.

But for once the mask was dropped, the naked truth revealed itself in her voice and before she had finished speaking she read his disgust and contempt in the expression of his face.

Hetty was so used to getting her own way, to over-riding and over-bidding anyone who stood in her path, that for the moment it was impossible for her to check her anger.

'Stella Marsden must stay here,' she asserted.

But she immediately regretted her outburst as Clive without another word turned and left her alone in her own sitting-room.

For a moment she was too astounded to speak.

Then she realised what she had done. Even now she could hardly believe that she had indeed lost and repulsed the one man she had desired in her whole life.

'He can't do without me,' she told herself.

Her confidence returned as she thought of the wonderfully equipped medical ward upstairs and the patients filling it, all of whom were being kept, fed and treated at her expense.

But her business-like brain, so well trained in the past,

117

remembered the papers she had signed, the conditions under which she had opened the convalescent home.

There was no mention of Clive's name in them, her contract was not with any particular man and she understood in a flash how slender a hold she had over Clive's gratitude.

She might tell him she was giving this or that to him only, but he accepted it impersonally on behalf of the sick and suffering.

'Just supposing,' she tortured herself, 'that he refuses to come here himself, that he sends another man, another specialist who understands what is required and merely carries out orders?'

'He wouldn't dare,' she thought, 'he wouldn't want to.'

But the fear was there, and when some minutes later she went upstairs to the ward it was to find that Clive had gone and without saying good-bye.

Something of Hetty's usual buoyancy seemed to leave her and that evening when dinner, taken *tête-à-tête* with Alice, was over she sat alone in her sitting-room and faced herself.

She was forty, a much-talked-of, much-envied woman, but she was terribly lonely. Even in those extra-ordinary years with Clement she had not known such loneliness as she was experiencing now.

She had a place in society, and that she could always retain so long as she had money. She had a circle of so-called friends chosen, she admitted to herself, for every reason save that of friendship and companionship.

'What more do I want?'

The answer came swiftly to her. She wanted Clive, she wanted him as a man. She would want him, were he a crossing-sweeper, were he the most utter outcast.

It didn't matter to her who he was or what his social position, she longed for his arms round her, for the feeling of his lips on hers.

She wanted to surrender herself, to be possessed as she had always possessed so much except love.

'I love nothing ... nothing,' she murmured suddenly, and was afraid of the implication within her own thoughts.

118

As she watched Stella leave the next morning, saw the ambulance drive away from under the great Gothic porch, she had a sudden fancy that something valuable, something precious went with her.

Then Hetty's common sense tried to reinstate itself.

'Stella is nothing more than a patient to Clive,' she told herself. 'You're giving her an importance which he would be the last to grant her. He is interested because she is really ill, because he has done one of his amazing operations upon her. There's nothing more—nothing.'

Yet however much she chided herself, the feeling of depression was there, the feeling of being left behind, outstripped, defeated in some race which she was not aware had started until she had found that she had lost it.

Alice found her hard to bear, for she vented all the restlessness of her emotions upon that patient, uncomplaining woman.

'I must get away for a change,' she told Alice. 'I can't stand this place any longer. Perhaps we are all on edge the fourth year of war, but at least one needn't stagnate. I shall go up to London—I haven't decided yet whether I'll take you or leave you here.'

Alice said little, she knew there was nothing one could say to Hetty when she was in this mood, she could only pray that it would pass quickly.

Guiltily, she felt that it had all started from the moment when she had come into the room and interrupted Hetty and Clive.

Yet how was she to know, to anticipate that Clive would act the way he did, that Lady Marsden would leave Trenton Park and that Hetty would take it as a personal insult?

Wearily Alice tried to concentrate on the housekeeping accounts, on the letters she had to type regarding the patients, but always her mind returned to the same problem—Hetty and the atmosphere of antagonism which now seemed to emanate from her towards everyone and especially herself.

Hetty changed into a smart and attractive dress before Mr. Vernon Wrighton arrived.

119

'Always look your best and always be smarter than the other person if you have a difficult interview in front of you,' Clement had said.

He had drilled Hetty into taking every possible advantage. She knew every move.

'Sit with your back to the light; make those who come to see you face it and sit low.'

'Always appear busy even if you are not.'

'Always be gracious if it costs you nothing, even to the most unimportant person.'

'I've never seen him before,' Hetty thought swiftly as Mr. Wrighton was announced.

He was a thin, short, insignificant-looking little man of about forty-five or fifty; he wore dark glasses and she was quite certain that he had left the inevitable Foreign Office black Homburg in the hall.

He carried a brief-case under his arm and he came forward with an unhurried gait across the long expanse of the library to shake her hand.

'Charming place you've got here, Mrs. Hayton,' he said.

He looked round him with an air of approval, and it was at that moment that Hetty decided she disliked her visitor.

He was too sure of himself, too suave. As she asked him to sit down on the sofa and offered him a cigarette she was seeking eagerly and swiftly for some point of vantage in what she felt certain was a fencing match ahead.

'You wanted to see me?' she said, as Mr. Wrighton seemed in no hurry to start the conversation. 'I don't think we've had the pleasure of meeting each other before to-day.'

'I have often seen you, though, Mrs. Hayton, and admired you—if I may say so?'

Hetty inclined her head. She was suspicious of compliments when they were paid in such a manner. She wished he would come to the point.

'I wanted to see you alone and privately,' Mr. Wrighton said. 'We cannot be overheard here?'

'Most certainly not,' Hetty replied.

She was surprised at the question, and it brought with it an intensified feeling of apprehension.

'Well, then, I call tell you the reason for my visit,' Mr. Wrighton went on. 'You were a friend, a very close friend I believe, of the Baron von Stronheim.'

Hetty stiffened. It had been convenient since the war started to forget how fervently she had championed the German envoys who had come to London before the war.

It had been fashionable before Munich to be more or less pro-German.

Certainly members of the German Embassy could be found in many of the most distinguished houses in London.

Hetty had made a point of giving large and much advertised parties for the Ambassador.

Baron von Stronheim had been sent to England on a special mission. Hetty was a little vague as to what that mission was, but undoubtedly he had received a great deal of attention both from the Press and from society.

He was a good-looking, distinguished man and he had welcomed very fervently any kindness Hetty was gracious enough to accord him.

She had entertained for him very largely all one summer: Cabinet Ministers, Duchesses, Peers, Members of Parliament and the Press were only too glad to be included in the parties she gave for Baron von Stronheim.

There were week-end parties at Trenton Park and she had even given the most popular *bal masqué* of the season especially for him.

She thought of him now, of that courteous, almost old-world manner beneath which lay a quick, imperious Prussianism.

At the beginning of their acquaintance Hetty had been deceived into believing Baron von Stronheim was what he appeared—a charming gentleman bored with politics and interested only in the society of lovely women.

Few people, she believed, could pierce that clever façade; but beneath it she learnt, as time passed, was a man fanatically devoted to his leader, a man whose whole life was one of intrigue, plot and counterplot.

It had amused her to discover this, it had been rather thrilling, rather exciting to feel herself run after and indeed courted by this man who in his subtle ruthlessness reminded her of Clement.

Now she felt a sudden chill at the sound of his name, but she answered Mr. Wrighton steadily enough.

'Yes, I knew Baron von Stronheim. You have news of him?'

'Nothing, I'm afraid, to his advantage,' Mr. Vernon Wrighton said with a smile. 'I believe he still holds quite an important post in the Nazi party although what it is need not concern us at the moment.'

Hetty waited. She had a feeling that a vast shadow was approaching her, was coming nearer and nearer and that in a moment it would envelop her.

'You had correspondence with the Baron?'

Mr. Wrighton was not looking at her as he spoke, but was undoing the straps of his brief-case.

'I'm sure I did. One usually corresponds with people whom one entertains,' Hetty answered lightly. 'May I ask on what authority you are asking me these questions?'

'Upon my own authority and to your advantage, Mrs. Hayton.'

'To my advantage!' Hetty echoed the words.

'Most certainly.'

Mr. Wrighton smiled and she felt it was the type of smile that the judges of the Spanish Inquisition gave as they watched their victims on the rack.

'On the 19th June, 1938, you wrote to the Baron, Mrs. Hayton.'

'Did I? I can hardly be expected to remember that.'

'You wrote to him from this house.' He took a letter out of the case. 'Yes, from Trenton Park.'

Hetty suddenly got to her feet.

'Where did you get that letter?'

'You recognise it, I see.'

Mr. Wrighton looked up, still smiling.

'That was a private letter.'

122

'Certainly, a very private letter,' Mr. Vernon Wrighton said. 'A letter written to the envoy of the German Government by a lady whose hospitality he had enjoyed, a lady whose adopted country, if not the country of her birth, was at that time not interested in the events of Europe.'

'From where did you get that letter?' Hetty repeated.

'I'm afraid, Mrs. Hayton, I've come here to ask questions, not to answer them. It is sufficient, let us say, that the letter came into my possession by unorthodox means. Nevertheless, at the moment it is in my possession.'

Hetty sat down in her chair. She was trembling.

'This letter, couched in very charming terms of affection,' Mr. Wrighton went on, 'carried in it some very interesting and doubtless edifying information.'

'I remember the letter,' Hetty said briefly.

'You remember, no doubt, the part in which you describe a conversation you had overheard between a Cabinet Minister and the Secretary of State for Foreign Affairs who had dined with you the night before.

'The conversation was brief, but it must have been of undoubted value to Baron von Stronheim to know exactly the views of the Secretary of State and, no doubt, of the Cabinet Minister, too, in the increase in German naval tonnage and our ability in this country to withstand attacks from the air.'

'That is all past history,' Hetty said. 'The letter, however valuable then, has no value today.'

'That is a matter of opinion,' Mr. Wrighton said; 'but I was just wondering what would be the view of my present chief at the Foreign Office and of the British Government at this moment towards the writer of this letter.'

'You are not, then, representing the Foreign Office?' Hetty said quickly.

'As a quite minor employee in that important Ministry, I am representing no one but myself.'

Hetty gave a little sigh. She was beginning to understand, to see daylight. She was no longer abjectly afraid, instead her brain took control and she gave a little laugh, scornful and sharp.

123

'So it's blackmail.'

'Exactly. An unpleasant word, but very comprehensive.'

'How much do you want?'

'I have been considering that on my way down,' Mr. Vernon Wrighton said. 'To begin with, my dear lady we have to take into consideration that you are very fond of this country. You have made for yourself an almost unique position here as a hostess.

'I can't believe that you would enjoy being dealt with under Section 18B or being exiled to that country across the Atlantic which you left some years ago and to which you seem in no hurry to return.'

'You evidently know a good deal about me,' Hetty said tartly.

Some part of her mind was almost amused now at his presentation of his case. The man had brains, she must admit that, but she wished she knew how that unfortunate letter had come into his possession.

'Never write letters.'

How often Clement warned her of that and she had been stupid enough to disobey him. Well, she must face the consequences she supposed, although she imagined they were going to be expensive.

'Well, what is your price? I don't imagine you can tell me much about myself that I don't know already.'

'We'll keep it strictly to business lines, shall we?' Mr. Wrighton said. 'Very well then. You'll forgive me if I state what I require in pounds, I find dollars so confusing.

'I want a hundred thousand pounds to be paid to me immediately; I want fifteen thousand a year for the rest of my life, and I want a promise in writing that you will never entertain in the future any envoy or representative of a foreign government.'

'I think you're mad!' Hetty snapped the words at him, jumping to her feet.

'On the contrary, my dear lady, I am exceedingly sane and strange though it may seem to you I have a great deal of patriotism left in me. It is women like you who are representative of no particular race or nationality who have done this country such immeasurable harm in the past.'

Mr. Wrighton's voice was that of a Prosecuting Counsel.

'You belong to the international set,' he continued, 'you have no loyalties, no patriotism, no feeling or emotion for anything except yourself. You live in London, you get your money from America, you dress in Paris.

'You are prepared to tell the secrets of all three countries, in fact to betray all those who have nurtured and cosseted you to the first good-looking German who comes along.

'I intend not to get rid of you—that's impossible—but to draw your teeth, to render you harmless. Those are my intentions.'

'And if I refuse?' Hetty asked.

'Then this letter will be placed with the proper authorities tomorrow morning. That's all—very simple. They may, of course, take up the attitude that you are an American subject—you are by marriage; then you will be discreetly sent home—for good.

'You could pick up the threads again in New York, you'll find many of your international friends there waiting for hostilities to cease. No doubt they manage to do an hour's work at the Red Cross when they are fortified with enough dry martinis in the Waldorf Astoria.'

Hetty thought of New York and shuddered.

There would be no pretending there, they knew her as well as they knew and would remember Clement. Her position gone, the legend she had built up round herself vanished, she would become a nonentity, a rich woman among rich women.

She knew then that whatever the price she must stay in England.

'Listen,' she said. Now that she was ready to begin to bargain she smiled, speaking in a voice that was both quiet and charming. 'Before we start to talk about the money, let's get this other clause settled, shall we? I'll give you an undertaking never again to entertain a representative of the German Government. Will that satisfy you?'

Mr. Wrighton shook his head.

'With world politics in the state they are,' he said, 'I

125

should be a fool to agree to such a suggestion. Who knows where our enemies or our friends will come from in the future.

'What I want to eliminate is the danger of social interference with what are national affairs. There have been too many pacts hatched at Mayfair luncheon tables.'

His eyes narrowed with disgust.

'It is women like you, who don't understand what is going on and who—as I have already said—care less, that do the harm, women who have no conscience or instinct to guide them. It is the crowd who go from Ritz to Ritz, hardly knowing what country they are in unless they look out of the windows, who spell danger not for themselves but for the men who die because of them—die on the beaches of Dunkirk and in the desert of Africa.'

Mr. Wrighton had not moved from the sofa and yet it seemed to Hetty as if he dominated the whole room.

Gone were the points of vantage; he was seated and she was standing, and yet she felt small, utterly small and humiliated to the point of exasperation.

That this man, this unimportant clerk, should put her in such a position was intolerable; that she could see no way out of it was catastrophic.

'But suppose,' she said, 'just suppose I give you my promise in writing and in five, ten years from now I break it—what then?'

'Then this letter will be brought to the notice of the authorities,' he said. 'I feel that even in peace time, even if we revert to our usual complacency and good-humoured tolerance of our enemies, we shall still have learnt something about spies, about the women who act as informers.'

Quite suddenly Mr. Wrighton dropped his formal manner.

'Good heavens, woman! don't you understand that if you were a man there's enough in this letter to hang you? How you could have overheard such a conversation is beyond my comprehension. The Foreign Secretary must have considered himself absolutely safe.

'I don't know whether you had a dictaphone in the room or whether you had your pretty ear to the key-

126

hole—whatever it was, there was no chance of your not understanding the value of what you were passing on to the German Government.'

He spoke with barely concealed anger.

'It was vital information and you supplied it at a vital moment in both countries' history. Who knows how much it affected the terms that were dictated to us at Munich?

'It isn't for me to judge that or for you. Sufficient to say that this letter incriminates you completely, you can't escape from it or from its significance.'

'And the money—why do you want the money?' Hetty asked. 'How dare you preach to me? you who are just a blackmailer, a man prepared to take money in payment for his silence.'

'That's my own business,' Mr. Wrighton answered. 'Sufficient to tell you that the money will not be used entirely selfishly, but will help the families of those men who have died that democracy, real democracy, may live.'

'It is too much,' Hetty said. 'I can't agree to any of the conditions.'

'You are going to agree,' he said; 'and as you are a sensible woman who has handled her own business extremely ably for some years, you will pay up and waste no time in squealing.

'I happen to know that a large amount of your money is in bonds. I will take those and I will take also some of your jewellery towards the hundred thousand.'

He smiled unpleasantly.

'It's going to cripple you for a bit, isn't it? and I want to do that; but doubtless Mr. Hayton's investments will double themselves in the boom which will succeed the war and then the paltry fifteen thousand a year you are paying me will seem unimportant.'

'It's a fortune,' Hetty said slowly, 'and how could I trust you not to ask more, how do I know that in a year's time you won't demand twenty thousand, thirty thousand a year?'

'You'll have to take my word for it,' Mr. Wrighton replied. 'I will give it to you if you like as an Englishman and a patriot. If you think it over, Mrs. Hayton, you will

127

see I have been very generous towards you. Things might have been much worse. You'd find Holloway unsympathetic, for instance.'

Hetty turned her back to him for a moment, looking down at the fire.

'Very well,' she said, 'there's nothing else I can do, I suppose I shall have to agree.'

But even as she spoke, her brain was working swiftly and avidly to effect a way out.

## 13

Mr. Wrighton replaced the letter carefully in his dispatch case, then he looked up at Hetty and said with a smile:

'I congratulate you, Mrs. Hayton.'

'Congratulate me!'

'On your self-control. Most women—you'll forgive me if I generalise—would have snatched at this letter or at least made some attempt to get possession of it. I had naturally taken precautions against that sort of thing, but I'm glad they were not necessary.'

'What precautions have you taken?' Hetty asked.

She spoke slowly, for only half her mind was attending to what this man was saying, the other half was speculating, scheming, searching for an avenue of escape.

'Well, anticipating what you have been wise enough not to attempt, I had the letter photographed. It was done very discreetly, of course, you needn't be nervous on that account.

'The man is one of the official photographers of the Ministry and documents of the most secret nature pass through his hands. Then I took the negative and the photograph and placed them in a very safe place.'

Mr. Wrighton saw Hetty's face and went on.

'Don't look worried, I know exactly what you're thinking. You are thinking that if I was killed by a bomb or run over by a bus that photograph might fall into strange hands. That would be unfair to you as you have agreed to my conditions.

'Thinking of all that—and you must admit I'm thorough—I have placed the photograph and the negative in a book in the shelves of my library.

'There are nearly five thousand volumes in that little library,' Mr. Wrighton continued with pride. 'I have collected them all my life and they are never touched by anyone but myself. I am too much of a book lover to encourage borrowers. Your secret is safe with me and me only. Is that fair?'

'You can hardly expect me to think that any of your methods are fair,' Hetty said coldly.

Mr. Wrighton looked at her as if he was disappointed that she did not appreciate his forethought and detailed planning.

'Well, I suppose it would be too much to expect you to praise me; all the same, I have tried hard to work this out to the $n$th degree of accuracy. And now, Mrs. Hayton, shall we look at your jewels?'

'Surely you don't intend to choose the pieces you want?'

'I'm afraid so. You see, I happen to be rather a connoisseur of jewellery; in fact, to let you into a secret, I was brought up in the jewel trade, my father was one of the big Amsterdam dealers.

'He always meant me to follow in his footsteps, but I showed so much unusual ability for my age that they decided the Civil Service should benefit by my services.'

Hetty had to clench her hands together to prevent her shrieking out at this pompous, self-satisfied bore.

She could see that he was enjoying every moment of this drama in which he was playing a leading part.

She could imagine that it must have taken him weeks, perhaps even months before he had the whole scheme worked out in his mind and before he came to see her.

It would have given him pleasure to wait like a cat playing with a mouse. Now he was savouring, almost relishing, the sensation of having her in his power.

The man was not evil, not the type of blackmailer who

129

merely battens brutally on his victims. This man was a very different breed.

She could understand that in his own way he felt that he was being intensely patriotic and she was even prepared to believe his hints that the money was to be expended on a good cause.

It would give him pleasure to dispense benevolence, the means for which he had obtained in unorthodox ways.

'What can I do? What can I do?' she thought frantically.

'My idea,' Mr. Wrighton was saying, 'is to pick out jewellery which I consider worth, say, thirty to forty thousand pounds. I have seen you at the opera, Mrs. Hayton, and I know that you have some very fine specimen pieces.

'Through the channels with which I am in touch these can be disposed of quite quietly and without comment.

'After all, by the time the war is over you will doubtless be able to replace such possessions and at the moment even you can have little use for them.'

Hetty felt herself tremble with rage at his impertinence, at the way he dared to dictate to her, but with a stupendous effort she checked the words that rose to her lips.

'Never get angry,' Clement had said, 'however provocative your opponent, however easy it may be to lose your temper. If you lose control, you throw away your last hope of winning the game.'

'It is indeed a lost hope,' she thought.

It seemed that Mr. Wrighton held all the cards.

'Your bonds,' he went on, 'are a different matter. Those undoubtedly you will have at the bank and I would suggest to you that to save any unpleasantness or any chance of questions you instruct the manager to send them here to you and I will come down and fetch them one day next week.'

Hetty still said nothing. She stood biting her lower lip.

'You'll forgive me,' Mr. Wrighton said, looking at his watch, 'if I suggest that we don't waste too much time. I would like, if possible, to catch the 5.30 train back to London.

'It is now nearly four o'clock and as soon as we have

130

examined your jewellery and you have signed the little paper I have here ready prepared'—he tapped the dispatch case—'it will be time for me to bid you *au revoir*.'

Hetty shuddered.

She could look into the future and see Mr. Vernon Wrighton saying *au revoir* down through the years, always taking a little more, always demanding something with that fearsome toothy smile of his which she felt would haunt her for ever. She must do something, must make a move of some sort.

'I'll go and get the keys of the safe.'

'I am content to wait, my dear lady.'

Mr. Wrighton folded his white hands over his dispatch case, which he laid somewhat ostentatiously on his knee.

Hetty walked with dignity from the room, but the moment she was outside she started to run up the staircase.

When she reached her own bedroom on the first floor she slammed the door behind her, then stood pressing her fingers to her eyes which were burning.

'What am I to do? What am I to do?' she asked herself again, but could think of nothing, nothing at all.

Slowly she dragged herself across the room, opened the drawer of her dressing-table and took from it the keys of her safe. She looked at herself in the glass.

It seemed to her excited fancy that she had grown immeasurably older in the last hour, then she turned away and walked slowly back along the corridor which led to the staircase.

When she reached it she went upstairs to the third floor where the jewel safe was housed. Hetty had had it specially built in the large wardrobe room where all her clothes were kept.

As she stepped on to the third floor landing, Watkins came out of her room. She looked surprised at seeing her mistress.

'Do you want me, Madam?'

'No, thank you, Watkins.'

'You're quite certain?' Watkins insisted. 'I was just going down to my tea.'

At that moment Hetty heard the servants' bell beginning to ring. Owing to war-time conditions and the alteration in the times of meals for the nursing staff, Hetty's own servants had tea at four o'clock.

As the bell clanged through the house a thought came to her. She remembered something which was hidden in an old jewel case at the back of her safe.

As Watkins turned to go, she said:

'Ask Barton to bring me up tea for two on a tray.'

'Up here, Madam?'

Watkins was obviously surprised.

'Yes. For myself and a gentleman to whom I shall be showing my jewels. I am giving some of them away for a Red Cross sale, the money is needed and we must all try to do our little bit in war-time.'

Watkins was impressed.

'It's very kind of you I'm sure, Madam, when you do so much already. I will tell Barton.'

'Not the silver things, of course,' Hetty said. 'He can lay those downstairs as usual. Oh no, I forgot, I'm going over to Lady Danvers' as soon as I'm free. Tell Barton one of the early morning trays will do.'

'Very good, Madam.'

Watkins went off on her errand and Hetty turned into the wardrobe room. It was a large bedroom which had been fitted with all the very latest accessories for clothes, suits and hats. At the far end, between the windows, stood the safe.

Hetty opened it and pulling out some of the pink leather and blue velvet covered cases found, as she had remembered, that right at the back there was a little jewel case in brown crocodile. It was the first jewel case she had ever possessed.

She opened it.

The top tray was filled with a miscellaneous collection of rings and brooches, mostly in paste and semi-precious stones, which had little value but which she kept from sentimental reasons, because they were the first jewellery she had owned,

She lifted out the tray and underneath was an envelope. It was sealed. She broke it open.

Inside were two small phials, both containing white, flat-shaped tablets.

Hetty looked at them carefully, then taking one from the envelope replaced the other, shut down the jewel case and put it away in the safe. She locked the latter and hurried on to the landing.

She had her foot on the top of the stair when she paused, someone was passing through the hall three stories below.

She looked over the balustrade—it was Barton, the top stair when she paused, someone was passing through the hall three stories below.

Hetty watched him cross the marble floor, then one hand holding on to the balustrade, she came downstairs one step at a time, very, very slowly.

At the end of George III's reign the owner of the house, wanting a grand staircase, had removed the rooms immediately above the hall right to the top of the house.

The staircase he had put in was very magnificent, photographs of it had more than once appeared in *Country Life* and it was quoted as one of the perfect examples of a Regency staircase.

Hetty reached the second floor, then the first, and started on the last flight into the hall.

The house was very quiet, the servants had all gone to their tea from which they would not emerge for at least an hour; the nursing staff would also be taking their tea round the wards. Hetty opened the door of the drawing-room.

Mr. Wrighton was waiting for her. He was standing in front of the fireplace and she knew by the eager way in which he moved forward that he had been impatient at her absence.

'I am sorry to keep you waiting so long,' she said.

She was conscious as she spoke of the small phial which she had taken from her jewel case, now hidden in her handkerchief and tightly clasped in her left hand.

'Will you come upstairs?'

'Do you keep your jewels in your bedroom?' Mr.

133

Wrighton asked. 'I wonder you're not afraid of being burgled.'

'No, I don't do anything as silly as that,' Hetty replied. 'I have a safe near my maid's room. I'm afraid it is on the third floor and we have no lift in this part of the house.'

'What a fine staircase,' Mr. Wrighton approved as they started to climb.

'Yes, isn't it?' Hetty replied. 'Everyone admires it, but I find it rather tiring at times—that is, when I want to go to the top of the house.'

'But you say that you have a lift?'

'For the luggage—yes, and of course the patients use it.'

They went on climbing, Hetty talking easily, smoothly. She pointed out several of the pictures as they passed them, but all the time her brain was rotating smoothly, calculatingly.

If only he hadn't had the precaution to take a photograph of the letter! The letter was there, hidden away it was true, but nevertheless at the mercy of anyone who by chance took a book at random from his shelves, and yet would there not be ways of buying those books, supposing, just supposing that. . . .

'Here we are at the top,' Mr. Wrighton said. 'I'm glad—it is a climb, isn't it?'

'I don't believe you are in such good condition as I am,' Hetty said.

She was breathing easily while Mr. Wrighton's breath was coming in quick jerks.

'It's an office life, my dear lady,' he said, panting a little.

He leaned against the balustrade where it bordered the landing. He looked down, then turned away.

'I feel dizzy!'

'I've ordered you some tea,' Hetty replied.

At that moment Barton approached from the baize door which led to the servants' quarters.

'Ah, here it is. Put it into the wardrobe room, Barton,' she ordered, 'and bring two chairs.'

'Very good, Madam.'

Barton did as he was told, but with an air of reproach

as if it was beneath his dignity to serve tea to anyone on the third floor. He brought the chairs, having set the tray down on the large table which stood in the centre of the room.

Hetty went across to the safe, swung back the heavy steel door and began bringing out the jewel cases.

'Here is my emerald set,' she said, 'and here are my rubies. They are always considered particularly fine.'

'Fine is the right word for them,' Mr. Wrighton remarked.

He opened the cases as she put them on the table, making little exclamations of delight. It was obvious that he loved jewels, as well as knowing something about them, he appeared to caress them, held the rubies up to the light, then turned to the emeralds.

'Let me give you some tea,' Hetty said. 'Do you take sugar?'

'A little.'

'I hope you won't mind it being saccharin, but I leave all my sugar ration except what is used in the cooking for the poor boys who are being treated here. They need it more than I do.'

She opened the little snuff-box which lay on the tray beside the tea pot. At the same time she tipped forward the phial that she held in her left hand so that two of the white tablets fell into the snuff-box.

She dropped the tablets with two of saccharin into a cup of tea and set it down on the table.

'I must show you my diamond necklace,' she said. 'I am rather hoping that you won't want to take that away from me, but I expect you will. The diamonds are really lovely; my husband spent nearly five years collecting them.'

She opened the velvet case in which the necklace was housed. Mr. Wrighton gave an exclamation of delight.

'They are indeed exceptional,' he said. 'Look at the fire in that centre stone.'

'I don't think I shall ever forgive you if you take it away from me,' Hetty said plaintively.

'I'm afraid you will never forgive me anyway, Mrs. Hayton,' came the reply.

Once again she was aware just how much this horrible little man was enjoying himself.

He wanted her to hate him, he almost regretted that she was not making more of a scene, being hysterical. Perhaps he even wished that she would plead with him, on her knees if need be.

'Well, you'd better see everything first,' Hetty said, turning towards the safe. 'Sit down and drink your tea while it's hot. It's no use being in too much of a hurry.'

'You're right,' Mr. Wrighton agreed, and he sat down as she had suggested.

With her back to the room Hetty heard him stir his tea and then drink.

For a moment she held her breath. It was many years since those tablets had come into her possession. Would they have lost their efficacy?

How well she remembered the first time Clement described them to her, once she had seen him use them and with tremendous effect.

She did not know what they contained. 'Knock-out drops' was what they were called and she knew that they were used by gangsters who wanted to rob someone in a night-club or a taxi.

Whoever took them became unconscious in a few minutes and remained so for a very short space of time. To an outsider the man appeared to have 'passed out' from the effect of alcohol; there were no ill effects save perhaps a headache and a dry tongue.

Oh God! would they work now?

Hetty turned round. Vernon Wrighton was replacing his now empty cup on the table.

She watched him and saw that even as he put it down his hand became paralysed, the cup tipped forward into the saucer with a clatter.

Then he leant back in his chair and made an effort as if to raise his hand to his head.

She moved towards him and as she did so he would have spoken; she saw an expression half rage, half horror cross his face before as if something had hit him his gaze became vacant; he gave one rasping snore and was unconscious.

He would have fallen from the chair had not Hetty pulled back his shoulders and let his head fall back; then she reached for his dispatch case.

She wrenched it open, took out the incriminating letter and thrust it deep into the bodice of her dress. She put down the case, ran to the door and jerked it open.

Outside the passage was deserted. She leant over the balustrade and looked down into the well of the hall. Everything was very quiet.

She heard something and started, then realised that what had startled her was the beating of her own heart.

'I don't care,' she almost spoke the words aloud. 'I've got to save myself, I've got to.'

She went back into the wardrobe room, put her hands under Vernon Wrighton's armpits and started to drag him across the room.

He was not a light man despite his size, but Hetty's determination and her frantic anxiety to be free of him would have managed someone far heavier.

She pulled him over the linoleum but his feet caught in the mat, crumpling it, then they were in the passage.

For a moment or two she had difficulty in raising him high enough to lift his shoulders on to the balustrade, then with one terrific effort she managed it.

She pushed . . . she heaved . . . she heard the sound of tearing and a button from his coat tinkled as it fell on to the bare boards. Something cold and calculating in her mind said:

'Remember to throw that after him, there should be no sign of a struggle.'

For one sickening moment she thought that he was going to slide back from the balustrade on to the floor. With a desperate effort she strained every muscle and held him.

His body wobbled, she balanced it and bracing herself gave one final shove. She had a last glimpse of his boots as she bent to pick up the button.

She heard the dull thud as he hit the floor three stories below. . . .

She straightened herself, putting up a hand to her hair, another to the neck of her dress; as she did so she heard the crackle of the paper between her breasts and knew she was safe.

Safe! But at what a cost! and what a part she had to play now. She opened her mouth to call out his name, to act the horror and concern of a woman whose guest, attacked by dizziness, had fallen from the top of a three-story staircase.

'Mr. Wrighton!'

Her voice came from her throat in a feeble cry and then she choked on the words, her heart seemed to jump so violently that her whole body palpitated from the shock.

Standing staring at her, her eyes wide and distended in horror, was Alice.

## 14

Hetty saw that Alice was going to scream, and she seized hold of her arm.

'Go to your room,' she said fiercely, but in a voice hardly above a whisper. 'Do you hear me?—go to your room.'

Alice goggled at her; she had turned deathly pale and her mouth hung open loose and wet.

'Go to your room,' Hetty repeated; then sharply she smacked Alice's face.

The report of her hand against the pale, cold skin was loud and sharp.

Alice did not speak, she merely made a sound—half groan, half sob; nevertheless Hetty imagined that she would obey.

There was no time to be lost; she gave Alice a push

down the passage which led to the back stairs and she herself ran down the front staircase.

As she moved she had a sudden sense of exhilaration. She was in control. She was mistress of the situation, she could overpower and dominate anyone or anything which crossed her path.

The thought came to her that this was how an airman would feel when he shot down an enemy plane—on top of the world, divorced from human frailty.

As she reached the first floor, Hetty glanced over the balustrade and saw that there was no one in the hall below, only that crumpled dark object lying spread-eagled on the marble floor.

She flung open the baize door which led towards the wing which had been given over to Clive's patients.

'Nurse! Matron!' she called.

A young nurse appeared from a bedroom immediately to the right of the door.

'Fetch Matron,' Hetty commanded her, 'and come yourself as quickly as possible. There has been an accident.'

The nurse ran along the passage, her starched apron rustling. Hetty stood still.

'I'll wait for them,' she thought, 'I won't go down alone.'

Just for a moment she felt afraid; it seemed as if a cold hand touched her elation and burst it like a bubble.

Supposing ... just supposing that she was suspected ... and there was Alice! Alice! her eyes distorted with horror! Murder—the word seemed to quiver in the silence of the hall!

Hetty thrust the thought from her; she saw Matron appear at the end of the passage and ran towards her.

'Oh Matron, thank goodness you're here,' she said, the tone of her voice, blended with just the right amount of relief, overriding an undercurrent of fear. 'There's been an accident—a terrible accident!'

Hetty went on repeating those words at intervals during the next twenty minutes. Over and over again she told her story.

'He felt giddy when he reached the top of the stairs,

139

and while we were looking at the jewellery he seemed to gasp for breath. He went out into the passage, I suppose in search of air. I didn't follow him for the moment, I thought as he felt ill he would like to be alone, then suddenly he gave a cry. It was low, rather indistinct, and as I reached the door I saw him falling.'

Over and over again she told the same story. Barton averred:

'The gentleman looked a bit queer when I brought up the tea.'

'He must have had a weak heart,' Hetty said more than once.

The nurses removed the body from the hall and at last, after a very long while it seemed to Hetty, she was free to go and find Alice. The police had been sent for, the local doctor was on his way up from the village.

It didn't give her much time, but she felt that she dared not leave Alice a moment longer to her own thoughts, to her own speculations.

'It was damnable luck her being there,' Hetty thought as she went upstairs again.

That feeling of being in supreme control had not left her; she was conscious, as an actress is conscious when she is playing a part really well, that her audience was with her.

There was no dissentient note, no one who had not responded as she had wished them to respond.

Alice! Her instinct warned her of danger, but danger from Alice was unthinkable—the woman adored her.

'It's all right, she would hang for me,' Hetty reassured herself.

Yet she was exasperated by the thought that her secret must be shared. Nothing was more dangerous. How much had Alice seen? Was there a chance that she had arrived too late?

Hetty would not deceive herself even to hope that this was so. Alice's face, her expression of horror, had told her the whole story.

She reached the first floor and stood outside Alice's room. Just for a moment she hesitated before knocking, then she raised her hand to rap against the smooth shiny wood of the door. There was no answer and impatiently she turned the handle. The door was locked.

'Alice,' she said, 'are you there? Open the door.'

There was still no answer and Hetty rattled the handle; then she heard steps, slow, heavy steps across the room and the key was turned.

Hetty entered the room and closed the door behind her, then she looked at Alice. She was still pale, but the vacant expression of horror had been replaced by one Hetty had never seen before.

Alice looked older but more resolute, there was an expression of strain on her face as if she had been through some tremendous experience, but she had regained control of herself.

There was, too, something else in her expression, something Hetty could not place and to which for the moment she could not put a name. As Hetty looked at her, she drew herself up and seemed by that simple gesture to grow immeasurably taller.

Neither woman said anything, but Alice met Hetty's eyes squarely. Hetty drew in her breath.

'Alice, my dear, what must you think of me?' she said caressingly. 'I must tell you what happened.'

'I don't want to hear.'

Alice's voice was deep and resonant, and seemed to come right from the centre of her being.

'But of course I must tell you.'

'I don't want to hear,' Alice repeated. 'I'm leaving this house now—tonight.'

For the first time Hetty looked round the room and saw that in a corner was an open trunk, beside it two suitcases. Alice's luggage!

How well she knew it; it had travelled with her on so many journeys. She had often laughed at Alice because she liked to have her trunk in her bedroom, even at Trenton Park and in London.

'You're like the servants,' Hetty had taunted her, 'ready to leave at a moment's notice.'

But Alice gently but firmly had refused to have her luggage taken away to the boxroom.

'I often do have to pack in a hurry,' she would say apologetically.

'It is as if she had always anticipated something like this,' Hetty thought to herself, before she turned to ask raspingly:

'Why are you going?'

'Need you ask that?'

'I insist on knowing.'

'Well, if you want the truth, I won't stay here with a murderess.'

Hetty gasped. It was so unlike gentle, quiet, hesitant Alice, this tall woman defying her, accusing her not in anger, but with a dignity which was even more frightening.

'You don't understand,' Hetty said quickly. 'That man was a spy, an enemy to this country. He revealed certain secrets to me and then threatened to do other things which would have harmed the Allied cause. Can't you understand, I was doing a patriotic act in getting rid of him.'

Alice said nothing, but Hetty knew that she did not believe her, did not for one moment credit the statements she had just made.

'I had to do it, don't you understand?' she cried shrilly.

Alice thrust her hands deep into the pockets of her tweed suit.

'I always knew you were hard and cruel,' she said, 'that you were a woman one could not trust, who had no heart, but I never suspected that even you could take the life of another fellow being—take it with your own hands and in such a way!'

Alice's voice sank to a whisper, just for a moment Hetty saw the horror in her eyes, then she grasped at her self-control and the strange mask of dignity and determination disguised her once again.

"But Alice! Alice, you can't leave me now.'

She held out her hands with an appealing gesture, with the smile which had so often in the past proved irresistible to both Alice and to other people who served her.

'I'm going,' Alice said uncompromisingly.

142

'But where will you go?' Hetty asked. 'You have no money.'

'That doesn't matter,' Alice replied. "I'll scrub floors, I'll beg from door to door rather than stay here with you.'

The words were brutal and Hetty felt almost as if Alice had struck her. Now she was afraid, afraid of this strange, ruthless person who had replaced a willing and loving slave.

'And what about me?' she asked. 'What about this ... thing ... you have seen? Can I trust you?'

'And if you can't,' Alice asked, 'will you treat me in the same way?'

Hetty said nothing and suddenly Alice began to laugh. It was a horrible sound, without humour, rasping and frightening.

'You're afraid of me!' she said. 'I never thought that I should live to see you afraid of me, you—the smart, all-conquering, all-powerful Mrs. Hayton, afraid of poor Alice—Alice who could never do anything right, who was kept on under sufferance, who was forced to be grateful for the crumbs that fell from the rich man's table.

'Yes, you're afraid, I can see it in your face and in the trembling of your hands—yes, your hands are trembling when they ought to be stained with blood.'

She laughed again and Hetty backed towards the door.

'You're mad!'

'Perhaps I am,' Alice answered. 'Perhaps I'm sane for the first time. Anyway, you're afraid of me, you don't know what I'm going to do. I don't know myself yet, I've got to think, to decide whether it is my duty to denounce you to the police.'

She stopped short, then asked abruptly:

'What did Mr. Vernon Wrighton know that made you decide to kill him?'

'Will you be quiet!' Hetty said. 'You're to stay here, I won't let you leave this house.'

'You wouldn't dare to stop me,' Alice retorted.

She stood in the centre of the room and suddenly she laughed again. The sound distorted her mouth, and her eyes behind their thick glasses no longer seemed mild and gentle.

Hetty turned swiftly, opened the door and ran out slamming it behind her. She put her hand up to her forehead and realised it was damp with sweat.

Alice was mad, she was certain of that, but what was she to do about it? She was shaking and her hands were icy cold.

'I've got to be careful, very careful,' Hetty thought, and looked up to see Barton approaching her.

'The police are here, Madam.'

'Tell them I'll be down in a moment,' Hetty replied. 'Tell Matron and Nurse—and Barton, I want some brandy, I feel rather faint.'

'I'll bring it up to your bedroom, Madam,' Barton said. It's not surprising you are upset. If you'll forgive me saying so, you have all our sympathy, Madam; it was a very unpleasant occurrence.'

'Thank you, Barton.'

Hetty tried to answer quietly, but every nerve in her body was suddenly screaming out to him to go, that she must be alone.

'I've got to be careful,' she thought. 'I've got to be careful. . . .'

It was some time later before the police left the house and she found herself alone once more and with time to think about Alice. They had left her apprehensive and not a little disturbed.

She had told her story in a straight-forward manner; but there had been an awkward moment when the Inspector had asked with whom the appointment had been made and she had been forced to say that Mr. Vernon Wrighton had spoken to Alice.

'Can we see Miss Farley?'

'I'm afraid she is out this afternoon,' Hetty replied, hoping that they would not question the servants and find that she had told them a lie.

'Never tell a lie if you can help it,' had been one of Clement's maxims. 'Always tell the truth in little things and only lie if it is absolutely essential.'

She must lie, Hetty thought, and yet how unnecessary, how needless all this was. If only Alice had not come on to the third floor at that particular moment!

Doubtless she had brought a message or had heard from Barton that she was having tea upstairs and wondered if she could be of assistance.

Any excuse trivial enough in itself might have brought her and with this result.

'Miss Farley knows as little about this man as I know myself,' Hetty said. 'He told her that he wished to see me and that he worked in the Foreign Office. When he arrived, he informed me that he was collecting a very special fund for the Red Cross and so I took him upstairs to see my jewels. I decided to let some of them be sold in such a worthy cause.'

The Inspector, an elderly man with an abrupt way of talking, said sharply:

"Do you usually show your jewels to anyone who comes on some charitable pretext?'

'I felt certain that Mr. Wrighton was quite genuine,' Hetty replied.

'Why?'

'He mentioned various people with whom he was associated,' she said, 'mutual friends.'

The Inspector took out his pencil.

'Can you give me their names?'

Hetty drew her breath. Another lie, and she had let herself be caught in it as easily as a fly became entangled in a web. She gave the names of various well-known people, choosing them at random.

'You had never actually met the man?' the Inspector insisted.

'No, never.'

He turned over a page of his note-book.

'You will forgive me suggesting it, Mrs. Hayton, but possessing jewels of such an unusual value it is extremely dangerous to show either them or the place in which they are kept to people of whom you know so little.'

There was nothing either in his tone or in his words to

imply that he suspected her and yet Hetty felt fear mounting within her.

The other witnesses were called, Matron, the nurse, Barton. Barton was excellent, corroborating her assertion that Mr. Wrighton felt breathless and giddy as he reached the top of the stairs.

'And now, Mrs. Hayton, we will go up to the scene of the accident,' the Inspector said.

As they reached the wardrobe room Hetty gave a sigh of relief. Watkins had already replaced the jewellery. Barton had taken away the tea things.

'Thank Heaven for a well-trained household!' she thought.

'This room has been altered,' the Inspector accused.

'I'm so sorry,' Hetty said. 'I didn't think to tell the servants that they must touch nothing. We all thought that as it was an accident. . . .'

'Quite, quite,' the Inspector said testily, 'but nothing should have been touched.'

'I'm afraid my maid thought it very imprudent to leave my jewellery lying about. I had spread it out on the table for Mr. Wrighton to see. He told me he was an expert in jewels as his father had been a big Amsterdam merchant.'

The Inspector made notes in his book.

'You will, of course, have to attend the inquest, Mrs. Hayton,' he said when finally he took his leave.

The doctor who had been called in had given his evidence. That the man had broken his neck owing to the fall, had been his verdict, but his giddiness and lack of breath were doubtless due to a bad heart and they would find out more about it when they knew his family history.

He was the local practitioner; Hetty knew him well for he was in attendance daily at the hospital, and he made things as easy for her as he could, promising that the body should be removed to a mortuary that evening.

He and Matron had also undertaken the task of breaking the news to Mr. Wrighton's wife or relatives if he had any.

'You are quite certain you can manage everything?' Hetty had said gratefully to them, and then had hurried away from Matron's sitting-room towards her own bed-room.

As she reached the first floor landing she hesitated, then crept across to listen outside Alice's door. Alice was still packing, she could hear the rustle of tissue paper, the sound of drawers being opened and shut.

There was only a little time now before the household would know she was going. Would they not suspect there was some reason for her hurried departure? What could she do? How could she stop her?

Hetty stood there beside the door listening, then she heard her name called. It was Matron coming down the passage.

'Oh, Mrs. Hayton,' she said. 'We have just got through to Mrs. Wrighton. She was very queer, very queer indeed.'

'Mrs. Wrighton?'

'Yes, the poor man's wife. Doctor got her address from the Foreign Office so we rang her up. She was naturally very distressed, almost hysterical, and then she said some-thing very strange.'

'What was it?' Hetty asked.

'She said "He told me he was going into danger, but I didn't believe him; I thought he was joking, that things like that didn't happen in England." What do you think she can have meant?'

'Is that all she said?' Hetty's voice to herself sounded as if it came from far away.

'Doctor asked her what she meant,' Matron replied, 'and she said her husband had mentioned something about a letter, but we couldn't quite understand and the line was very faint.

Anyway, Doctor's going down to see her tomorrow. He thought it was better and I expect the poor woman will want to come back here to arrange about the funeral.'

'He's going down tomorrow?'

'He thought it best,' Matron said. 'Poor woman! I can quite understand her being upset; this must have been a terrible shock, but I don't understand what she meant about danger. She can't have known this was going to happen unless he often had these heart attacks.'

'Perhaps that's what she meant,' Hetty said, but her voice was unconvincing.

She felt as if the very walls were closing in upon her closer ... closer. ...

## 15

All day Clive was conscious of something at the back of his mind.

He tried to ignore it, to deny what it suggested when it obtruded into what he was doing, but it was there and deep down within him he responded to it as a boy will respond to the call of the sea.

Now that the day's work was done and the last patient finished with, he could face the fact that the moment for which ostensibly he had been waiting all day had come.

Outside his house in Harley Street the car was waiting for him, the car which was to carry him down to Miss Oggie's.

Slowly Clive collected together the typewritten sheets which held the history of his last patient, then he pressed the bell and his secretary came in.

Miss Harris had been with him for nearly fifteen years, she was small, thick-set and exceedingly plain.

Clive had engaged her because he felt sorry for her, he knew she would find it difficult to get a job and impulsively this had overruled all other considerations, even the excellent references of other applicants for the situation he offered.

He had never regretted his decision.

Mary Harris had proved a perfect secretary and her jobs in Clive's house far exceeded those to which she had nominally been appointed.

He had no idea how much she did do, for she mothered him quietly, engaging the servants, seeing to his clothes, arranging the rooms and the flowers so that he was seldom troubled with domestic details.

He only knew that bachelorhood for him was a comfortable state in which there were few crises.

'We've finished now, I understand,' Clive said, as Mary came up to the desk and he held out to her the typed sheets.

Mary in return handed him a card on which were written the calls he was expected to make during the evening. Clive glanced at it casually.

'Must I really call again at Lady Evelyn's?' he asked. 'She was quite all right this morning—more nerves with her than anything else.'

'Her nurse rang up half an hour ago,' Mary said. 'I told her you would do your best.'

'How I dislike society patients!' Clive said. 'They are more trouble than all the rest put together.'

'You couldn't live without them,' Mary answered. 'Have you any idea how much you are owed?'

'Not the slightest,' Clive replied.

Money always bored him and he left his financial affairs entirely to Mary. She told him what was due to him. He looked at her incredulously, then whistled.

'As much as that?'

'Quite as much and more if I hadn't already written off a number of bad debts, but don't for one moment imagine that you will get it all.'

'I'm quite certain I shan't,' Clive said. 'All the same, if I was paid, what a lot I could do with it.'

'Spend some more of it on the ungrateful poor, I suppose.'

Clive turned to her quickly.

'They're not ungrateful and I'd rather treat a poor person for the thanks he gives me than any of your duchesses and millionaires for a hundred guinea fee.'

'I know, I know,' Mary said; 'but how do you expect I'm going to pay the rent, the rates, the taxes, the servants' wages, and incidentally myself?'

She smiled as she spoke and Clive was not the least perturbed by her outburst.

He knew Mary so well and this was almost a monthly occurrence when she told him off and tried to make him be more conventional, more provident in matters that concerned his position and money.

They both knew it for only a game, they both knew that while Mary chided Clive, underneath she admired and respected him simply because he did not care about the social prizes which could so easily be his now that his position in the medical world was assured.

'I'm hopeless, Mary,' Clive said. 'I wonder why you bother with me.'

'I often wonder that myself,' Mary answered: 'but don't stand there arguing—get off to your next appointment, wherever that may be, otherwise there will be little chance of Lady Evelyn seeing you tonight.'

'I shall go to Oggie's first, and then on to the Children's Home at Stepney. If you want me, you'll know where to find me.'

As he reached the door Mary stopped him.

'By the way,' she said, 'Lady Evelyn is supposed to be a millionairess!'

'You are nothing more or less than a money-grubber,' Clive accused her.

He was still laughing as he came out of the front door and got into the car waiting outside.

He always drove himself, it was far less trouble and, apart from that, he did not feel like paying the wages of a chauffeur.

He lived very frugally and yet was seldom out of debt, and the reason for this was that every penny he could spare was spent on the children he attended.

Only Mary knew how many holidays to the sea, new clothes, better surroundings, extra grocery, milk and eggs were owed to Clive's generosity.

Sometimes he would be almost afraid to tell her when he committed himself to some fresh extravagance over a destitute family or a child who had been badly injured.

'You're heading for the bankruptcy court if you go on like this,' she would say tartly.

But somehow she managed to keep things going and

150

strangely enough the rest of the household seemed to like her and to accept her orders.

He had grown so used to having Mary about him that he himself never noticed her ugliness although often new patients would say to him:

'Is that your secretary I spoke to when I came in? Poor woman, can't you of all people do something for her face? She's not a good advertisement for you.'

It always made Clive angry when people spoke like that, yet he had to admit that there was something in what they said. Mary was astoundingly ugly, her head was, in fact, not far from being a deformity.

She had been born with a harelip and it had been badly operated on. Her eyes were weak and often red and inflamed as if she had been crying.

But she had a morbid, almost fanatical horror of operations and Clive knew she would never consent to another.

Only he realised what a difference work had made in Mary's life. Before he engaged her, she had gone from job to job, always ultimately being turned away because either her employer or the people with whom she worked couldn't stand her looks.

She had become acutely conscious of herself, introspective and agonisingly shy.

The responsibility that Clive had heaped upon her, her awareness that he relied on her absolutely to do the job fully and to the best of her ability had changed her whole outlook.

Now she basked in his success, taking a reflected glory from him which set her looks and the unkind criticism of them in their right perspective.

'I am Mr. Ross's secretary,' she would announce to strangers.

'Not Mr. Clive Ross!' they would exclaim incredulously.

When she acknowledged that was so she would feel herself someone of importance that could not be denied, someone who really mattered.

As Mary tidied up Clive's desk after he had gone, arranging his pencils and pen on the silver tray, putting the block on which he wrote prescriptions back in the drawer.

She noticed that he had been scribbling on the blotter—'doodling' was what they called it in America.

She pulled out the top sheet of blotting paper; Clive had made an untidy mess of it.

Mary could imagine him listening to some patient droning over her symptoms, making too much of little pains and yet holding Clive's attention save for the almost unconscious movement of his pencil.

S. S. S. That was what he had written over and over again, entwining them together, S's of all shapes and sizes.

Mary wondered what they portended, what drug of treatment was in his mind, then she crumpled the piece of blotting paper in her hands and threw it into the waste paper basket. . . .

Clive drove through the traffic quickly. He felt light-hearted, gay, as he turned into the narrow streets which led towards East London.

It was nearly three days since he had seen Stella Marsden; she was improving and Oggie was pleased with her.

He had been half afraid when he took Stella to Oggie's that they might not get on. Yet strangely enough they seemed to be settling down together.

Could anything be more extreme? Miss Oggie with her lifelong devotion to the poor, her amazing gift of healing, her championship of socialism and loathing of what was termed colloquially 'the idle rich?'

On the other hand—Stella.

Clive felt something strange within him when he thought of her, the sensation not unlike a sweet weakness was too strong to be denied, he had to acknowledge it.

'Am I crazy?' he asked himself out loud, and was relieved that his voice sounded angry although there was no anger in him. -

He was no prude, he was not as many people thought a woman-hater, he merely knew little about them. Few people were aware of the struggle he had had to get started in his career.

His father and mother still lived in Scotland in the tiny stone croft which, with the patch of land behind it, was all they possessed in the whole world.

His father, the only son of the Minister of Glendale, had been a sickly boy owing to a fall in his early youth which had more or less crippled him; But he had married the woman of his choice and never regretted it nor had she.

Their life had been a hard one. Often they had been hungry and yet so far as Clive could remember they had always been happy.

His father was not ambitious, neither was his mother—not for themselves. For their son, their only child, they were determined on one thing—he should have the best possible education.

Somehow they managed it and there had been other people willing enough to help when they realised that Clive had exceptional ability.

The Minister had taught him Latin; the doctor had given him the run of his library and unconsciously decided his whole future.

Clive had trudged six miles every day, wet or fine, rain or snow, to the school over the hill which was slightly superior to the one in Glendale itself.

His father and mother had been rewarded for any sacrifices they had made on his behalf.

They still lived in the old croft; nothing would induce them to move although it was a very different place in these days from what it had been when Clive was a boy.

He had refurnished it, he had insisted on having it connected up with the main water and main electricity which now fed the village.

His mother still did most of the work herself, but Clive knew that the labour-saving devices, the cooker and refrigerator that he had installed saved her much trouble and exertion.

He only wished he could get up to see them more often, but the journey to Scotland meant leaving his work for several days at least and he seldom granted himself a holiday.

No, he had had little time for holidays all through his life, no time to make friends with people of his own age, to enjoy the light, boyish flirtations which are so much a part of adolescence.

He had grown up unnaturally serious, shy and old for his years—and his shyness had remained with him, where women were concerned, even after he had tasted success and had become sought after for his looks and his personality as well as for his skill.

Clive was no fool; he was well aware that many of his women patients found him attractive.

They made it very obvious, but once they had done so Clive always managed to shelve the responsibility of their illness on to some other doctor.

'I've no time for women,' he told himself more than once, and then acknowledged it was something deeper than that.

Because he had never known attractive women in any way except when they were sick or in pain, he had created for himself an ideal woman who, hidden away in his heart, was a kind of solace when he was lonely.

Perhaps the imaginary woman was in many ways a part of the adoration he had always had for his mother.

Clive could remember his mother as being beautiful and she had, too, a quiet gentleness which had made him feel that whatever else happened in the world home was an inviolate sanctuary.

The woman Clive would love must be like his mother, and yet he wanted something more than a maternal love, something deeper, more fundamental, something which he had never found among the women who sought him out.

Clive found it hard indeed to remember that his patients were women until they thrust their sex upon his attention.

A patient had always remained to him something sacred, he had never got over the thrill and the excitement of knowing that he could help someone who was suffering.

Yet, of course, he met all types of women.

Clive thought of the shallow, rotten women with whom he sometimes came in contact, women who were prepared to take all from life and give nothing.

Women who allowed their lust full rein, but who were offered what most of their sex crave—a home and chil-

154

dren, offered it because of their features, the colour of their hair, the blue of their eyes!

Ugly, sometimes loathsome characters were forgiven or ignored because of a pretty face.

'It is not fair,' Clive thought, 'and some women have everything . . . everything. . . .'

But had they? His thoughts veered back to Stella. Here was a woman whom the world looked on as having been born with a silver spoon in her mouth, who excited the envy and the admiration of other women.

Ever since it was known that Clive had operated on her he had been inundated with questions as to how she was. His patients questioned him about her, even those who did not know her were curious.

'Is she really as lovely as her photographs, Mr. Ross? She always looks so sad, but she ought to be happy.'

'I've always admired her and wished that I was like her somehow.'

'Oh, women! women!' Clive thought. 'Setting up for themselves idols.'

Film star or society beauty, what did it matter so long as they had one thing, the one thing all women apparently craved—glamour, attraction, or should one call it, in the jargon of Hollywood, sex appeal?

There was indeed something, he acknowledged to himself, which made Stella different from other women.

He thought of her with her pale face and heavy, tired eyes, of her hands lying listless over the white sheets of the bed, of her hair brushed back plainly from her forehead, and knew that even unadorned she was still lovely, still appealing with something which was irresistible and inexplicable.

'What was it?'

He wished he could define it to himself, but he could not; he only knew that now at this moment he wanted to see her, to talk to her. And she hated him!

She would never forgive him for having dragged her back to life when she wanted to die.

Usually he felt irritated with people who wished to

155

evade their responsibilities. He felt angry, as if they besmirched something beautiful in their desire for death.

Clive could not put it into words, but inside himself he believed that life was wonderful—an adventure, of course, with its ups and downs, its joys and sorrows, its tragedies and miseries—but still wonderful, still real, dazzling, transcendent, something to be prized and treasured.

He thought of the times when he had brought a baby into the world half choked, lifeless, smothered, and how working until the sweat poured off his forehead he had finally made it breathe.

The child should live, should know all the glory of life, life that was desirable however low and sordid the position into which one was born.

That older people with brains and common sense, with individuality and means with which to work should deliberately throw away that precious gift of life was to Clive incomprehensible.

But he knew that the desire to 'let go' was in itself a disease.

He had not studied melancholia or depression in any great degree; now he found himself thinking of it, watching for it among his patients, snatching at a thread here and there and considering new ideas, new suggestions for treatment.

Stella had not been a hard case, but Clive did nothing by halves.

Interested, he was determined to go on, to make his research more and more thorough, to save people from themselves.

As he worked he saw always Stella's face and he heard her voice saying over and over again

'I want to die . . . I want to die.'

To what had he brought her back? That was what he asked himself as, on the last lap of his journey, he turned down a long street with clanging trams and squalid, crowded shops.

'What can I offer her?' he asked himself.

He had asked the question as a doctor and now it became a personal one.

"What can I offer her?"

Clive had a sudden vision of Marsden House with its long galleries and grand staircases, its panelled rooms and polished floors, its curtained beds and the stained glass of heraldic windows . . .

Trudging towards it footsore and weary he saw a ragged, hungry schoolboy.

'I must be mad!' he said aloud.

## 16

As Clive was let into Oggie's flat by Liza, there was a burst of laughter from the kitchen.

'It's them girls,' Liza explained. 'Miss Oggie's teaching them cooking and the mess they make you wouldn't believe.'

Clive smiled as he put down his hat and gloves on a chair. He knew that the girls referred to were some of Oggie's patients who had been injured when a bomb dropped on their school. It was one of those occasions when he had had a tussle with the other surgeons whether the limbs should be amputated or not.

As usual, he had won and now it was up to Oggie—for he had passed the responsibility on to her—to see that these children were able to use their arms which had been saved after so much argument.

Oggie had her own methods of making them use their muscles; teaching them to cook was one of them.

They loved it and would make every effort to knead pastry, to stir puddings, to beat up an egg, all of which brought their muscles into play just as well as any exercises ordered by the text book.

Clive walked across the sitting-room and knocked on the door of Stella's bedroom. When she said, 'Come in,' he entered.

'Oh, it's you.' She looked up from the book she was

reading and he fancied that her expression brightened at the sight of him.

'Weren't you expecting me?'

'We are always expecting you,' she answered solemnly. 'At least, Liza is. She counts the hours to your next appearance.'

'And you?'

He could not forbear asking the question.

She looked at him with an expression he could not fathom.

'What am I expected to answer to that?'

'Only the truth. Surely you know you must always tell your doctor the truth?'

He was conscious that they were both fencing with each other, that behind the trivial, superficial words with which they conversed there was so much left unsaid.

It seemed to him as if all this had happened before and was quite unimportant, that there was another deeper and stronger tension between them which could not be denied.

Then suddenly a wave of shyness swept over him.

He was aware how out of place Stella looked in this bare, shabby little room. Since he had last seen her she had added a lot of her own things.

There was a bedspread, which he had never seen before, of antique lace backed with blue satin; there were lace pillows behind her head and against the expensive simplicity of her satin bed-jacket there glittered a great acquamarine clip, which sparkled as she breathed.

'I'd better tell Oggie I'm here,' Clive said abruptly.

'There's no hurry.'

Arrested by her voice, he turned towards the bed.

'You are better?'

'I thought it was about time you asked that question. Much better, although I hate to admit it.'

'Why?'

'Because it proves you right. Don't you dislike people who are proved right when it would have been much easier if they had been in the wrong?'

'You must thank Oggie, not me.'

158

'I do. I have thanked her, and that reminds me of something I want to ask you about.'

'What is it?'

'Oggie and her charities. She's got all the children of the neighbourhood working to send that child you operated on a month ago—Jean something—away to the seaside.

There's nothing radically wrong with her now, but Oggie wants her to have a holiday and would like some of her family to go too. I wrote out a cheque and what do you think Oggie did with it?'

'I know the answer to that one,' Clive smiled. 'She tore it up.'

'Actually she put it on the fire, but why? That's what I can't understand. Why shouldn't I help? I'm one of her patients too and yet she won't take a penny from me. Do you know what I'm paying here?'

'Three pound a week, isn't it?' Clive asked.

'Exactly. Can you imagine anything so ridiculous? She just covers the cost of my food and the washing of the bed linen; she won't take a penny for her own services.'

'Haven't you learnt Oggie's views on money by this time?'

'I've heard them all,' Stella said; 'but however much it may irk her, the fact remains that some people have money and others haven't. What am I to do if she won't take any of mine?'

'Give it to those who will.'

'You're as bad as she is,' Stella exclaimed angrily. 'Can't you understand that I can't stay here on those terms?'

'I'm afraid you've got to, unless, of course, you feel strong enough to go back to Trenton Park.'

Stella made a little grimace.

'Not on any terms. How is your friend Mrs. Hayton?'

'I believe she is very well,' Clive replied.

He stiffened as he spoke and Stella realised that the subject was unwelcome.

He walked restlessly across the room and the thought came to her that with his magnificent physique it was not surprising if women like Hetty Hayton ran after him.

Nurse Benson had hinted more than once while they

were at Trenton Park that their hostess was intrigued by Clive Ross.

Oggie had spoken with scathing contempt of the women who chased him, and Stella could believe that it was not always easy to avoid patients who thought that a good-looking man was fair game.

'I wonder what he really feels about women?' she asked herself, and was surprised at her own question.

Men, she believed, had long ceased to interest her. Never again would she be fool enough to be taken in by one, to invite that tingling in her veins, that breathless warmth which made one long for the touch of a man's lips, the strength of his arms. That was over and done with.

Even now she could not bear to read a love-story, to think of the approach of a man to a woman; it was too poignant, too real. It recaptured too vividly Bertram and all that he had meant to her.

She had only to think of him to remember how her heart would beat quickly as he approached, to feel again the thrill of his touch, the passion which had inflamed her when his mouth found hers.

Sometimes Stella would taunt herself with the pictures of what might have been had she surrendered herself and become his mistress.

At least they would have had the happiness of belonging one to the other and things might have been very different. He might not have been sent abroad, he might at this moment be at her side.

Vain imaginings which merely tortured her, and yet she could not escape but must endure them at night when she could not sleep, when a picture in a magazine, a casual sentence, or the sound of music would recall Bertram vividly to all her senses.

Some movement of Clive's now, perhaps just his silhouette against the growing dark outside the window, made her heart start as if in sudden pain.

Bertram: the thought of him came to her swiftly. Without thinking she said:

'Oh, if only we could be rid of our bodies!'

160

Instantly Clive was the doctor again.

'You are in pain?'

Stella regretted her impulsive words.

'What I was referring to was not physical, but don't let's talk of it. I'm tired of myself, I'm tired of lying here day after day.'

'We're getting you well. Very shortly you will be able to go away.'

'Where to?'

'Anywhere you like. To your own home.'

'I suppose you mean to Marsden House,' she corrected. 'That will be nice for me, won't it?'

She spoke bitterly, dropping her reserve and behaving as she phrased it to herself, 'like a spoilt child, petulant and disappointed.'

She did not know quite what she had expected, but she somehow had the idea that Clive would have some further plan for her.

It wasn't anything definite, nothing actually formulated in her mind, and yet now, ridiculous as it seemed, she was hurt.

'Why can't I make you happy?'

Clive spoke abruptly, breaking in on her moment of self-pity. She answered him frankly.

'No one will ever be able to do that again, but perhaps a few may consider me, may do their best to make me comfortable.'

'I have tried to do that.'

She felt the reproach in his voice.

'Am I ungrateful?' she asked. 'I suppose I am. To tell you the truth, I feel lost. Oggie tells me the world to which I once belonged is finished, that after the war there will be no place for the type of woman I was forced to become.

'The world I know will be swept away and, as it seems, there's no place for me here in this one. I must hang betwixt earth and sky—an unenviable position.'

'I see—a poor little rich girl, in fact.'

Clive was surprised at his words even as he said them; it

161

was hardly the way that even fashionable doctors spoke to the important Lady Marsden.

Stella, indeed, did not look important at this moment, but a child, a lost, unhappy child.

'But is it only my money?' she asked him. 'Isn't it something else, something in me?'

'Good Lord, no!'

He was wise enough to recognise the danger signal which began by thinking oneself different.

He had seen it so often—in the unemployed who came to believe they were unemployable because of some fault in themselves, in women like Mary who began to doubt their own normality because their features were unusual, in fear-driven men and women of all classes and all stations in life.

Clive leant over the brass rail at the end of the bed; clasping his hands together, he spoke earnestly.

'Listen to me,' he said. 'You are no different from anyone else. There's nothing wrong with you. What has happened is merely that public opinion has created for you a superficial personality.

'There's you as you are yourself and there's you as the public sees you—a Jekyll and Hyde if you like.

'If you were a film star, you could blame your Press agent; as you are not, you must blame the power of money blended with the background, the position and the name which are also yours.'

'And if I don't want all these things?'

'You can't escape the responsibility of what, after all, is part of yourself,' Clive answered. 'Men have tried to do that since the beginning of the world and invariably failed. Look at T. E. Lawrence, for instance. It doesn't answer to run away, there's no escape in deliberate evasion, it merely adds another burden to one's own back, the fear of being found out.

He paused and his voice softened.

'Oggie may be right, the world you have known may have ceased to exist, but there will be a place for you in the new world if and when it is created.'

'I think it is frightening,' Stella said passionately. 'I hold no brief for what I hated, but this sweeping away of everything familiar may in the end prove only eliminative—a desolation of destruction.'

'That is the wrong way to look at things,' he replied. 'We have got to adjust ourselves to the change, and maybe to the loneliness of the future if by the sacrifice of self we can achieve a better world for the majority.'

'And you think it will be better?' Stella challenged.

'When I think of the children I have treated down here, when I look at the streets in which they have been bred and brought up, when I learn of the poverty, misery and disease which has always been attendant on their families, I wonder if anything could be worse.'

Stella was silent, then in a very low voice she said:

'You and Oggie make me feel ashamed.'

'Who is taking my name in vain?'

Oggie spoke from the doorway, and both Clive and Stella started for they had not heard the door open. She came into the room, vast and ungainly.

'Liza told me you were here,' she said, 'but I couldn't get away for the moment. We were making a cake and very good it's going to be, too.'

'You've done wonders with those girls,' Clive said.

'They'll be all right,' Oggie answered. 'It was as much mental as physical, doctors croaking over their arms, telling them it was unlikely they'd ever be much use to them. If I had my way no doctor or nurse would be able to enter a patient's sick room without wearing a muzzle.'

Clive laughed, but Oggie watching him had the feeling that his mind was really elsewhere. She looked at Stella. There was a touch of colour in her cheeks and yet she did not look happy.

'What have they been talking about?' Oggie wondered.

Because she loved Clive she felt angry that Stella should not respond to him more eagerly.

'Damn her! Damn all women!' she thought.

She saw herself slim and attractive as she had been at seventeen. If she could have met Clive then, or someone like him!

Instead, all her life had been one long work of transmitting the normal passions within her into the channels of self-sacrifice and self-denial.

'Sex works in funny ways,' Oggie thought grimly.

Now over sixty, she was content, fired with the spirit of her mission—a one-man crusade which she led herself.

Yet there had been times when she must fight against the flesh, times which had lost their sting in the passing years, but which nevertheless remained as scars.

Bitter, agonising hours in a Gethsemane had made her strangely gentle with the weaknesses of others.

But only God and Oggie knew how hard it had been at first; only He knew the bitterness of the nights when she had cried out for something more, when the desire within her had asked not self-sacrifice, but fulfilment.

Now in her old age all the love for which her body had been starved through the years had centred itself on one person—Clive.

She loved him, it seemed to her, in every way—passionately, as a young woman might love a man, possessively, as a mother for a son, adoringly, as a student for a master.

She admitted this love to herself frankly and without subterfuge—she had learnt long ago in a very hard school not to be hypocritical—and because she loved him, she wanted his happiness.

It would have been easy to die for him, in the common parlance of dying for those one loves; it was far harder to live for him, to deny him some of the things he asked of her.

To know that he was attracted, if not yet in love with this woman who lay beneath her roof, but of whom she was not yet sure.

Stella puzzled her. At first she had been blindly prejudiced by her background, her money, her title, the type of society she represented.

Then Stella's weariness, her antipathy to Clive, her utter indifference to what became of her had not added to Oggie's dislike, but rather had caught her in her weakest spot—her sense of pity.

To be so lovely—for grudgingly, but truthfully Oggie

164

acknowledged Stella's beauty—and to gain so little seemed pitiable. To rouse something which had never been aroused before in Clive and not to know it—that too seemed pitiable.

Without realising it Oggie gradually developed an affection for Stella.

Pity was her Achilles' heel; whenever she most wanted to be unresponsive, to be hard and impregnable to argument or appeal, it was her sense of pity which let her down.

Now because she was worried about Clive she was disagreeable.

'Lady Marsden is better,' she said. 'She will soon be leaving here; in fact she will soon be able to do without me—or a doctor.'

She meant to hurt herself, but succeeded only in hurting him, and as she realised what she had done she could have bitten out her tongue to save the pain in his eyes.

Then suddenly the telephone in the next room shrilled across the silence.

'I'll answer it,' Oggie said.

She went out of the room, leaving the door open. Stella did not look at Clive or he at her, they were both listening.

Somehow when the shrill bell ceased it still seemed to hold their attention, it was as if they were both instinctively aware that the call was of importance.

'It's for you, Doctor, from Trenton Park.'

Clive moved as if he had been waiting for the summons. Stella could hear what he said.

'Hello. Oh, it's you, Matron. I'm sorry you've had so much trouble in getting me ... What? I can't hear ... What time? . . . After lunch . . . And the doctor's there? ... Yes, I'll come down at once ... A letter? I'm afraid I can't hear ... Yes, I understand, and the police have it ... Very well, I'll be down within the next two hours. Good-bye.'

Clive replaced the receiver, then he stood for a moment staring at it.

'I've got to go,' he said.

He made no attempt to go back to Stella's room; instead he picked up his hat and gloves. Oggie opened the outside door for him.

As he passed her she broke a rule of fifteen years standing, a rule never to ask Clive questions unless it was absolutely necessary.

'Who is it?' she asked apprehensively, her voice low.

'Mrs. Hayton,' Clive replied. 'She's dead.'

Without saying good-bye he hurried down the stone staircase, his footsteps echoing sharply and resonantly through the dark well of the building.

## 17

Clive bought a paper at Waterloo station. On the front page a paragraph was headed:—

'Famous Society Hostess Found Dead.'

He started to read, then crumpled up the paper and threw it away. Hailing a taxi, he gave his address.

The taxi set off down the sunlit streets which were almost empty of traffic so early in the morning. Clive sat back in the seat and shut his eyes.

He had had very little sleep the night before. When he had got to bed, it was already in the early hours of the morning and the sleep which he needed eluded him.

He found himself wondering what Hetty's death was going to mean to him, how much her last action would affect his career.

Her letter was an indictment against himself and Alice. Two people she had supposedly been fond of in her own warped way. Love was not an emotion one could attribute to Hetty.

Clive could imagine her making her plans to destroy them even as she planned to destroy herself. She had made certain enough of her own death.

A small phial of morphia tablets was found beside her,

lying with the letter the writing of which had been her last action previous to committing suicide.

It was in keeping with Hetty's character that she had done it theatrically.

She had dressed herself in one of her loveliest evening dresses, a dress she had last worn in London at a grand spectacular party she had given to end the season of 1939.

It was of white satin, bridal in appearance, and she wore her famous diamonds so that in death they glittered like living things against the pallor of her cold skin.

She had lain down on her bed to die, her head against satin pillows, a huge bunch of white lilies lifted from a vase and arranged beside her.

The whole scene might have seemed pathetic to those who were not hurt or injured by her act. The little Irish girl who had journeyed across the Atlantic bare-footed had come to the end of her story.

She had meant her funeral pyre to be impressive, even beautiful, but she had succeeded only in making it grotesque and in poor taste.

Clive had taken one last look at her this morning before he left Trenton Park. The early sunshine coming pale and golden through the windows had dimmed the fire of her diamonds.

Something else was also dim, fading and dispersing a few hours after death—the personality of the woman who had managed to conquer society, to force the most important and most influential people in the land to accept her hospitality.

The name of Hetty Hayton would soon be forgotten.

Clive had the feeling as he looked out on the morning mists covering the gardens that the impression Hetty had made on the world would last just as long as the mists which were already moving away before the rising sun.

She was unimportant; her only power had been the power of money; and now in death she became herself, an empty, shallow, unsatisfied woman.

He tried to understand that last defiant gesture of hers, the way she had dressed up and worn the jewels that she had valued and loved so dearly.

She loved them not for themselves—Hetty had very little real appreciation of fine things; art treasures, jewellery, paintings, even clothes meant nothing to her save that they symbolised the spoils of success.

Diamonds added to her own power and prestige—houses, estates, gardens, all possessions came into the same category—they were a background, a costume in which she acted her part.

And so in dying she had tried to die triumphant—the leading lady against an appropriate background. But instead of appearing beautiful beside the dignity and finality of her death, her possessions became tawdry and ridiculous.

The play was over, the curtain had been rung down sooner than was expected; who cared that the part would never be played again?

Hetty Hayton had held the stage, she had dominated everybody and everything to such an extent that *she* was the play, and it was a failure.

Other people could give her nothing because she asked only for personal power—friendship, sympathy, understanding were things for which she never had time. Even love was a thing she had never understood.

She had desired Clive as she had desired position, power and jewellery, and because he had not reciprocated that desire she strove to injure him.

The letter she left behind was a bestial one, Hetty at her worst.

Hetty when the thin veneer of education slipped from her, when the airs and graces that she had acquired because they were necessary wore thin to show her as she was, uncivilised, cruel, heartless.

She had known only too well that the letter she wrote would damage Clive irretrievably, would prevent Alice from finding other employment.

She had known also that it was inevitable that it should be handed to the police before Clive arrived to claim it.

Clive could imagine her writing that letter, sitting at the beautiful little Queen Anne walnut writing-desk which she always used, writing quickly and forcibly with a gold pen which she dipped into an ink pot of Sèvres china. She must have thought to herself:

'If I can't have him, I'll make it difficult for him to have anyone else.'

'She also,' Clive thought, 'meant to damage and destroy Stella.'

Why had she been so jealous of the woman she hardly knew and who had spent such a short time under her roof? His own heart supplied the answer.

Hetty had known that he was interested in Stella, because she herself was interested in him, had wanted him and found him indifferent.

Thinking back over the times they had met, of the things they had said to each other, Clive understood at last many conversations which at the time he had dismissed as unimportant and pointless.

Now he understood. Hetty had wanted him as a man and had been angry and bitter at his refusal to consider her as a woman.

She had always repelled him.

He did not care for the type she represented, for her strong, obtrusive vitality, her voice which rose loud and strident when she was annoyed or excited, her too gushing manner which was in strange contrast to the imperious way in which she ordered people about.

Not in any circumstances would Hetty Hayton have attracted him, and yet this woman of whom he knew very little save that her house had been used to heal his patients was able with a few strokes of the pen to injure and defame him.

When he arrived at the nearest station to Trenton Park the night before, he found a car waiting for him. Matron had had the foresight to send it, knowing how difficult it would be to get a taxi so late in the evening.

Inside he found a note suggesting that he should go first to the police station as there was a letter there which he ought to read.

He went; and when he had seen the note handed to him apologetically by the Inspector, who was a decent country-

169

man, Clive had understood Matron's reluctance to break the news to him herself.

The letter was written to him, but with typical cunning Hetty had made sure that no misguided person should keep the letter until Clive's arrival.

On the envelope she had written, *To be opened after I am dead*; but inside, *To Clive*.

Before he had read further, Clive had been conscious of Hetty's scent, the one she always used. It had come up to him in a great wave from the thick white paper that he held in his hand.

It recalled her very vividly—flashing, glittering, chattering, a restless woman with whom one never felt at peace or at ease.

It was difficult to believe she was dead and dead in such circumstances.

Then Clive had read on:

*I have taken morphia. You will think this strange, but life holds little interest for me now. Once I believed that things might be very different both for you and for me; once I thought that there might be a wonderful future for both of us together; but that dream has gone and I cannot face such desolation alone.*

*You will understand there are so many things that cannot be put on paper, cannot be written. If only I had thought of this before I let myself get fond of you, things might have been different; but now it is too late and there is nothing more to say.*

*I have had a second worry, too, but I have not troubled you with it. You have seemed to be uninterested in any of my doings lately or perhaps I have merely fancied your indifference.*

*Alice has slowly been going off her head; she has illusions, believes that crimes are being committed and that she sees them. I have done my best to spare her, but I am afraid that now I am gone she will find things very different and at least she should be kept under strict surveillance.*

*I am very tired and the rest ahead of me may be enjoyable. I doubt it; but sometimes when you are talking to*

*Stella Marsden, remember me. It is stupid to mention in this letter how hurt I was at your taking her away from here.*

*I quite realise, of course, that you didn't want us both to be under the same roof; nevertheless, we might have found a great many things in common—and you can guess why.*

*Good-bye Clive*

*Hetty.*

Clive read the letter through without showing any emotion whatsoever, then he handed it back to the Inspector.

'I'm afraid it will have to be produced at the inquest, sir,' the Inspector said gruffly.

'Of course,' Clive replied,

He had known immediately on arrival at Trenton Park exactly what other people's reactions were likely to be after reading Hetty's letter.

Matron was polite as always and yet he fancied there was an unusual coldness in her tone.

She had judged him and found him guilty—guilty of leading a woman astray, of letting her fall in love with him and then having no further use for her.

The reference to Stella was the most damning of the lot. 'Off with the old love, on with the new.'

He could imagine with what enjoyment this would be seized upon by those who relished gossip—the dirtier and the more harmful the better. He could imagine, too, the people who would say:

'Two rich women, but of course Stella was the better catch of the two.'

Clive writhed inside and yet outwardly he was cool, calm and courteous, his usual self. Matron had taken him upstairs to her sitting room where the local doctor was waiting for him. When the two men were alone together, Dr. Gordon said:

'I'm sorry about the letter, Ross. You understand that I would not have allowed anyone to see it if it had not been read before my arrival. Matron and the servants and some of the nurses had all seen it, there was nothing I could do in the circumstances but hand it over to the police when I reported the death.'

'Of course you did the right thing,' Clive said. 'I understand.'

'I'm sorry about it, though, damned sorry!'

There was genuine feeling in the Doctor's voice and Clive held out his hand.

'Thank you,' he said.

He found out exactly what had happened. Hetty's maid, Watkins, had gone to call her as usual at nine o'clock in the morning.

The door was locked and thinking her mistress was tired and wanted to rest, she had gone away and waited for the bell to ring.

It got later and later and still there was no sound from Hetty's room.

Finally Watkins had gone in search of Matron and after a long consultation and repeated knockings on Hetty's door they had eventually sent for the estate carpenter and instructed him to break in.

By the time he had done so it was two o'clock in the afternoon. The doctor was sent for, but he was many hours too late.

In the meantime a further complication had arisen owing to the fact that Alice was not to be found. All her luggage was packed and left in her room with the exception of a suitcase which she must have carried herself.

No one had seen her leave the house and she had disappeared.

The servants, on finding her room empty in the morning, had thought that she had gone to London for Mrs. Hayton; it was not such an unusual occurrence although generally one of the cars took her to the station.

It was only after Hetty's letter had been read that her disappearance caused comment and the police decided that she must be found immediately.

It was not hard to trace where she had gone. The station reported that she had taken the early morning train to Leeway, a seaside town about twenty miles distant.

The boarding-houses and hotels were searched and by

172

seven o'clock that evening Alice was on her way back to Trenton Park.

Clive was there when she arrived. She looked to him much as usual save that she was obviously desperately tired. The police had already told her what had happened.

She made little comment, only when Clive held out his hands to her in welcome did her self-control seem to relax.

'Oh, Mr. Ross, I am glad to see you.'

'I'm glad to see you, Alice,' Clive said. 'Have you had anything to eat or drink?'

Alice looked vague.

'I don't think I have.'

'Not all day?' Clive asked.

He rang the bell for Barton. He ordered her a meal and some black coffee.

Alice sank down into a chair in front of the fire as if she was too exhausted to refuse anything he suggested for her. Clive went outside to where the plain-clothes detective was waiting.

'I'll look after Miss Farley,' he said.

'Is there anything you want?'

'We shall want a statement from her.'

'But she must have something to eat and drink first,' Clive said. 'Don't you think it would be wise to ask the inspector to come up? You can telephone to him and I expect you would like something to eat yourself. Barton will look after you.'

'Thank you, sir.'

Clive went back to Alice, but he made no attempt to get her to talk until she had had something to eat. Then when Barton had taken away the empty tray, he said:

'Mrs. Hayton is dead. You know that, don't you?'

'The policeman told me,' Alice replied. 'They don't think I killed her, do they?'

'Why should they think that?' Clive asked.

'I only wondered,' Alice said, in a quiet, dull voice. 'He said something about a letter and I thought it would be like Mrs. Hayton to accuse me of murdering her.'

'I think she has made me the culprit,' Clive said quietly, and he told Alice what was in the letter.

173

'But it's cruel! It's wicked!' she exclaimed, showing animation for the first time since she had returned. 'How dare she do such a thing?'

'Why should she say that about you?' Clive asked.

'I wasn't thinking about myself,' Alice said scornfully. 'But you, to accuse you, when I know. . . .'

'Thank you, Alice,' Clive said quietly, 'but it doesn't matter.'

'It does matter,' Alice protested. 'Don't you understand why she has done this? Haven't you heard what happened yesterday?'

'Dr. Gordon did mention it,' Clive said. 'You mean about the accident when that strange man fell over the banisters.'

'Accident!' Alice exclaimed. 'It was no accident.'

'What do you mean?'

Alice told him, told him in tones of horror which made him believe at first that she was suffering from the delusions that Hetty mentioned.

Then, with the full force of his intuitive sense that never let him down, Clive knew she was speaking the truth.

'This complicates things tremendously,' he said. 'I don't know quite what to do about it. What were you going to do?'

'I hadn't decided,' Alice answered. 'You will think that weak of me—cowardly, and I suppose in some ways that is what I am. I have always been afraid of taking the initiative, I have always obeyed orders.

'When I left here early this morning, I felt that if I didn't go away I should go mad. That woman scared me, not because of any injury she might do me, but because suddenly she seemed to be the personification of all that was evil.'

Alice's voice was eloquent of her feeling.

'I had watched her through the years, you see, watched her as she climbed higher and higher, making use of this person and that and then not only throwing them away when she had finished with them but trying to damage them, to hurt them if she could.'

Alice's hands were clasped together until the knuckles were white.

'She hated anyone to know anything about her,' she continued. 'If she could obtain a favour from anyone, she would; but she would loathe that person ever afterwards, she would pray for his death, she would go out of her way to do him an injury.

She looked at Clive with her tired eyes and he understood a little of what she must have suffered.

'It took me a long time,' she went on, 'to begin to understand the workings of Mrs. Hayton's mind. I saw her day after day; I saw her generosity to charities, the public kindnesses she would do, the cheques that she wrote when it suited her purpose.

But I saw, too, her horrible, incredible meanness to little people, people who had never done her any harm, but who perhaps quite inadvertently had learnt something about her and had become, in her mind, dangerous.'

Alice drew a deep breath. Then she said slowly and distinctly:

'What Mr. Wrighton knew I don't know, but it must have been something pretty terrible for her to take the course she did.'

'But how could she have had the strength to push him over the banisters?' Clive asked. 'There were no marks on him as if he had been subjected to violence or Dr. Gordon and the police would have noticed it.'

'He was unconscious,' Hetty said. 'I'm quite sure of that.'

Clive sat thinking.

'Did anyone suggest that it might not have been an accident?' he enquired.

Then he got to his feet.

'Will you wait here while I go and discuss what happened with Dr. Gordon? He is having dinner with Matron. I won't repeat to him anything you have just told me until you give me permission; I just want to know exactly what occurred yesterday evening.'

Alice agreed and Clive, after apologising to Matron,

saw Dr. Gordon alone. He was only too ready to chat about the tragedy of the day before.

'I went to see the wife this morning,' he said. 'She lives just outside London. A very nice woman, obviously very fond of her husband and desperately upset at what had occurred.

'I would have brought her back with me only she preferred to wait till tomorrow, when their eldest son will be on leave. He has been sent for, of course. They are coming down together.'

'Did she give an explanation why her husband should have come here?' Clive asked.

'No, nothing reasonable,' Dr. Gordon replied. 'She said he had mentioned a letter that he wanted to discuss with Mrs. Hayton and he had said that his journey was dangerous. What he meant by that I can't conceive; in fact, jokingly as he left he said,

"If I don't come back, take care of yourself, old woman."

'He had a kind of dry humour apparently, and his wife just laughed, having no idea that he meant it seriously.'

'And the letter?' Clive insisted.

'She only knew there was one. She inferred that he liked being mysterious, the type of man who pretends to know more than he does. He was very proud of being in the Foreign Office and from what I can gather was rather inclined to talk as if he had the confidence of the whole War Cabinet.

'Anyway, she confirmed what I suspected, that he suffered from heart trouble—going up three flights of stairs must have been too much for him.'

Clive thanked Dr. Gordon and went back to Alice. She listened to what he had to say, then in her usual hesitant way she remarked:

'There must have been something that he knew and there was a letter.'

She sat still, staring into the fire, the flames glittering on her spectacles, and then suddenly she started.

'When was the question of the letter first mentioned?' she asked. 'Did Mrs. Hayton know about that?'

'I don't know. I suppose Dr. Gordon might have told her.'

'Go back and ask,' Alice begged. 'Please, Mr. Ross, ask Dr. Gordon if anyone mentioned the letter to Mrs. Hayton.'

Clive did as he was bid. He found the doctor in Matron's sitting-room and put the question.

'I'm sorry to sound like the detective in a crime novel,' he said, 'but Miss Farley is very anxious to piece the events of last night together.'

'Do you think she is suffering from delusions?' Dr. Gordon asked.

Before Clive could reply Matron interrupted.

'I think that is nonsense, if you ask me,' she said in her firm voice. 'I have had a great deal to do with Miss Farley since we have been here and I have always found her most reliable.

'She is shy, of course, and at times becomes rather flustered when too much is heaped upon her shoulders, but apart from that she is a most sensible woman.'

'I agree with you,' Clive said. 'But can you remember about the letter?'

He spoke to Dr. Gordon, but again Matron answered him.

'I told Mrs. Hayton myself,' she said. 'I came straight from the telephone after both Dr. Gordon and I had spoken to Mrs. Wrighton. She was standing on the landing at the top of the stairs, and now I think of it she was just outside Miss Farley's room.

'She started when she saw me and I remember thinking that she couldn't have heard me coming because I was wearing rubber-soled shoes.

' "Oh it's you Matron!" she exclaimed.

'I told her that we had rung up the poor man's widow and repeated her remark about her husband going into danger. I also said that he had mentioned something about a letter. Mrs. Hayton looked upset. I thought it was due to the shock of Mr. Wrighton's death. You don't think it was anything I said, do you, Mr. Ross?'

177

'May I leave that question for the moment?' Clive asked. 'until I have taken the answer back to Miss Farley.'

He left Matron and Dr. Gordon sitting over the fire and had the idea that as soon as his back was turned they would start talking about him. He felt a violent distaste for the whole thing.

He thought of the man Wrighton, of whom they knew very little, lying in the police mortuary, of Hetty lying upstairs garbed in her splendour, of Alice waiting for him in front of the fire, her future, like his, problematical because of a letter written by a malevolent, bitter woman who had taken her own life.

He went dowstairs and gave Alice the information he had received from Matron.

'I knew it!' Alice said excitedly. 'Don't you understand? It's so obvious what happened. There was a letter, a letter that Mrs. Hayton had written. Mr. Wrighton got hold of it. He blackmailed her and she killed him!'

She paused, then continued slowly as if choosing her words.

'She thought her secret would die with him, but Matron brought her the news that his wife knew about it too. Then she was mortally afraid. She had been afraid of me, afraid of what I had seen.

'She was still more afraid of what was in the letter and of yet another person knowing about it. And so she killed herself, killed herself, it appears, quite unnecessarily because if I had kept silence no one could ever have known.'

Alice Farley looked at Clive, then slowly and mirthlessly she laughed.


18


All day Stella had felt that something was wrong.

Ever since Clive left her abruptly the night before to answer the telephone Oggie had been strange.

She answered questions erratically and all through

Stella's treatment that morning she had been brusque and unresponsive to the point of rudeness.

Stella would have liked to ask her what was the matter, but some pride within herself forbade it, or perhaps it was because Oggie had an outstanding dignity of her own, a dignity which made it almost impossible for anyone to be rude or impertinent to her.

It certainly owed nothing to her appearance—that was often laughable; it owed nothing to her position in life, for no one was more simple and humble with the resignation of a saint who has no use for earthly possessions.

Whatever it was, it was something very real which impressed itself on all with whom Oggie came in contact.

Stella found herself watching the old woman and asking herself what was this particular quality in her which commanded respect and emanated from her like a living force.

She could imagine Oggie controlling crowds, ruling a nation; she was that type of woman, because Nature had endowed her with leadership.

Quite suddenly Stella knew the answer to her question.

It was the good in Oggie which commanded attention; not staid, inactive goodness, the type emulated by tight-lipped spinsters who had never faced the reality, the cruelty or the wonder of life, but rather the good which is the true reflection of life itself—giving, living and loving.

At last she could understand a little of Oggie's immense concentration, the whole-hearted power and passion that she gave to her work, and that the patients she treated became part of herself because of the living force that she directed towards and into them.

Stella could feel that force when she was being massaged.

It was like lying beneath the warm rays of the sun, it beat into her, it drew out a response despite her every effort to withstand it.

Always, after her body had been in contact with Oggie's hands, she felt more alive, possessed almost by a sense of exhilaration.

Gradually, after some time, the strength of it would fade, yet much remained to build her up day by day, to

179

give her besides physical health a spiritual urge and a desire to come alive.

'I feel as if I had been dead a long time!' Stella said once aloud.

As she said the words she knew that they were the truth.

She had been dead—dead ever since she found out the truth about Philip, dead through those long years when she must act the part as his wife, must take her place in the glittering shallow world with which she had so little in common.

She had died again for a second time that morning in Bertram's flat.

Yet now she was forced to admit that actually only a very small part of herself had blossomed beneath his love—a superficial bloom, exotic, brought to fruition by artificial heat, having few roots and very little strength to survive.

'If I had loved Bertram enough, would I have forgiven him?' she asked herself.

She was afraid of the answer because it revealed her own shallowness, her own lack of depth.

Oggie was so different; she was a woman too and yet everything about her seemed fundamental, her every thought, every action came from the depths, was honest and true.

It was difficult to think of frivolous things in connection with Oggie and yet this did not exclude an exquisite sense of humour.

Sometimes Stella would find herself laughing helplessly at the stories Oggie told her of the people or the children round about, stories of rough Cockney humour which she began to see was part of the greatness and grandeur of the British race.

Sometimes Oggie would bring her near to tears with a description of some pathetic family struggling against disaster and privation.

Then before she could appreciate her pity to the full she would find herself laughing at some ridiculous aspect of it which Oggie would describe in her own inimitable way.

'Don't make me laugh, I haven't said yet how sorry I am for them, how dreadful it all seems to me,' Stella said once.

'They don't want your pity,' Oggie said, 'any more than they want charity. They want justice, the opportunity to live and breathe like human beings. You can't understand that—why should you? You've never known any life save that which you have viewed through a plate-glass window.'

'That's not my fault,' Stella said, stung by the contempt in Oggie's last words.

'Isn't it?' Oggie asked quietly. 'You've got free will, I suppose, like everyone else.'

Wearily Stella had closed her eyes against further argument; nevertheless she had felt humiliated and ashamed.

It was true, she had accepted the life in which she had found herself, hardly believing there was any different, any other in which she might feel more at home.

She could see herself, a pale ghost wandering down the years, letting so much pass her by because she was foolish enough to be afraid.

That was the truth. She had been afraid to rebel, to revolt, to speak her mind, to be like Oggie leading a clean, cleansing, invigorating crusade.

'We are two women,' Stella thought. 'The world would think that I have everything, that I am important; and yet how insignificant, how contemptible I am beside Oggie!'

She found after the first day that there was no reason to pretend to herself an interest in the woman under whose roof she lay.

She was interested, interested to the point of enthralment, and curious too, but Oggie would not speak of herself. Stella tried various ways of enticing her confidence, but always she was disappointed.

There was some innate reserve in Oggie beyond which it was impossible to penetrate. That reserve prevented Stella from speaking about Clive.

She had a feeling that Oggie's anxiety concerned him; she longed to know why he had left the evening before without saying good-bye. It was unlike him, for Clive was invariably courteous.

'Will he come today?' Stella had wondered.

She was surprised to realise how much she was looking forward to seeing him.

'It is because I'm curious,' she thought.

But she found herself going over the conversation they had had the night before, rehearsing another in which she could express her views, prevail upon him, maybe, to decide her future.

'How bored I am with myself,' she said aloud suddenly, as Oggie was taking away her luncheon tray.

'Are you? I'm not surprised,' Oggie said. 'There's little enough you have to be interested in.'

She walked out of the room and shut the door sharply behind her.

Stella smiled, but it was an effort. It was like Oggie to be so blunt; Stella knew her opinion of a social existence and of the people who led it.

Stella felt lonely. As she had said to Clive, this hanging betwixt earth and sky was an unenviable position.

What would happen after the war? What would become of women like herself? Could she work? Should she? And if she did, what at?

And yet hadn't Clive said that there must be a place for her in the new world?

Wearily the questions asked themselves over and over in her mind. Pictures from the past came back to taunt her, memories of the great parties held at Marsden House and in Philip's London residence.

Of the bills they had paid for the luxurious, out-of-season food, for the bands which had cost hundreds of pounds, for the clothes she had chosen for herself at sums which would have supported Oggie's patients for their whole lives.

And with it all she had had no pleasure out of it.

Some of those parties, Stella felt, had been the hysterical swan song of a dying era.

They dared not face the rumblings of the gigantic storm gathering over Europe and Asia—the burning of the German Reichstag—the invasion of Abyssinia—the marching

182

of Blackshirts and Brownshirts—the steps which led to Munich and beyond.

How could anyone have been so foolish as to ignore the signs, the portents, the writing on the wall?

Yet they had gone on dancing, eating, drinking and loving—each person, it seemed to Stella, possessed by his or her personal greed, each content to hold tightly to the slogan 'Let's laugh and be merry for tomorrow we die.'

And tomorrow had come!

Stella thought of the horrors which had come to Europe with the dawn of that tomorrow.

Paris, which she had known so well, under the heel of the Nazi storm troopers; the mimosa of the South of France breathing its fragrance over armoured cars and camouflaged tanks; the lovely, quiet coast of Brittany built over and fortified by the invaders.

So many places she had known brutalised and ruined, so many people she had known lost or remaining only a memory with those left bereaved.

War such as had never been known before in the history of mankind, a war of ghastly devastation and desolation, but one which people like Oggie and Clive believed would bring in a new world—a world very different from the old one.

She wondered if they were right and felt once again an utter lonliness sweep over her.

She felt as if she was the only person outside it all, a stranger in a land so strange that there was no familiar landmark she could recognise as her own.

The afternoon was passing slowly.

More than once Stella looked at the clock, hoping that there would be some excuse for Oggie to come in, for Liza to bring coals for the fire, to pull the curtains and shut out the twilight.

But it was only her mind that moved quickly, the hours went slowly enough; and then suddenly when she felt she could bear it no longer, could be no longer alone with her thoughts, her own unhappiness, there came a knock at the door.

'Come in,' she cried eagerly.

183

It was Clive.

She was so glad to see him that she made no attempt to hide her pleasure. For the first time she held out her hands spontaneously.

She was aware instantly that something was wrong; she could not put a name to it, but as he asked after her health she felt her heart begin to beat.

What could have happened? What was the matter?

Why did Clive look so ... there was no word for what she wanted to say; he looked tired, but no more than usual; he looked serious, but then he habitually did ... he looked—was drawn the right word?

Then while she searched for her own thoughts he moved across the room to stand in front of the fireplace, his hands deep in his trouser pockets.

'I've got something to tell you,' he said abruptly.

Suddenly Stella found the word for which she sought.

He looked forlorn, a little boy left out in the cold. Quite unexpectedly she felt her heart go out to him in pity and in tenderness.

She saw him no longer as the efficient, famous surgeon, the ruthless healer who had forced her back to life against her desires; instead she saw him as a man in trouble, a little boy who was half afraid and yet whose courage would not let him down.

'How his mother must have loved him,' she thought suddenly.

In a flash it came to her that she had always longed for a child of her own. She had not known until that moment the ache there had always been within her.

'If I had a child,' she thought, 'I should not be asking what part I had to play in the new world—I should know. My work would be there, creating a citizen of the future, giving him a better chance, a better outlook than I have myself.'

Just for a moment she saw the son she might have had, whom she still might have, a little boy with his jaw stuck forward defiantly, his hands deep in his trouser pockets. . . .

'What is the matter?' she asked and heard her own

184

voice, quiet and calm, speaking above the tumult, the hurry of her thoughts.

'Something rather terrible has happened,' Clive replied. 'I don't know quite how to tell you about it and yet I must because you yourself are involved.'

'Why should he mind this so much?' Stella thought. 'Is it because of me?'

'I can only regret,' Clive was saying, 'that your name should ever have been dragged into what at the very best must be an unsavoury business. I can only regret with all my heart that I ever sent you even for those few days to Trenton Park.'

'Trenton Park?' Stella questioned. 'You mean something has happened there, that Mrs. Hayton has made trouble?'

'Mrs. Hayton is dead.'

Clive spoke sternly, as if for a moment he sat in the seat of Justice, and then he went on to tell Stella everything, everything, that is, so far as she was concerned.

He and Alice had sat late the previous night talking as to what they should do about the truth of Vernon Wrighton's death. Finally they had come to a decision. They had decided to say nothing.

Hetty was dead, she had died as an act of reparation for the sin she had committed.

It was only Alice who knew the truth, and if there was a sensational murder case, the revelation of what had occurred could hurt and injure only Alice and not the woman who had escaped by administering justice with her own hand.

What would be the point? Clive argued, and Alice had been only too thankful to have, if nothing else, a breathing space for the moment.

She was a mass of nerves and Clive had advised her to stay quietly at Trenton Park, to tidy up the affairs of the household and the hospital.

He knew that the familiar tasks would keep her busy.

He hoped that Hetty had had the good sense to leave Alice something in her will.

If she had not, he had every intention of seeing the solicitors, of doing what he could to get her at least a just recognition for the years she had spent in Hetty's service.

He also meant to bring home very forcibly that Hetty's last action would leave Alice in a precarious position as regards employment.

There was still some hope that the whole letter would not be published in the papers, but the Coroner's Court would be a public one and the newspapers would not miss such a juicy piece of scandal.

Already one of the servants must have talked. In the early editions of the evening papers there were references to the letter which had been left by Hetty's bedside.

It was only a question of time, Clive thought, before the whole story was revealed to the public.

He gave Stella a copy of the letter. As he waited, watching her expression as she read it, he thought how much better she looked since she had come here to Oggie.

There was a faint natural colour in her cheeks and her eyes were bright and shining.

There was indeed little to remind him of the woman who had tried to die before and after he had operated upon her, or indeed of the woman he had once met on the staircase of a famous London house.

How well he could remember that woman.

He was feeling nauseated and angry at what he had encountered upstairs and then on the landing he had come face to face with Sir Philip Marsden's wife.

She was looking amazingly beautiful, but her beauty was one which had little appeal for him at the first glance.

He was repulsed, by the sophisticated elegance of her skin-tight black satin dress, by the absurd fantasy of the hat which she wore, by the diamond bracelets which bound her arms and found an echo at her throat and in her ears.

'The best-dressed woman in Society'—that was how the papers described her.

Then as he had spoken to her, meaning to rebuke her for the neglect of her dog, he saw the pain in her eyes, he saw a woman suffering and humiliated, and the pity of it left him speechless.

There was nothing he could say, nothing he could do, and he had gone away thinking of the agony he had seen amid such pompous splendour.

A woman suffering! He wondered now if this letter would make her suffer as he was suffering.

Stella held it out to him and as he took it from her he realised that once again a great change had come over her.

She leant back wearily, the momentary animation which he had surprised in her when he arrived was gone, instead she said dully:

'There is nothing we can do to prevent this being published, I suppose?'

'I have taken the matter up with my solicitors,' Clive replied, 'and I have also been in communication with the Medical Council. I will see your solicitors, too, if you think they can help in any way.'

'I should imagine it is unlikely—the law will take its course,' Stella said. 'You have no other suggestions?'

There was a coldness in her voice, something else, too, which seemed to Clive like contempt and which stung him.

'I'm afraid not,' he said.

Then as he folded the letter and replaced it in his pocket he added;

'May I say once again how sorry I am that you should have been involved in this?'

'It is very unfortunate,' Stella said,

There was a finality in her tone which told Clive as surely as if she spoke aloud that she dismissed him.

He went towards the door. As he reached it he looked back.

'I will keep you informed of what happens.'

'Thank you.'

Her tone was as distant as if she spoke to a servant. Clive shut the door quietly behind him.

Stella lay very still. Now at last the early winter twilight was beginning to fall, the coals shifted themselves in the grate, otherwise there was no sound.

After a long while the door opened and Oggie came in. She pulled the curtains and switched on the light.

'Are you ready for your tea?' she asked.

Stella could tell by her tone that she was upset, even more upset than she had been this morning.

'Yes, please,' she answered, 'and can I have the evening papers?'

'What for?' Oggie asked.

'I want to read the charming things they will say about Mrs. Hayton.'

'Mrs. Hayton!' Oggie's whole bulk quivered with rage. 'If that woman was alive I'd strangle her with my own hands. That she should dare to try and ruin a man whose whole life has been one of service to others—

'She, was a useless parasite, a social climber whose only achievement in life has been to gain notoriety by feeding those who will eat and drink anywhere so long as it is free—yet she can damage and defame a good man, a man like Clive Ross!'

Stella smiled cynically.

'Poor Oggie!' she said. 'Do you really believe that there are good men? If you do, you are very easily misled. All men are the same, all men fall when a woman beckons.'

Stella spoke bitterly, her voice rising.

Then to her own horror she found that she was weeping, the tears pouring uncontrollably from her eyes.


19


Liza brought in Stella's breakfast and put it down silently. She made no sound but crept from the room like a wounded animal.

Stella could see by her swollen eyes that she had been crying and she debated within herself whether to ask the child what was the matter.

Later Liza returned with the morning papers. She put them down as was her custom beside Stella, then turned to go.

'Is anything the matter?' Stella asked gently. 'Have you had bad news?'

Liza shook her head dumbly and slipped out of the room.

'What is the matter with her?' Stella wondered. 'Has Oggie been angry with her?'

She picked up the *Daily Express*, opened it, and learnt the reason for Liza's tears. There was a picture of Hetty in her Court dress on the front page; above it a caption in large print said:

'DRAMATIC DISCLOSURES AT INQUEST ON SOCIETY HOSTESS.'

Stella read on. The letter to Clive in which she herself was mentioned was printed in full; the Coroner's somewhat caustic comments were given prominence.

When she had finished reading the report in the *Daily Express*, she took up the other papers. All of them had something to say in a more or less sensational degree regarding the inquest.

However much notoriety Hetty had obtained in her lifetime, in death she had certainly achieved the prominence she loved.

Her famous jewels and the treasures at Trenton Park were described in detail; her rise to fame soon after she arrived in England, the amazing parties she had given and the important people who had attended them were all recorded, all set down for the delectation of a public which feeds on thrills and scandal.

Slowly Stella read every word regardless of the fact that her breakfast grew cold.

One of the papers gave a picture of Clive and a short paragraph described him as a famous surgeon, mentioning the names of well-known people whom he had attended in the past two or three years. Her name was amongst them.

She looked at the photograph.

The camera had caught the sharp line of Clive's jaw, the breadth of his shoulders, and he looked very unlike the average doctor—a handsome man who might easily captivate a silly, frivolous woman's heart.

'All men are the same!'

She heard her own voice, saw Oggie's expression of anger, and felt the hot tears blinding her.

'Why did I cry?' she wondered now, and knew if she was truthful, it was because yet one more idol had crashed.

She had believed in Clive, she had begun to rely on his strength, on the rock-like quality of his character, and now he, too, had failed her.

He like all the other men she had known was weak, foolish and unable to resist temptation.

She had believed him different—why she could not say except that he did not resemble in any way either of the men she had known so intimately in the past.

His idealism had seemed to radiate from him, she believed that he had indeed dedicated himself to his career, to the healing and saving of others.

But she had been mistaken—fool that she was!—and she laughed bitterly as she thought how Philip would have sneered at her.

He had warned her once about Bertram and she had not heeded his warning. How right he had been!

'Never expect from people more than they are capable of giving.'

That was what he had said and yet she had gone on expecting to find gold among the dross.

How vain, how idiotic, to imagine that she would be more successful than other people had been!

All the women she had known had sooner or later bewailed the unfaithfulness of their men, had something of which to complain, for which to seek the sympathy of their kind.

Well, Bertram should have taught her a lesson—never, never to expect anything from men save treachery and hypocrisy.

It was the wanderings of a sick fancy, of course, she realised that now, which had made her trust and believe in Clive.

Didn't they always say that men when they were ill clung to their nurses? Sometimes they were even fools enough to marry the women who had attended them through their illness or who had soothed their convalescence.

Well, apparently women also lacked common sense.

Sick in body they clung to their doctor. Laughable to think of it—that she, Stella Marsden, who had been taught so many hard lessons in her life, should have begun to believe in the integrity and the honesty of a stranger simply because he had the power to heal her.

Stella looked down at Hetty's pictured face on the paper.

The woman was good-looking, there was no denying that, but she looked for all her prettiness ill-bred and hard. Hers was not the expression of a gracious, loving woman.

There was, too, a look of triumph on that pictured face. The photographer had taken Hetty when she had good reason to feel triumphant.

She had just been presented at the Court of St. James's, had made her curtsy to the British, King and Queen.

At that moment she had reached the Mecca of all good Americans who, the cynical aver, go to Paris when they die, but who find Paradise as they walk up the red carpets at Buckingham Palace.

That was the real cause for Hetty's air of triumph, but to Stella it was as if the dead woman looked back at her from the newspaper with a challenge which was personal.

'I've won!' she seemed to say, and Stella found a hidden meaning for that assertion within her own heart.

Yes, Hetty had won—in her death she became the conqueror.

Stella, an unwilling foe, was defeated and routed. Her last idol was shattered, an idol erected slowly and with great difficulty within her lonely, desolate heart.

Clive was Hetty's chosen man—her beloved—perhaps her lover. Stella shrank from the thought.

The future seemed to her one of utter blackness and misery.

She tried to think of one friend, even one person whom she could love and trust—but she could think of no one.

191

Oggie came in later in silence and took away the breakfast tray and then started Stella's treatment.

All the time she worked, her brows were knitted together darkly and her mouth was tightened ominously. Stella felt as if the sympathy and the healing power which usually radiated from her were missing.

She herself was unresponsive. It was as if neither of the women was tuned in to the other and the vibrations which flowed between them were discordant.

After a time the silence was broken by casual remarks.

They spoke of the weather, of what Stella would have for luncheon, and yet both of them were well aware of the newspapers lying at the foot of the bed and of what they contained.

The day passed slowly, so slowly that it seemed to Stella as if each tick of the clock was an eternity of time.

She told herself that her mind was preoccupied with other things, that she must cease to think of Clive or the mess in which he had involved himself; but her mind refused to obey her.

Over and over again she picked up the newspapers to read them. Soon she could have repeated every paragraph by heart.

Once she remembered Philip reading something faintly disparaging about himself in one of the newspapers and throwing it down with a laugh. Stella had been indignant.

It was in the first months after her marriage when, unawakened to the truth, she still loved him, and when whatsoever concerned him concerned her also.

'How can they say such things!' she cried hotly. 'How dare they!'

'Why shouldn't they?' Philip replied. 'They have to sell the paper and it is always easier to amuse the public with "the evil men do" than to bore them with the good.'

'Why should that be so?' Stella asked wonderingly.

'Because every man and woman is a Pharisee at heart. We love to say, "Thank God I am not as other men", and we only get that satisfaction when somebody else is found out.'

192

'We should be sorry,' Stella exclaimed. 'Are we really such brutes?'

'Not brutes,' Philip said, 'but not very civilised as yet. Don't you realise that all humour is based on sadism? Read the comic papers, listen to the jokes at a music hall, and you will find we laugh at another fool's misfortunes. But not for a moment do we forget to cry about our own.'

It was true, Stella thought now, the world liked misfortune.

If Hetty had died and left all her millions to a hospital, there would have been a few short lines of obituary and then she would have been forgotten.

By implicating other people in her death, by dying sensationally and horribly, she was front page news, a nine days' wonder.

Stella could imagine the articles that would appear in the Sunday newspapers, articles which would invite controversy.

'Should Those About to Die Tell the Truth?'

'Is a Social Life Spiritual Suicide?'

'Are Letters the Best Farewell?'

And there would be more photographs of Hetty, more photographs of Clive, and lastly photographs of herself.

Without actually saying so, the newspapers were making it obvious that she and Hetty were rivals for Clive.

It was the sort of triangle that the public enjoyed—two beautiful, wealthy and notorious women vying with each other for the Scottish boy who had risen from penury to become a famous surgeon.

Two women in love, and one had died because of that love.

Stella thought of Clive and wondered if he would be sorry now that he had not let her die in the factory, when they had brought her to him crushed and bleeding from beneath an overturned machine.

He had forced her to live.

She remembered the ghastly pain, the agony of creeping back to consciousness after the operation, the horror in her own mind when she had realised that she could not escape, that her misery, her loneliness, her sense of defeat were still with her.

Clive in making her live had called forth an avalanche on his own hand. Perhaps there was justice in it, a just retribution.

Stella found no relief from her own thoughts.

She opened a book, but after holding it in front of her for nearly a quarter of an hour found she had not read a single word.

She looked at the clock, lay still for a few minutes then looked again. Would the day never pass?

She found herself listening and quite suddenly knew for whom she was listening—for Clive. Would he visit her to-day, and if not today, tomorrow or the day after?

She wanted to see him, she admitted that to herself. Despite everything, despite the contempt she felt for him, she wanted to see him.

'It is because I can tell him what I think,' she thought, and knew that in the past there had been a sense of exhilaration and excitement in fencing with him.

But supposing he didn't come? She had made it clear enough, when he had told her about the letter, what she had felt.

She could remember the icy silence, the coldness of her voice, hard and bitter as it had been so often in those long years after she had learnt about Philip.

She had never been able to control the tones of her voice so that they did not express her innermost thoughts. She had tried, for she realised that they betrayed her, gave her away when she most wished by her reserve to mystify the outside world.

She had enjoyed in the past hearing people speak of her as an enigma.

Once in a cloakroom she had heard two young girls discussing her, daughters of women she often entertained.

'She's lovely,' one of them said. 'I wish I had a figure like hers.'

'And a face too,' the other added with a laugh. 'But she's strange, though; I don't think she gets much fun out of life.'

'Oh but she must!' the first exclaimed with girlish enthusiasm. 'Think of owning Marsden House! And her clothes! I thought I should die with envy when I saw her in that chinchilla cape the other night.'

'Do you know what Johnnie calls her?' the other girl asked. Stella, listening behind a concealing mirror, wondered who Johnnie might be.

'No, what does he call her?'

'He calls her "the Icicle" and the other day he said she was one of those women which even the fires of hell couldn't melt.'

Stella had remembered who Johnnie was by now—an impetuous young man in the Household Cavalry who had pursued her at every party in the last six weeks.

'Oh, I don't believe a word of what Johnnie says. I think Lady Marsden's lovely and I bet she has a lovely time. It just makes her all the more exciting and glamorous to be a bit stand-offish. I wish I could behave like that, instead of which if I like someone I just fling myself at them. I can't help it, I try not to, but I get so excited.'

'You'll have to take lessons from the Icicle, my dear.'

They both giggled and before they saw her Stella had gone away, amused and not displeased at what she had heard.

Thank God nobody did know of the feelings and emotions that battled and throbbed under a cold exterior!

Well, she supposed her reputation would stand her in good stead in the future; she would need to be enigmatical if she was to hold her head high despite all the things that would be said about her now.

'So that's what Stella Marsden's been up to all this time,' she could hear her acquaintances sniggering and giggling. 'My dear, and we thought she was so ill!'

'Of course he's good-looking but only a doctor. Surely that's a bit of a come-down after Philip?'

'Do you think she meant to marry him? And Hetty Hayton, of all people. Fancy even considering a man who had been hers!'

Stella could hear it all, hear, too, the comparisons that would be made between herself and Hetty.

'Stella's younger, but she always seemed to me so cold and frigid—except, of course, one heard stories about her and Bertram Armstrong.'

'Hetty's parties were fun and Stella's were often like morgues. Hetty at least had welcome on the mat for all and sundry, but Stella was so choosey!'

'Oh well, she's not been so particular where this fellow was concerned!'

At parties, at cocktail bars, restaurants and canteens, wherever two or three of the people she had known before were gathered together, the conversation inevitably would take the same course—Stella and Hetty and Clive Ross.

Two women and a man! How ridiculous—a plot which has been used over and over again by every aspiring dramatist, by every ambitious novelist! Two women and a man—and she was one of the women.

Stella reached out her hand and pressed the bell.

She heard it ring sharply in the flat and a moment later the door opened.

'Did you want me?' Oggie asked.

'For God's sake come in,' Stella said. 'I'm going mad. How can you leave me here hour after hour with nothing to do but to think, to worry about myself and the future. I'm ill, I'm your patient, haven't you any consideration for me?'

Oggie came over to the bedside.

'You poor child,' she said and her voice was soft again, her hardness and her anger had gone.

'Shut your eyes,' she commanded.

Stella felt the touch of her hands on her forehead smoothing back the hair, mesmerising her into peace, disentangling the twisted tension of mind and muscles.

'Oh, Oggie,' she whispered. 'I'm so desperately lonely.'

She slept that night but not without the help of a sleeping draught. The next day Oggie was able to spend more time with her.

They talked of many things, but neither of them could bear to mention the subject that was uppermost in both their minds.

'There's nothing to say,' Stella thought: 'nothing.'

She had a feeling that Oggie was suffering and yet since that first morning when she had been dark and foreboding the older woman had said nothing and given no indication of her feelings.

'She's certain to hear from Clive,' Stella thought.

She knew, too, that she was waiting, waiting for him to visit her.

The day passed and the day after that, and yet another day.

Her thoughts veered from contempt and anger to a kind of blind desire to see him, to talk with him, to make him bring forth some explanation.

Now she was not angry, she had the feeling that Clive alone could give her the clue to the problem, could explain everything away.

She could not bear to read the newspapers while, as she had anticipated, they mouthed over the scandal, chewing the whole subject over and over again until there was nothing left but a nasty taste in the mouth.

Yet somehow it was still harder when the subject died, when there was nothing to fill the pages but the war news and the speeches of M.P.s.

'There's nothing in the papers,' Stella said petulantly the sixth day after the inquest.

She was aware that she meant nothing about Hetty's death rather than news of the Russians' advance printed in extra large headlines.

Nothing had been heard from Clive, nothing at all.

'I think I ought to be allowed to get up soon,' she said to Oggie as the afternoon drew to a close.

'We shall have to ask the Doctor,' Oggie replied.

'Well, let's ask him then,' Stella said impatiently. 'He seems to be neglecting us at the moment.'

'He should be here tomorrow,' Oggie said soothingly.

'But I want to know now,' Stella exclaimed, and suddenly she felt angry.

Why should she wait patiently for Clive to condescend to come and see her?

She was Stella Marsden, rich and important enough to

197

command the attention of the very best surgeons in the land; she wouldn't be neglected like this. Clive should attend to her and attend to her properly or she would find someone else who would.

She thought of the attention she had had in the past, of the time when her appendix had been removed.

The general practitioner who then had hovered round attentively had been decorated only the year before for his services to the Royal Household; the surgeon who had performed the operation had a name as famous as Clive's, if indeed not more so.

There had been nurses specially chosen for the privilege of looking after her; her room, the best in the nursing home, had been filled with bunches of flowers—so many had been sent her that many of them had been dispatched immediately to a hospital.

She remembered the telegrams, the letters, the telephone calls, the stream of cars carrying famous and important people who waited outside the home during the afternoon to leave cards, to inquire.

'Lady Marsden is ill' . . . 'Lady Marsden is better' . . . 'Lady Marsden is convalescent.' . . .

But not until she had finally gone home had anyone relaxed, had the doctors ceased to visit her or the nurses left her side.

That was the way to be treated, Stella thought, instead of lying here in a slum, neglected, uncared for, wretched and forlorn. She felt her sense of injury grow and grow.

'Telephone Mr. Ross at once,' she commanded Oggie.

Oggie hesitated. Stella knew that she was longing to do as she suggested, she wanted to talk to Clive, wanted to find out what he was doing, feeling, thinking.

'How fond she is of him,' Stella thought and was suddenly sorry for this poor old woman. 'I wonder if he knows. I wonder, indeed, if he cares.'

How much love to be expended on one man—Hetty dying for him, Oggie caring for him so much that her old face seemed suddenly to have lightened at the mere thought of speaking to him.

'Fools! Fools!' Stella cried out in her heart.

She was aware that there was something hysterical in her own emotion.

'I'll ring him up,' Oggie said suddenly and decisively.

She got up from her chair and went to the telephone.

'Leave the door open,' Stella called after her.

She looked at the clock. It was a quarter-past six. Clive should have finished his consultations by now.

She heard Oggie dial the number, heard the clink of the telephone, and then she found herself waiting, holding her breath. Oggie was speaking.

'Can I speak to Mr. Ross, please? Yes, it's Miss Oggie. Oh, it's you, Miss Harris. Can I speak to the Doctor? . . . Didn't I know what? . . . No, I haven't heard from him at all since last Tuesday . . . No, he never visited Lady Marsden, he hasn't been here at all . . . What can't you understand? What has happened?'

There was a long silence. At last Oggie spoke again.

'Perhaps he is wise . . . You say they agreed . . . It's unusual, of course . . . Well, I suppose he's a big enough man to do what he wants. What do they say at the hospital? . . . I can well believe that . . .

'Thank you, Miss Harris. Yes, if you would, Lady Marsden wants to get up. I could, of course, take the responsibility . . . Yes, I'll discuss it with Lady Marsden and let you know . . . Good-bye, Miss Harris.'

Stella heard Oggie replace the receiver, then there was a pause so long that she could bear it no longer.

'Oggie.' she called. 'Oggie, what has happened?'

Her voice was sharp. Oggie came slowly into the room. She was unashamedly wiping her eyes.

'What has happened?' Stella repeated.

'Doctor Clive has gone abroad,' Oggie replied. 'At this moment he is with the 8th Army in North Africa.'

## 20

'Nurse Start.'

Stella jumped to her feet and slipped the letter she was reading into her apron pocket.

'Yes, Sister.'

'The patient in Number Two bed wants a drink of water and the one in Number Ten should be coming round soon from the anaesthetic.'

'Yes, Sister.'

Sister gave Stella a severe glance as if she suspected her of idling although she could not be certain. Stella quickly poured out a glass of water and hurried into the ward.

She was greeted by shouts of joy from the children nearest the door.

'Come and tell us a story, Nurse. . . . Tell us another story, Nurse. . . . You promised, you know you did.'

She gave the child who was needing it the glass of water, turned her pillows, tucked her in cosily, and then she went across to the ones who were calling her.

'Shush!' she said. 'You know you mustn't make such a noise, some of the children are asleep and you will get into trouble with Sister if you wake them.'

'I hate Sister, she's an old pig!' a small, plump girl announced solemnly.

Stella tried to look severe while inwardly she reciprocated the sentiment.

'If you will all be very quiet,' she said, 'I will tell you a story, but you mustn't make a fuss if I'm called away in the middle. You must remember you aren't the only children here.'

'We know that right enough,' a rather pert little girl with pigtails remarked, 'and you aren't the only nurse either. Let that stuck-up Sister do some of the work herself.'

'Shush!' Stella said again.

'Lazy old toad!' ejaculated the fat child.

'Now if you are going to be naughty I shall go away,' Stella admonished.

Instantly there was silence although there were sly smiles on the three faces looking up at her and she herself was conscious of twitching lips and a sense of humour which would not be controlled.

She could not help it, she told herself, if the children were really fond of her and Sister Mason resented it.

She resented a good many things about Stella, that was obvious by her manner, although there was nothing Stella did that she could actually find to complain about.

There had never been a more willing and tireless nurse in the children's ward—Matron had said that when she had congratulated Stella on her six months' service in St. Anthony's Hospital.

'I knew that anyone Miss Ongar sent me would be good,' she said, 'but we are very proud of you, Nurse. You have done marvellous work and the doctors all feel that the children's devotion to you goes a long way towards helping them to recover their health.'

'Thank you, Matron,' Stella answered quietly.

But she felt the tears sting her eyes. She was so proud, so exceedingly proud that she had not failed.

She had been afraid when Oggie had suggested to her that she was well enough to take up hospital work.

They had been talking of the future and Stella, knowing her own loneliness and bitter because of the sense of betrayal which lay within her heart, had cried out,

'But what am I to do, Oggie? What is there for me? I'm alone in the world, nobody wants me. If I die tonight, a few acquaintances would give my obituary a passing glance, otherwise no one would care, no one at all.'

She looked across at the older woman, at her greying hair, at her kind, tired face and huge ungainly body, and she felt how strong she was, how impregnable against the trivial and petty difficulties of everyday life.

'Oh, Oggie,' she breathed suddenly, 'teach me to be like you—help me.'

Oggie had understood.

'Men have failed you, my dear,' she said, 'and women, too. At the moment you are bitter, although that bitterness will pass. You have got to work out your own salvation—we all have to. In the meantime you will find happiness again if you turn to children.

'Children never fail; when one is unhappy there is no comfort in the world like being with them. They are engrossed in themselves, they live in a world which is very real to them, a world of fantasy.

'For them things are so simple. People are good or bad, black or white, there are no half shades, no greys and near-blacks, no off-whites or any of the hundred and one subtleties which make life such a complicated business that sooner or later it breaks your heart.'

Oggie sighed.

'Sometimes,' she continued, 'I feel as if you have never grown up. You are very childish, my dear, in the way you look at people—you expect so much of them.'

'Don't say that,' Stella begged. 'Someone else once said the same thing to me and I have always hated to think it is true.'

'It isn't a bad fault,' Oggie said, 'but so often you will find yourself disappointed. And because they have failed you in one thing, because of your disappointment, you will turn away from them and miss something far greater and far more marvellous.

'Judge people by their own standards, not yours; accept them for what they are, as a child does, asking only kindness and love.'

Oggie had been right; children had brought a happiness to Stella that she had never believed existed in the world.

She had been frightened at first, frightened to assume a new personality, to enter St. Anthony's Hospital as a probationer.

Oggie had insisted that Stella should hide her identity.

'They will be prejudiced against you,' she said firmly. 'You will start at a disadvantage. They will believe, however untrue it may be, that you are a society woman slumming, that you are taking an interest merely because it has caught your fancy for the moment. If you go there, you must go as yourself, the real Stella who has never yet had a chance to live.'

Stella had been only too eager to agree. With a touch of humour she and Oggie had decided that she should call herself 'Stella Start.'

'It sounds rather like a film star,' Stella laughed, 'but once they look at me they won't suspect that I have any connection with Hollywood.'

It would indeed have been difficult for many people to recognise her.

She was very thin when she was finally well enough to get up; and without any make-up on her face, with her hair swept back plainly from her forehead and with the severity of a nurse's cap pinned over it, she looked very unlike the glamorous, much-photographed Lady Marsden.

Oggie had spent the whole time of her convalescence teaching her about nursing.

When she told Matron that Stella was experienced she spoke the truth; Stella knew far more than the average nurse who had had a year or more's training in hospital.

Every evening Oggie had taught her from the text books, had instilled into her the theoretical part of medicine.

Every day she went with Oggie to her patients, learning to wash and change the bed linen of the sick, to dress wounds, to treat accidents, to attend to babies from the moment of their birth.

She had nearly three months at this, three months while she stayed on with Oggie, helping her, working with her.

The work was hard; sometimes Stella was so tired when she got home that she couldn't eat before she tumbled into bed to sleep soundly and dreamlessly until the morning.

She was amazed at what Oggie could do and not feel tired.

At first she excused herself on the plea of weakness from her wound, but later she knew that the older woman had a tremendous strength, a strength which came mostly from her power of determination, from her almost fanatical desire to do more and still more for those who were suffering.

Finally the day came when Stella was to enter the hospital. She felt exactly like a child going to school for the first time.

In fact, the plain cheap trunk which contained her uniform, the only worldly belongings which Oggie would permit was not unlike the outfit of a schoolgirl.

All her personal things had been sent back to Marsden House, the soft nightgowns of chiffon and lace were replaced by flannel pyjamas, the sheer silk stockings which she had delighted to wear and which had been sent over in their dozens from America before the war were substituted by black lisle thread.

The cotton dresses, stiff aprons, hard collars and belts were very different from the gowns of satin, georgette and velvet designed for her by the greatest dressmakers of the day.

Yet Stella was proud of her new trousseau, proud because she knew for the first time in her life she was going to be useful.

This pride, however, did not keep her from feeling nervous.

She, Stella Marsden, who had met crowned heads, Ambassadors and diplomats without feeling in the least degree excited or even interested, trembled because she must meet the searching eye of the elderly woman who ruled the great hospital over which she presided with a rod of iron.

'It just shows,' Stella thought to herself, 'what a difference a background and a position make to one's self-confidence. Now I am just me I feel I am a nobody.'

She was indeed a 'nobody' those first few months in the hospital. Oggie had warned her that she would be no more or less than the 'dog's body'.

She was right; the newest probationer was at everyone's beck and call, invariably in the wrong, unceasingly blamed and scolded.

More than once Stella had felt she could not bear it,

could not stay on, and then grimly she had begun to find her feet.

After a few weeks when it was easy to get panic-stricken if she was asked to do something she did not understand, when she forgot an order or Sister Mason accused her of idling, she became sure and confident.

She knew what she had to do and the children loved her. That was what mattered more than anything else.

'I want my Nurse, my own Nurse,' wailed one small girl when the doctor came to see her. 'I don't want you,' she said to Sister who put out a calming hand, 'you're ugly. Go away.'

This might have been satisfactory, but unfortunately it made Sister Mason dislike her more than was necessary.

Sister Mason was of the old school, she disliked nurses who were not robots, prepared to give complete efficiency to their work but without a trace of individuality.

But Sister Mason was the only fly in the ointment.

Stella loved the hospital, the clean wards, the faint smell of disinfectant, the children's beds each containing its tiny patient in a bright coloured dressing-jacket.

There was only one thing which destroyed her happiness, one thing of which Oggie had warned her but against which she could not be sufficiently armoured—her own pity.

She suffered with the children.

When they were in pain, when they were unhappy, she found it impossible not to yearn over them.

She found herself worrying about them and even against all rules would come creeping down to the ward at night when she should have been asleep in her own quarters.

The night nurses did not mind, they laughed at her half affectionately.

'Thank goodness you've come, Start,' they would say. 'Number Seven is yelling her head off—it's you she wants. See if you can get her off to sleep. She's been sick again, poor child.'

Stella would go along to the bed—a miserable little face would light up at the sight of her, thin arms would reach out for her neck, and then while she kissed and cuddled the child she would tell a story or sometimes croon a song.

Once Matron came into the ward when a child who had been desperately ill had gone to sleep in her arms.

Stella had been unable to move, she had sat there frozen with horror wondering what would be said. Matron had come through the ward, had looked at her, then stopped at the end of the bed.

She had glanced down at the sleeping child, at Stella in her plain warm dressing-gown.

For a moment Stella had thought she was going to speak, but Matron had moved away. Stella had crept back to bed to lie shivering with fear.

What would happen to her in the morning? Would she be sent away?

Would she—a far worse punishment—be moved from that ward to another one or sent to help in the laboratory or kitchens?

The morning passed and the afternoon—nothing was said. Finally she had to see Matron on another matter altogether. She went along the corridor apprehensively.

Quite suddenly the humour of it struck her, she was as nervous as a girl of eighteen, she—Stella Marsden who once had had the whole social world at her feet.

'I don't care,' she thought defiantly to her own inward mocking. 'This means so much more than anything I have ever done in my life before.'

Matron said, 'Come in.' Stella entered the room and stood waiting. 'Well, Nurse?'

Stella delivered her message. Matron took down the details.

'That will be all, Nurse Start.'

'Thank you, Matron.'

As Stella reached the door Matron's voice recalled her.

'You mustn't get over-tired, Nurse. It is essential that a nurse should always be at her best at all times during her hours of duty. Late nights are not always conducive to this.'

'Yes, Matron.'

That was all, but Matron's eyes had twinkled and Stella could have flung her arms round her and kissed her.

She understood. A blessed woman who understood that rules are made to be broken, that there is always an exceptional case which can be explained to those who are human and kindly.

The hospital itself was an old building, ugly and out of date. Three sides of it were bordered by busy roads full of traffic.

In the heart of Dockland, great warehouses had to be served, there was the constant noise of trams and traffic, of drays and lorries. It was bad, Stella thought, for the children's health.

Sometimes she imagined how perfect it would be if they could look out of the windows on to green fields, on to woods and valleys, on to lawns sloping down to a silver stream.

Some of the children had never seen flowers except on barrows; few had been in a green field; the nearest they knew to the country were the dirty playgrounds, many of them now dug up to create air-raid shelters.

Soon after Stella had arrived at St. Anthony's she had sent an order to Marsden House.

No one at the hospital had any idea that she was responsible for the great bunches of flowers and the huge hampers of fruit which arrived weekly.

She had given instructions that her name was not to be mentioned.

She was afraid that if people started to exclaim over the generosity of Lady Marsden they might, in thinking of that much-photographed lady, compare her even inadvertently with quiet, unobtrusive little Nurse Start.

'An unknown donor' was the person who gave flowers and fruit. The same person sent at Christmas-time enough toys for every child to have one and for every ward to have its own Christmas tree.

'It's about time someone paid some attention to us,' one of the nurses had said. 'I've been here six years and I've often thought I'd joined the army of the Lost Legion.'

'Why don't we get more gifts?' Stella asked.

'We're not a fashionable hospital,' somebody remarked. 'The hospitals that are get Royalty as patrons and then all the society nobodies who want to be seen shaking hands with the big-wigs give generous cheques.

'But St. Anthony's was started by subscriptions from the poor people themselves and we have very few big names on the list of patrons.

'I think Matron likes it that way, she's one of those simple-minded people who don't know that snobbery pulls strings while goodness gets chucked in the dustbin.'

'That's true enough,' many of the nurses laughed, while Stella sat silent.

She thought of the big charitable appeals she had headed, appeals which always had to be made palatable by being served to the public with a ball, an Albert Hall concert, a midnight matinée.

How easy it would have been for her or for any of the women she had known to write a cheque, to give generously because their hearts were touched.

But they had not given unless they had something in return—an evening's enjoyment, the chance of showing off a new dress, of wearing their diamonds, of being presented to Royalty.

How petty, how trivial, and yet children suffered and went on suffering because of such things.

Today Stella had achieved something which had been very near to her heart for many months.

As she told the children in the ward the age-old story of Hansel and Gretel, she was conscious all the time of the letter in her apron pocket.

A letter which told her that her efforts had at last been rewarded, that the innumerable communications she had had with the various Ministries had been successful.

Her story finished, she got to her feet.

'Now, children, be very good and very quiet,' she said. 'I'm going out this afternoon and when I come back I will try to bring you something really nice.'

'A present?' one of the children asked.

'What is it?' inquired the fat child. 'Chocolate?'

The little girl with the pigtails looked at her scornfully.

'Go on, greedy, isn't that like you—wanting to eat Nurse's sweet ration? You keep it for yourself, Nurse; she's fat enough already.'

'Now, be good,' Stella said, 'and if you aren't—no stories for at least a week.'

'Oh, Nurse, you couldn't be so cruel,' they cried.

Once outside the hospital Stella hurried towards a bus stop and got a bus which dropped her at the end of Oggie's street.

She had already telephoned to say she was coming and Oggie was waiting for her in the tiny sitting-room.

The two women kissed each other and then Stella, unable to curb her enthusiasm, cried:

'I've won, Oggie! They've written to me that the Ministry of Food will move out of Marsden House within a month. We've got our own way. Now we can begin.'

Oggie clasped her hands together.

'I never thought you'd do it. Quite frankly, dear, I didn't think you'd got a chance.'

'Nor did I, to tell the truth,' Stella said. 'I was afraid they'd hang on to it until the end of the war, but they have been awfully decent about it.

'They said they believed that the premises were eminently suitable for a hospital and as it was to be a permanent one they would not stand in my way.'

'And now what are we going to do?' Oggie said. 'What is the next step?'

'That is for you to say,' Stella answered. 'I've been so concerned with getting the people out that I haven't had time to think of what I'm going to put in. It's for you, Oggie, to tell me what you require. The house is there, the money is there—Oh, Oggie, it ought to be the most perfect hospital in the whole world!'

Oggie shook her head.

'I'm not clever enough to advise you on that,' she said. 'You'll have to get hold of Dr. Clive.'

Stella felt herself stiffen. She got up and walked across the room to stand staring down at the fire.

'Have you heard from him?' she asked.

'Never a word,' Oggie replied, 'but he sent me a message by Mary Harris.'

'What was it?'

'It was very short. He just said, "Tell Oggie to carry on", that was all.'

Stella said nothing. From the moment they had begun to speak about Clive her voice had sharpened, had become cold and distant. She could never speak about him naturally.

Oggie was aware of this and he was the one subject on which the two women could not speak easily.

'She doesn't trust him,' Oggie thought.

She was hurt that anyone—and especially Stella—should disparage the man whom she admired above all others.

But she was wise enough to know that arguments are never convincing when feelings are involved.

Sooner or later Stella would find out her mistake, would understand that Clive was not as other men, but until she did there was nothing she could say or do to influence her.

Now she sighed and getting up she walked across to Stella and put her hand on her shoulder.

'You know my feelings about Clive Ross,' she said. 'I'm not going to force them on you, but if there is one man who understands what is wanted in a hospital for children it is he.

'He talked of it so often, dreamed of the day when he would be able to have the improvements, the facilities, the treatment rooms which were so much needed. If you are going to give the children anything, my dear, give them the best.'

'We can't get hold of Mr. Ross,' Stella said petulantly; 'we don't even know where he is.'

'Mary Harris will know well enough.'

'Didn't he ever make any plans, draw them up and set them down on paper?'

'It's an idea,' Oggie answered quickly. 'There's no reason why he shouldn't have done so. Mary would know for certain. Shall I get hold of her?'

'Yes, please do,' Stella said. 'There's no harm in asking her, and if he hasn't, letters won't be much help to us one

210

way or another. There must be other doctors, men who have taken on his work.'

She knew by the expression on Oggie's face that she felt no man could take over Clive's work and do it satisfactorily but at the same time Stella felt that the old woman's attitude was rather ridiculous.

Clive was not the only doctor in the world and although the hospital she wished to create in Marsden House would in some ways need his special type of treatment and manipulative surgery, there were many other facets which were not dependent upon him or any particular doctor.

'Poor old Oggie, how she loves him,' she thought to herself. 'He might have written to her.'

She played with the idea that she would write to Clive, upbraiding him for his neglect of the woman who had served him so well and who loved him so deeply, and she imagined his surprise at receiving a letter from her.

'I dislike him,' she told herself, and knew the words were untrue even as she formulated them.

She still felt a deep resentment, a sense of injustice which she was well aware she could not justify but which nevertheless persisted in her mind.

She had believed in him even as once she had believed in Philip and Bertram, and he, too, had failed her. She still felt nauseated at the thought of him and Hetty Hayton.

She had done so much, experienced so much since Hetty's death that she could almost forget that Hetty had died or had left a letter which involved her in scandal and gossip.

What did it matter when she went nowhere and did not hear gossip, when in the little world in which she now lived there was no one who was interested in her as she had been or in Hetty Hayton?

Yet at the same time she could not forgive Clive, could not help but feel that in some way he had betrayed her.

It was stupid, it was ridiculous, and yet there was a wound which would not heal, which persisted in aching despite all her efforts to forget or ignore it.

But what did Clive, what did anybody matter beside the

fact that she had got her own way at last, that she could create a place of healing and of happiness for children at Marsden House?

Memories of Philip, memories of her own lost youth would be swept away by their laughter, by the sound of sturdy feet and limbs restored to health clattering down the wide staircase and across the parquet floors.

The formal gardens, where so few people walked or enjoyed the fragrant splendour cared for by a dozen gardeners, would at last justify their existence. The greenhouses, the orchards and the woods would no longer be desolate, no longer neglected by their bored, overwealthy owner.

'I've found something to do at last,' Stella thought, 'and it is a job worth doing.'

She smiled suddenly and Oggie, looking at her, thought with a sense of satisfaction that she had never seen her look more beautiful.

## 21

'I thought of using this room as a store-room,' Stella said as she opened the door.

Oggie gave an exclamation.

'But it's much too good for that! I should make it one of the dormitories or even a playroom. There's masses of room for storage downstairs and this gets all the sun.'

Then she saw Stella's face and her voice changed.

'Why?' she asked abruptly.

'This was my husband's bedroom,' Stella replied and her voice was hard.

Oggie put out a hand and laid it on her arm.

'Listen, my dear,' she said. 'Those things are past. Let them be past—forgotten.'

'Is that possible?' Stella asked quietly.

Oggie nodded her head.

'I remember a very wise old man whom I used to nurse

many years ago. He was bedridden and in the most appalling circumstances owing to the cruelty and greediness of some of his relations.

'Once, when I was looking after him, a niece came to see him and I remember so well how she talked of small, unimportant things, while I was certain that all the time she was itching to get down to bedrock, to the cause of the quarrel, between the old man and his relatives.

'You know the type of person who glories in other people's rows, in other people's unhappiness—well, she was that sort. At last she plucked up courage to begin and she said:

' "Seeing you lying here, Uncle Joe, I can't bear to think of those who have brought you to it."

'That was a good opening for him to state his point of view, but my old man just looked up at her and I think he saw very clearly how much she was looking forward to hearing the more juicy bits of the quarrel. I remember he smiled and then he said:

' "Well, don't think of them then. I don't. Wouldn't give them that satisfaction."

'That was all he would say on the matter, and I laugh now when I think of her disappointment, but his advice was good. Don't think about your enemies or those who have hurt you—don't give them that satisfaction.'

Stella stood very still and then suddenly she smiled, capitulating completely.

'Very well, then, we'll make this room one of the dormitories. As you say, it gets all the sun.'

Oggie felt Stella's hand squeeze her arm and was conscious of a wave of love and affection sweeping over her towards the younger woman.

She said little, but as they moved about the house her eyes watched Stella.

She had a beauty which was different from that which had been hers before; her face was thinner, more spiritualised; she had lost that cool, aloof air which had been so characteristic of her; instead there was a new warmth, a new maturity.

213

She was more vulnerable, too, but that was inevitable as she became more human.

The last armour that she had erected against her own sensitivity was down and in the future it would be still easier to hurt not her pride, but the spirit within her which seemed to radiate like a shining light.

As they reached the top floor of Marsden House Stella looked at her watch.

'Mary Harris ought to be here soon,' she said. 'I think we'd better go down. Goodness knows if there will be anyone to answer the bell.'

'I understand she has notes, plans, and all sorts of things to show us,' Oggie said.

'So she tells me,' Stella replied. 'It's exciting, isn't it, Oggie? It's funny, but I like this house at the moment better than I have ever liked it before. I can half regret living here myself.'

She looked up the uncarpeted passage, at the walls empty of pictures and decorations, through the open doors into the vast bedrooms which were stripped of every furnishing, ready for the painters and decorators who were coming in on the morrow.

'I think you will love it still more when it is inhabited,' Oggie suggested.

Stella smiled.

'Won't it be fun, Oggie? I don't remember ever in my life being so excited at planning anything. Just think of the children who are going to get well here, think of the miracles we are going to accomplish.'

'We?' Oggie raised her eyebrows at the word.

'We,' Stella repeated firmly. 'Don't try to pretend that it hasn't anything to do with you. You know quite well that the whole idea is really yours. It originated because you showed me how much it was needed.

'Indeed I'm not certain you didn't plan the whole thing and mesmerise me into doing it. You're an old witch when you want something, we all know that.'

Oggie laughed.

'I set out to cure you. All I can say is that I've succeeded.'

'And I've never told you how grateful I am, have I?'

'Is there any need?'

'No, of course there isn't. You know I'm grateful, more grateful than I can express in words.'

'There's someone else you should be grateful to as well.'

Oggie sensed rather than saw the shadow that passed over Stella's face.

Always in every conversation the shadow of Clive stood between them, a ghost at every meeting, all the more potent because they seldom spoke of him.

Now Stella turned towards the stairs.

'Come on,' she said quickly, 'we must go down. I'm sure Miss Harris has been standing on the doorstep for hours.'

Oggie sighed, but she said no more. She wondered if Stella would ever be able to speak of Clive without resentment, to acknowledge the debt of gratitude which should be his because he had saved her life, because of the operation he had performed on her.

She might so easily have been a cripple; instead, it was hard to believe that the accident had taken place, that it was a miracle that she lived.

'Maybe it will come right,' Oggie thought.

She acknowledged that her heart was torn between these two people—Clive whom she loved, to whom she had given a professional allegiance and the whole-hearted adoration of a pupil for a master, and Stella whom she had grown to love despite herself.

Only now could Oggie look back and realise how she had shrunk from having Stella in her flat, a woman who stood for everything she most despised.

Like so many reformers, Oggie regarded society with an exaggerated importance; to her it was indeed the proverbial 'red rag to a bull'.

Nothing was too bad, too fantastic, too exaggerated for her to believe about society and the women like Stella whose names were incessantly in the newspapers.

But Stella, lost and unhappy in a strange world, had caught Oggie in her most vulnerable spot—her pity.

She was sorry for Stella and that, of course, was fatal,

215

for she began to mother her and her hatred of the type which Stella represented crumbled and died.

She loved Stella now—that was the plain truth.

She loved her as she might have loved her daughter had she had one; she loved her as she loved the few friends with whom she had a bond in common, an interest shared.

'She has altered,' Oggie excusingly told herself when she thought of her past animosity.

Yet she could not help wondering, if she had come to know other people, other women in the same status of life to which Stella belonged, whether she would not have liked them also, have discovered in them many redeeming features.

It was disconcerting to have the hatred of a lifetime taken away from one and replaced by a compassionate love and understanding.

'It is a lesson to me,' Oggie thought, 'and one, thank God!, which I am not too old to learn.'

In this difficult, turbulent world there was no room for personal hatreds, only for compassion, pity and sympathy.

'I may have helped Stella,' Oggie ruminated with her usual self-honesty, 'but she has also helped me. I, too, had my hard spot, was becoming a bigoted old woman in many ways.'

Humbly she acknowledged her faults and then suddenly the thought came to her that she would die happy if she could see, just for a short while, Clive and Stella united, happy with each other, perhaps with a family of their own.

She was so certain that they were made for each other, these two incredibly good-looking young people who had both suffered in their own particular way, who had both—as the poor people put it—'been through the mill.'

Oggie remembered her fears, her horror when she had first realised intuitively that Clive was personally interested in Stella.

Now she acknowledged that she had been wrong whereas he had known so surely the gold which lay under the dross.

Clive had been right, as he had always been, but Oggie

216

no longer wanted to shake Stella because she would not acknowledge Clive's righteousness; instead she felt afraid because of her obstinacy.

One day she would know the truth but might not that day be too late? Clive with the Eighth Army was in danger—supposing he was killed?

Even the thought of Clive dying, and it was a thought which occurred frequently, was enough to make Oggie's heart stand still for a moment.

Then she felt certain with that clairvoyance which had been her special gift since childhood that Clive would not be killed. He would come back finer and better for the experience.

'Perhaps he went ahead too fast,' Oggie thought.

It was hard for her to admit that anything might improve Clive, but she knew she touched the truth in admitting it.

Maybe Clive had become too fashionable, too much the miracle worker in that particular section of society where the ordinary could become glorious, the unimportant spectacular.

He was too good for that world where publicity was half the battle; but nothing could be too good for the men of the Eighth Army fighting and dying for freedom. It was fitting that Clive should be amongst them.

He had longed to go abroad at the very beginning of the war, but he had been pursuaded by the hospital and the Medical Council to stay where he was. His experimental work alone made him invaluable.

Funny the vapourings of a petty, frustrated woman, should make them change their minds.

'Well, perhaps in the long run it would prove "all for the best," ' Oggie told herself.

She was certain, though she had no tangible reason for her certainty, she would be proved right.

As she came down the great staircase of Marsden House, Oggie found herself saying a little prayer for Clive's happiness and for Stella's. They were, she knew, insolubly linked in her mind.

Mary Harris had arrived and was waiting in the small

morning-room, which was the only room in the house that had not been dismantled, because Stella had arranged to leave it as it was and to use it as a sitting-room for a Matron.

She pushed the door, hurried in to greet Mary, and then saw that she was not alone.

'I hope you don't mind,' Mary said after she had shaken hands with Stella and Oggie, 'but I have brought Miss Farley with me. I have only just discovered how good she is at drawing plans. I have never been able to draw a straight line in my life, but Alice has made sketches from Mr. Ross's notes. I felt I'd never be able to explain them to you myself so she has accompanied me to act as interpreter.'

'How kind of you,' Stella said quickly, wondering vaguely where she had heard the name before.

'Alice is working with me now,' Mary Harris went on, speaking to Oggie rather than to Stella. 'Mr. Ross arranged it before he went abroad. She has been a tremendous help, I can tell you.'

Then Stella remembered. Alice Farley!

Of course—Hetty Hayton's companion, the woman who had been spoken of in that last damning letter as being mad or deranged. She felt herself stiffen.

All the pleasure with which she had greeted Mary Harris and the sense of enjoyment which had been with her all day vanished.

Somehow everything seemed to darken and the sordid misery of the past sprang up to her grip again.

She wondered if her feelings were obvious to the other woman as Mary Harris drew out a file from her dispatch case and Alice Farley unrolled her plans.

'Of course,' she said shyly in her quiet voice, 'I had never seen Marsden House when I did these, I just tried to work out an ideal hospital as Mr. Ross had planned it. If after I have seen the house you would like me to try to fit his ideas into this building, it would be quite easy. But first Mary will read you his notes.'

Stella suddenly felt as if she could not bear to hear Clive's ideas read out to her.

It was what she and Oggie had planned when they had heard that Mary had some idea of the kind of hospital Clive had always wanted.

Now she regretted that she had allowed herself to be convinced that Clive's ideas were the important ones.

As she had thought so often, there were other authorities—child specialists, matrons of hospitals who had spent their whole lives caring for children.

Why not consult them? Why worry about Clive? It seemed to her the whole thing was ridiculous; any notes he had made might easily be out of date.

Either she should have been firm enough to refuse to consider anything in his absence or else she should have demanded that he give her first-hand information of what was right and reasonable.

Mary was talking, explaining this or that item, showing Clive's notes, recalling what he had said about the disadvantages of the various hospitals he visited.

Somehow Stella could not take it all in.

She was conscious of Oggie listening intently, her eyes shining as they were wont to do when anything was mentioned regarding Clive; of Mary Harris, ugly to the point of caricature and yet animated and excited because she was doing something for the employer she adored.

She knew there was Alice Farley—Stella could hardly bear to look at her—an undistinguished, unobtrusive, middle aged woman.

How much did she know, how much did she hide away regarding Clive and Hetty Hayton?

Stella felt again the horror she had known when Clive first told her of the letter Hetty had left behind, felt the anguish and desolate sense of insecurity that for the third time the rock to which she had tried to cling had proved false and crumbling.

Then had come the utter loneliness of which she felt an echo now.

'It's no use,' she thought, 'I can't really mix with anyone. I am outside, apart from these other women. They have a bond in common, a very close one—Clive.'

Abruptly she got to her feet.

'Suppose before we go any further Miss Harris and Miss Farley come round the house. Oggie, you've seen it already, so why don't you sit here comfortably in front of the fire? It's no use trying to plan which room should be fitted with what until the two newcomers have a general idea of the building.'

Mary Harris agreed while Alice followed meekly in her usual, self-effacing way. Stella led them through the rooms one by one.

It was funny, she thought, how cold and bare her own bedroom looked without the great four-poster bed, without the carved furniture and silk curtains.

It was just a bleak, barrack-like place without atmosphere, without anything to remind a stranger that she had lived and slept in it, had known a swift passing happiness and many long years of disillusionment and tragedy.

'Surely emotions should imprint themselves on the walls?' Stella thought.

Then told herself cynically that it was only if they were the emotions of great personalities.

'What a perfect place for a hospital!' Mary kept exclaiming over and over again.

When they came at last to the great picture gallery she uttered a cry of pleasure.

'It's too perfect! Oh, if only Mr. Ross was here, if only he could tell us exactly how to arrange it. I'm so frightened that we shall do something wrong. It would be such a pity to spoil even in the smallest detail anything so splendid.'

Stella said nothing, but Alice Farley in her quiet hesitant manner ventured almost the first remark she had made since she went round the house.

'Don't you think it would be wiser, Lady Marsden,' she inquired, 'if we asked Mr. Ross to get special leave? Even in twenty-four hours he could give you a very good idea of what was wanted.'

Stella did not answer.

'Have you got your plan?' Mary Harris asked Alice.

'No, I left it downstairs,' Alice replied. 'Shall I get it?'

'I wanted to show Lady Marsden how this would fit in

with Mr. Ross's idea of a special gymnasium for deformed limbs,' Mary said. 'Wait a minute, I'll fetch it.'

'Let me,' Alice interposed.

But Mary had already gone and they could hear her feet running down the passage.

It seemed to Stella now she was alone with Alice Farley that an awkward constraint fell upon both of them. She searched her mind for something to say, but Alice spoke first.

'It is a pity Mr. Ross can't be here,' she said.

Stella felt a sudden impulse of anger. It was almost impertinent of this woman to harp upon Clive's presence to her.

She felt that she was insulted; she felt, too, obscurely, deep down within herself, that she was hurt. Without thinking, without considering, she struck back blindly.

'It's a pity Mrs. Hayton is not here, too, to help us.'

As she spoke she regretted the vulgarity of her words, but it was too late, they were spoken.

Alice made a gesture as if she was distressed, then quite quietly she replied:

'But Mrs. Hayton knew nothing of Mr. Ross's ideas. Although she gave her house to be a hospital, all the arrangements were made by Matron—in fact, it is doubtful if she had any idea of what was done in the wards or for the well-being of the patients.'

'Really!' Stella spoke politely.

She was ashamed now of her outburst and was thankful that Alice was answering her seriously and with surprise.

'But then, you see,' Alice continued, 'Mrs. Hayton hardly knew Mr. Ross.'

Stella said nothing and Alice looking at her face, seemed to see there both incredulity and derision.

'Oh, Lady Marsden!' she said. 'You didn't really believe those terrible things Mrs. Hayton wrote in that last letter, did you? I thought no one who knew Mr. Ross would credit them for a moment. It was because she was such a bad woman that she tried to hurt him with her lies even after she was dead, and it was all lies—every word of it.'

'How do you know?'

Stella had to ask the question, something told her that this was important, very important.

'How did I know!' Alice repeated. 'But of course I knew. I was always with Mrs. Hayton, I knew all that she did. I wrote most of her letters for her and posted those she wrote herself.

'I saw from the very beginning that she was attracted by Mr. Ross, but he did not like her—I was certain of that. She kept asking him to her parties, but he didn't accept one of her invitations.

'Then came the war and she made Trenton Park into a hospital, not because she cared for the sick and suffering—Mrs. Hayton never cared for anyone but herself—but because she wanted Mr. Ross.

'I knew why she did it, but it amused me to see how oblivious he was of the truth.'

'He must have known,' Stella said.

'He hadn't the slightest idea until that night at Trenton Park when you were there, the night we heard that your friend, Major Armstrong, had been killed.'

'How did he know then?'

Stella felt as if she must hear the end of this story.

It was as if something which had been in the dark and threatening at the back of her mind was thinning, getting clearer, almost transparent; in a moment she had the feeling it would vanish altogether and she would see the light.

'Until that particular night,' Alice said, 'Mr. Ross had never stayed at Trenton Park, he had always refused. He would come down, see the patients and go back immediately afterwards either by car or by train.

'On that occasion Mrs. Hayton persuaded him to stay. She gave me my orders and I knew at once what she was after. She told me to put him in the Lilac Room.

'The last time that room had been used had been by Baron von Stronheim—a German who was her lover.'

Alice paused and Stella said nothing, she stood with her eyes on the older woman's face.

'I admired Mr. Ross. I knew what Mrs. Hayton was like and I was worried for him—afraid if you like, and all

222

through the afternoon I thought about the Lilac Room which was so near to hers.

'They had dinner together downstairs and when I heard her order special wines I knew what she was up to. I had watched her methods before, they were not very subtle.'

Alice's voice had sharpened, now she continued:

'While they were having dinner the message came through from the War Office that your friend had been killed.

'I was not such a fool that I didn't realise it would be more tactful for me to keep the information until the following morning, but I had a good enough excuse for doing what I did.

'Mrs. Hayton had told me to tell her informant at the War Office that she wanted to know at once about Major Armstrong. I went in to tell her the news.'

As Alice paused Stella felt that she was reliving that moment.

'They were sitting in front of the fire and I had the feeling that Mr. Ross was uncomfortable, perhaps apprehensive, anyway he seemed glad enough of the interruption, although Mrs. Hayton would have killed me there and then if she had had the power.

'As soon as I told them about Major Armstrong, Mr. Ross insisted on going to tell you himself and when he had gone Mrs. Hayton turned on me.'

Alice almost seemed to shiver at the memory.

'I would hate to tell you what she said. It didn't worry me very much, I'd heard her often enough when she couldn't get what she wanted the moment she wanted it, but she gave herself away pretty frankly.'

Alice's voice dropped.

'She told me what I had suspected—in fact, had known—that she meant Mr. Ross to be her lover, and when I looked at her, uncontrolled, spitting her words of fury at me like any fish-wife from the East End, I determined that if I could prevent it I would.

'She believed that Mr. Ross would come down to her after he had finished talking to you. I was dismissed and I went upstairs.

'I rang the bell for the housemaids and I told them that the fire in the Lilac Room was smoking badly. It was at that moment, for I had stuffed a great bunch of flowers up the chimney.'

There was a faint smile on Alice's lips as if she relished her little revenge on the woman who had abused and decried her so often.

'I told them,' she went on, 'to move Mr. Ross's things into another part of the house. While they were doing it I stationed myself on the landing outside your room.

'When Mr. Ross came out, I told him that his chimney was smoking and I hoped he wouldn't mind using another bedroom. Of course it meant nothing to him, and then, I waited for him to go downstairs. But what do you think he did?'

'What did he do?' Stella asked.

'I think he was feeling disgusted already with Mrs. Hayton. He had heard the way she spoke to me when I brought in the news of Major Armstrong's death, he had heard her try to dissuade him from seeing you. I think, also, he had already begun to be afraid of her—if not of her, of her intentions.

Anyway, when I told him about the bedroom, he said:

' "I think it is time you and I had a talk, Miss Farley. You look dead tired. I'm going to prescribe for you. Have you got a sitting-room anywhere about here?"

'Well, of course I had and I took him along to it and having settled himself down in a chair in front of the fire he talked for nearly two hours.'

Alice gave a sigh of satisfaction before she continued:

'Once or twice I wondered what Mrs. Hayton was thinking, but most of the time I was so interested in what Mr. Ross was saying that I couldn't worry about anything else. When the clock struck eleven he got to his feet.

' "I'm going round the wards now to see that the night sisters haven't gone to sleep," he said. "After that I shall turn in. Good-night, Miss Farley, and thank you."

'He shook hands with me and I had a feeling that he was thanking me for a little bit more than the hospitality of my chair in front of the fire.

'Anyway, I know that when he came back from the wards he went straight to his new bedroom. If Mrs. Hayton waited for him downstairs, she waited in vain.'

'And after that?' Stella breathed.

'You went away from Trenton Park and he only came down once, without any warning. Mrs. Hayton was out and anyway he didn't ask to see her. She was furious, when she came back, to find she had missed him.

'But I had an idea that even if she had been in the house he would have gone before she had been told. The night he stayed was the last time she saw him.'

'Is that the truth?' Stella's voice was hardly above a whisper.

There was no need for Alice to answer, Stella had only to look into her eyes to be sure that every word she had spoken was the truth, unvarnished and unadorned.

She had a sudden insane desire to put her arms round Alice's neck and kiss her, but she remembered that she had only just met this woman for the first time. Instead she heard herself murmur:

'I'm glad to know what really happened.'

'I only hope no one will believe Mrs. Hayton's monstrous lies, but I was certain anyone who knew Mr. Ross well would not be taken in by them.'

Stella felt her own voice choke in her throat.

'I believe them,' she wanted to say; 'I believed them and they have been troubling me ever since,'

But she did not speak the words. Instead, with a sense of relief, she heard footsteps on the uncarpeted passage and knew it was Mary Harris returning.

Stella turned towards the open door.

As she did so she looked at Alice Farley and saw on her face an expression of anxiety, the anxiety of someone who wants to put right what is wrong, to mend and repair the damage done by wanton and spiteful hands.

Impulsively Stella put out her hand and touched her arm.

'Thank you,' she said gently. 'Thank you so very much for what you have told me.'

## 22

The four women finished their luncheon and Oggie and Mary lit cigarettes.

'Five minutes,' Oggie said, 'and then we must get back to work.'

'There's an awful lot to be done,' Alice remarked.

'Don't say it!' Stella begged. 'I feel the three weeks' leave I've got won't be nearly enough.'

'You can always apply for more,' Oggie told her. 'Matron is very sympathetic with this project of yours.'

'Quite frankly, I don't want to ask for more,' Stella replied, and added, half shyly: 'To tell the truth I hated leaving the hospital even for three weeks.'

At that moment the telephone rang. Stella got up to answer it and the others lowered their voices but went on talking. After a moment Stella called across the room:

'It's a personal call for you, Mary, from Scotland—Glendale I think the operator said.'

Mary Harris started to her feet.

'It must be from Mr. Ross's parents,' she exclaimed. 'I wonder what has happened?'

She took the receiver from Stella. Good manners made the other three women talk among themselves although all were conscious of curiosity and interest in this unexpected telephone call.

When Mary returned to the fireside, her face was serious.

'I have bad news,' she said. 'Mrs. Ross is very ill, in fact there is little chance of her living more than a few days. The doctor has diagnosed a very virulent form of cancer, but she is too old and too frail for there to be any chance of a successful operation.

'They have cabled Mr. Ross, but they don't know

whether he will be able to get there in time. Mrs. Ross has asked to see me and I must go to Glendale at once.'

She paused and it was obvious that she was fighting with her emotions. After a moment she said:

'I have always been very fond of Mrs. Ross. She has been more than kind to me ever since I started to work for her son. We shall all miss her and he most of all.'

There was a silence and then to hide her tears Mary picked up her bag. 'I'd better be going.'

Oggie spoke first.

'I am sorry, Mary,' she said, 'really sorry. I have never met Mrs. Ross, but I've heard a great deal about her. She is a fine woman and a wonderful mother. I only hope Dr. Clive gets there in time.'

'Dr. Murdoch, who was speaking to me,' Mary said, 'asked me to bring a nurse to help with the night work; I'll try to get hold of one when I arrive in London.'

'There is a nurse here,' Oggie said quickly. 'Why not take her?'

She put her hand on Stella's arm. Stella felt herself quiver and then was conscious only of the heavy throbbing of her heart.

Mary Harris looked surprised, then she replied:

'But of course—I never thought of Lady Marsden. That would be perfect if she will come.'

'She would be glad to come,' Oggie said.

As if in a haze Stella heard her own voice echo,

'I shall be glad to come.'

As she spoke she wondered how Oggie had known that her feelings towards Clive had altered within the last hour.

How had she known? As if in answer to her question she heard her own voice saying earlier in the day:

'You're an old witch when you want something, we all know that,'

Witch or not, she knew at that moment Oggie gave her a chance to redeem the past, to find again the happiness she thought she had lost for ever.

From that moment it seemed to her that she had no time for coherent thought, only for action—

She got together her uniform, hurried with Mary to the

227

local station, arrived in London, drove in a taxi across the city to King's Cross, stopping on the way only to pick up a suitcase for Mary.

There was no chance of getting a sleeper, but they were fortunate enough to find two corner seats in a carriage and covering themselves with rugs which they had taken the precaution to bring they settled down and tried to sleep.

Mary succeeded, but Stella was awake for a long time thinking over the events of the day.

She wondered at the strange pattern of events—the unexpected appearance of Alice Farley, her explanation of the relationship between Clive and Hetty, the news from Scotland, the demand for a nurse, and Oggie's clairvoyant understanding which had resulted in her being where she was at the moment *en route* for Clive's home.

She was half afraid of what lay at the end of her journey.

Yet at the same time she felt that everything that happened was inevitable, was leading her step by step towards some unavoidable dramatic climax.

She had a feeling that she neared the end of a journey of her own, a journey which had started with her marriage to Philip.

Why she felt this she did not know except that for the first time for many months she felt at peace within herself.

The last vestige of doubt and distress had vanished; she could think of Clive and think of him without reserve.

Now she acknowledged in all honesty that he had been at the back of all her thoughts and only some tiresome perversity of pride and hurt sensibility had kept her thinking that she hated him.

Dear Oggie! She had understood; that amazing intuition of hers had proved itself right once again! For Alice's explanation had destroyed the bonds of misery and distrust with which she had bound her own heart.

Stella felt cramped but in shifting her position she loosened the rug so that she had to cover herself again to keep out the cold.

She smiled as she readjusted the coat she was using as a

pillow at the thought of how she had travelled in the old days.

Her own special silk sheets, monogrammed and embroidered, had been arranged by her lady's maid before the train started; bunches of exotic hot-house flowers had scented the compartment.

There had been a special light-weight rug for her to stand on, and her dressing-table fittings were arranged before the mirror so that everything was at hand—bottles, brushes and boxes, all engraved with her monogram surmounted by a jewelled coronet.

A piquant contrast indeed to the minimum amount of serviceable things packed in the small plain black suitcase which was hers today.

To the nurse's uniform, trim, dark and unassuming, which she wore instead of specially designed travelling clothes and a mink coat.

The old life was over, Stella thought, and knew that as long as she lived she would never go back to it. She had learnt to use her money wisely on essential things—on hospitals, on saving life, on people who needed help.

The endless selfish round of pleasure-seeking had died with the war and had been replaced by sacrifice and selfless service.

There might be a few of the international nit-wits who would seek when victory was won to put the clock back, but they would be few and far between.

To those who had suffered bereavement, privation, and the terror of bombardment there had come the compensation of enlightenment and a new purpose in life.

She was one of these lucky ones and never again would she be forced to look at the world through the plate-glass windows of wealthy indifference. She had suffered—suffered terribly, but she thought:

'How much happier I am!'

It was the truth; she was happier and at this moment her happiness was undimmed because of what she had learnt that morning.

She looked at Mary Harris sleeping on the other side of

the carriage and felt small and ashamed. Mary had trusted Clive implicitly without the need of explanations.

'She knew him better than I did,' Stella thought, but felt the excuse was feeble.

How could I have doubted him? How could she have suspected that he could have had anything in common with a woman such as Hetty Hayton?

'One day I'll tell him I'm sorry,' Stella thought, and fell asleep.

The journey to Glendale was long and tiring. They missed the connection at Inverness and had to wait for a slow afternoon train which got them into the tiny station just as dusk was falling.

'I don't suppose there will be anyone to meet us,' Mary said, 'although I did wire the doctor which train we were coming on.'

But her fears were unfounded. Dr. Murdoch, in an ancient and very dilapidated Austin, was waiting for them. It was cold and after shaking hands quickly he bundled them into the back of the car and covered them up with a rug.

'How is Mrs. Ross?' Mary asked.

'She is very weak,' he replied. 'I doubt if she will be with us by the morning, but she is hanging on in the hope that she will have one last look at young Clive.'

'Is he coming?' Mary questioned.

'I have sent him two cablegrams,' Dr. Murdoch answered, 'but I have had no reply. We can only hope that he will get them.'

The car, wheezing asthmatically, took them down the sharp incline from the station and into the narrow village street with its houses of solid grey stone verging abruptly on the roadway.

'If you had come earlier,' Dr. Murdoch said, 'I hoped to take you to my own home for a bite of food and a wash, but it's getting dark and I think I'd better be taking you straight to Mrs. Ross. You'll be relieving Jeannie McCulloch. She's been with her night and day since she was taken ill and the woman's on the verge of a breakdown.'

'What about Mr. Ross?' Mary asked. 'How is he taking it?'

'He has been very quiet and good,' Dr. Murdoch replied. 'But remember he is over eighty. He sits beside the fireplace watching his wife and saying little. If he outlives her it won't be for long.'

Mary sighed.

'It's Mr. Clive I'm worrying about,' she said. 'What will he do without them?'

'Young Clive will have to do as others have before him,' Dr. Murdoch replied, 'though there's never been a boy that's had better parents than he.'

Stella could not help smiling at the way he referred to Clive as 'young,' but she realised so well how to the people in Glendale who had watched him grow up he would always be a boy, perhaps a little irresponsible and head-strong—

She felt how strange it was that Clive should appear in so many different aspects to so many different people.

To Oggie he was a kind of god; to his colleagues he was an irritant, a revolutionary who had gone ahead despite all their dismal croakings, all their efforts to prove him at fault.

To the children whom he treated he was the jolly friend, the cheery uncle who made them laugh and who never failed to conjure them back to health by some magic of his own.

Now in Glendale she found another Clive—who was only a boy, who had loved this small place with the great mountains towering over it.

'And what is he to you?' a voice asked to her heart.

As she peered out of the car through unpolished windows, she caught a faint glimmer of the river as they drove beside it.

Here Clive must have paddled and bathed as a boy, have watched the salmon, silver in the spring, leaping the falls.

He would have climbed the mountains, seeking in the heather for grouse nests and later watching the chicks with their parents dust themselves on the rough, unfrequented roads.

The air, fresh with the peaty fragrance of the moors,

was as strong and invigorating as Clive himself, and Stella felt perhaps it too was ready to sweep away all inhibitions and hypocrisies.

Suddenly the car stopped.

'Here we are,' Dr. Murdoch exclaimed.

Stella followed Mary and found herself walking up a narrow pathway to the door of a small croft. The house was tiny, but when they were inside it was cosy enough.

There was a small sitting-room on one side of a passage and on the other a bedroom through the open door of which she could see a woman lying in a big wide bed. Dr. Murdoch beckoned them to enter.

As they did so, an elderly woman rose and came towards them.

'They've come, Jeannie,' Dr. Murdoch said. 'Now you can be off home and mind you get at least twelve hours' sleep or I shall be prescribing for you.'

'I'll not be troubling you to do that,' Jeannie McCulloch answered with a broad Scots accent. 'I expect the ladies would like to put their suitcases upstairs.'

'I expect they would,' Dr. Murdoch said apologetically. 'You show them, Jeannie.'

The woman led the way up a staircase, which was little more than a ladder, to a tiny attic bedroom. There were two beds and a dressing-table in the room—nothing else.

'I'm afraid it's rather primitive,' Mary said as Mrs. McCulloch left them, 'but it's not as uncomfortable as you might imagine. There's always hot water and there is electric light. It cost Mr. Ross a great deal of money, but he insisted on it and we'll be thankful of it now.'

Stella put down her things and taking off her hat smoothed her hair.

'I'd like to wash,' she said.

'The bathroom's next the kitchen at the back,' Mary answered; 'I'll show you.'

Stella washed and then slipped into her indoor uniform. The crisp starchiness of her white apron, her stiff cuffs and belt gave her confidence.

The doctor was still waiting for them in the sick room,

but one glance at Mrs. Ross told Stella that she was past the help of any doctor, however skilled.

Mary bent to kiss Mrs. Ross, then greeted her husband who was seated by the fire.

He held her hand, but looked up at her with a puzzled expression on his handsome old face. Clive was very like him, Stella thought.

'I'm glad to see you, my dear,' he said to Mary. 'What did you say your name was?'

'His memory is getting very bad,' Dr. Murdoch explained as Mary answered softly.

Stella moved the pillows of her patient and made her as comfortable as she could while Mary went into the kitchen to find something to eat after their long journey. Dr. Murdoch looked at his watch.

'I'm going home,' he said, 'but I will be back very shortly.'

He spoke seriously and she understood that he felt, as she did, that for Mrs. Ross the sands were running out.

'I may find a telegram at the house,' he murmured as he turned towards the door.

Alone with the old couple Stella put some peat on the fire and adjusted a cushion behind Mr. Ross's back.

'Thank you, my dear,' he said, and added: 'Where's Clive? The boy should be home by now. He always stays so late on the river. It's too dark to fish.'

Stella understood that his mind was wandering.

'He'll be back soon,' she answered soothingly. 'Don't worry.'

'He's a good lad,' the old man mumbled, 'but he always was unpunctual. His mother will be worrying about him.'

Stella moved across to the bed. Mrs. Ross looked up at her with tired eyes and her lips moved.

'Clive.'

'There's no news from him yet,' Stella said gently, 'but Dr. Murdoch thinks there may be a telegram.'

She saw that the old woman understood. Her mind was not wandering, she was merely conserving her strength— waiting for her son to come to her.

The evening dragged on. Mary came in, sat for a little

233

while holding Mrs. Ross's hand, talked to the old man who still could not remember who she was, and then went to bed.

'There's no point in us both sitting up,' she said to Stella. 'I'll go and get some sleep and perhaps I shall be able to relieve you later on.'

Stella thought it was unlikely, but she was all for Mary resting. There was no sense in their both keeping watch and Dr. Murdoch when he came back agreed with her.

'What about Mr. Ross?' Stella asked. 'Can't we persuade him to lie down?'

The doctor shook his head.

'Ever since his wife has been ill he has sat in that chair and slept in it too. He wouldn't understand if you asked him to go to another room and I don't advise you to try.'

A sudden spasm crossed Mrs. Ross's face and the doctor hurried to her side.

Her breathing grew laboured and more than once during the next two hours Stella felt she was dying.

But each time she rallied, each time it seemed as if some tremendous will power within her kept its tenacious hold on life.

'Clive ... Clive,' she whispered, but still he did not come.

After a time she seemed to doze. The doctor went into the sitting-room and lay down on the sofa. Stella sat by Mrs. Ross's side, watching her and the clock.

Three o'clock ... four o'clock ... the room was warm and more than once Stella felt her own head beginning to droop.

She got up hastily to heap more peat on the fire, to move the medicine bottles, to do anything rather than allow herself to give way to the utter drowsiness which crept over her.

At five o'clock there was the sudden sound of a car outside. Mrs. Ross heard it almost as quickly as Stella and opened her eyes.

Her lips moved and once again Stella knew that she was saying her son's name.

She heard Dr. Murdoch go to the door; there was the

sound of voices and one of them she recognized with a leap of her heart.

The door opened and Clive came in.

He went straight across to the bed and took his mother's hand in his. Stella saw the sudden light in her face, the expression of love and adoration which transfigured her.

'I came as quickly as I could, my darling,' Clive said. 'I flew from Italy. It has been a long journey, but I am here at last.'

He bent and kissed his mother on the cheek and then raised her hand to his lips. Unobtrusively Stella moved a chair behind him so that he could sit close to her.

'You're late, young fellow. You always were unpunctual, but this time you've worried your mother.'

It was old Mr. Ross speaking from the fireplace.

'I'm sorry, Father, I couldn't help it.'

'Help it! Of course you could help it! That's boys all over, always the same excuse when they get into trouble.'

Old Mr. Ross mumbled for a little while to himself, then his head dropped forward and he was asleep. Clive began to talk to his mother.

What was said was for her ears alone and Stella moved out of earshot into a dark corner of the room. Dr. Murdoch sat down on the other side of the fireplace.

From where she sat Stella could see Clive in profile. She had forgotten how big he was, how clear cut his features.

Now she watched him talking gently and soothingly, every word a caress, every movement of his lips revealing his love for the woman to whom he spoke.

'How gentle he is, how tender!' Stella's heart cried out.

She knew then that she would give up her hope of Heaven itself, should it be possible, for Clive ever to speak to her like that, to offer her that same love, that same adoration.

She knew at last that nothing mattered beside her love for him and what she prayed might one day be his love for her.

That was what all the suffering in her life had been

235

for—that she should learn the supreme lesson of love which meant self-sacrifice and the giving of oneself.

Had she not suffered so intensely, had she not passed through so much turmoil and tribulation, she would never have recognised the wonder of such love as Clive's, have understood it when it came.

Now she saw it in all its glory and fell on her knees humbly asking in passionate supplication that it might be hers.

She felt her whole being yearn towards him and then suddenly she saw him cease speaking—saw him make a convulsive movement before becoming very still.

At the other side of the room Dr. Murdoch got to his feet. He walked quickly towards the bed and as he did so Clive put down his head and laid his forehead against his mother's hand.

Stella understood. Mrs. Ross had waited for her son and then had been content to go. . . .

Some time later Stella drew the sheet over Mrs. Ross's face. As she did so, she looked down and saw there an expression of happiness which was quite indescribable.

The lips were curved in a smile and it seemed to Stella as if many of the wrinkles of age had vanished, leaving a face curiously young, a face at peace.

Stella drew the sheet over slowly, then she went towards the door.

She felt as if she must have a breath of air, away from the hot stillness of the room in which death lay.

In the sitting-room she could hear voices and knew that Clive and Dr. Murdoch were looking after old Mr. Ross and that Mary was making them tea in the kitchen.

Stella opened the front door. The cold air struck her. She shut the door behind her, and stood looking out over the valley.

The dawn was just breaking. The river, winding down the valley, was molten silver and in the distance beyond the roof tops of the village Stella could see the crested waves of the sea.

Slowly the deepening light swept away the darkness,

the stars faded, the sable of the sky gave way to a pale primrose.

The sun was rising, in another moment the whole glory of the dawn would be there. During the night there had been a slight fall of snow and a frost.

The valley was white and as the first rays of the sun rose above the moors every blade of grass and patch of heather glittered and glimmered as if by some magic transformation.

Stella drew in her breath. It was cold, but she felt as if her body was tingling in anticipation.

At that moment the door behind her was opened. She knew who it was without turning and she stood very still, waiting . . . just waiting.

She was aware that he looked at her and heard him give an audible gasp of surprise. She imagined that for a moment he thought he was dreaming before she heard him speak her name.

'Stella! Why are you here?'

She didn't answer, and he stood looking at her. She had pulled off her cap without realising she had done so, and the first rays of sunshine were on her hair and in her eyes.

She had no idea how beautiful she was, or how the strange pounding of her heart had brought a radiance to her face which he had never seen before.

'To find you here is unbelievable,' he said at length in a low voice. 'Do you know what my mother said to me just now—a few seconds before she died?'

'What . . . did she . . . say?' Stella asked, her voice almost a whisper.

'She has always been fey where I am concerned,' Clive answered, 'and she said: ' "You've found love, my son— you will be very happy." '

Stella stood looking at him, unable to speak.

She felt as if her breath was constricted in her throat. Clive came a step nearer and her heart seemed to turn over in her breast.

'Do you know why I went away?' he asked in his deep voice. 'Not because I cared about the scandal, or what people thought or did not think, but because I could not

237

face the condemnation in your eyes, the contempt in your voice.'

'Forgive . . . me,' Stella pleaded breathlessly, 'please . . . forgive me.'

'Mary told me in her letters what you have been doing,' he went on. 'How you have started a new life under a new name, how much the children in the Hospital love you, what happiness you have brought to them. Why have you done this?'

Clive waited, and it seemed to Stella in that moment that she knew the answer, so clearly, so blindingly that it might have been written in letters of fire. She hadn't known the truth herself until now.

Very softly so that he could hardly hear she answered:

'So that . . . I could be . . . worthy of . . . you.'

'Stella! My darling, how can you say such a thing?'

Clive swept her in his arms.

He looked down at her and saw in her eyes not only a glory to which he dare not put a name, but the trust which he thought had gone for ever.

'My unhappy little love, I thought I had lost you,' he said unsteadily. 'I love you more than I thought possible to love anyone. Everywhere I see your face and I hear your voice. I have longed for you until I could hardly bear not to return to England to see you again. But I was afraid, desperately afraid you still distrusted me.'

'I was . . . so blind, so . . . stupid,' Stella murmured.

With his arms round her and his face near to her, she was conscious of a joy rising within her which was unlike anything she had ever known before, a joy so poignant, so thrilling that it was like a physical pain in its intensity.

'Your name means star,' Clive said, 'and to me you have always been like a star, out of reach, but making me yearn for it, making me long to find for myself the love and beauty it signifies.'

His arm tightened and he said brokenly:

'I love you, Stella, I love you so desperately. Could you ever care for me a little?'

He bent his head as he spoke, and as if he broke under

238

the strain, without waiting for her answer he found her mouth.

For a moment his lips were gentle and tender against the softness of hers.

Then as a flame leapt within her they were joined by an ecstasy so wonderful, so glorious and so spiritual that it was not of this world.

For a long time they stood still, then when he took his lips from hers they were both trembling.

'Clive ... Clive!' Stella's voice was that of a child who had found security after a nightmare. 'I love you ... be kind to me ... I didn't know what love was ... I've never felt like this ... before.'

She was so beautiful in that moment that he could only stare at her, seeing the soft trembling mouth, the unshed tears in her eyes.

'You'll never be lonely or unhappy again,' he vowed. 'I will look after you, protect you and worship you until I die. Will that be enough?'

'It will be all I'll ask of life,' she answered. 'We'll be together ... Clive, working together ... and reaching towards ... the stars.'

She could say no more, his lips were on hers again, but now fiercely demanding and possessively passionate.

With a little murmur of unutterable happiness, she surrendered herself completely into his keeping.

They were one—they were indivisible.

'You are mine, my darling, star of my heart,' Clive murmured against her lips.

And she knew this, at last, was what she had been seeking all her life.

It was love.